Inside the Privet Hedge

A NOVEL

NEVA COYLE

Inside the Privet Hedge

A NOVEL

BETHANY HOUSE PUBLISHERS
Minneapolis, Minnesota 55438

Published by Bethany House Publishers
A Ministry of Bethany Fellowship, Inc.
11300 Hampshire Avenue South
Minneapolis, Minnesota 55438

Printed in the United States of America.

Library of Congress Cataloging-in-Publication Data

Coyle, Neva, 1943–
   Inside the privet hedge / Neva Coyle.
      p. cm. — (Summerwind ; 2)

    1. Fathers and daughters—California—Fiction. 2. Orange
industry—California—Fiction. 3. Young women—California—Fiction.
I. Title. II. Series: Coyle, Neva 1943–   Summerwind ; 2.
PS3553.O957I57   1996
813'.54—dc20   95–45869
ISBN 1–55661–547–7   CIP

Summerwind Books

A Door of Hope
Inside the Privet Hedge

NEVA COYLE is Founder of Overeaters Victorious and President of Neva Coyle Ministries. Presently she is the Coordinator of Departmental Ministries in her church. Her ministry is enhanced by her bestselling books and tapes, as well as by her being a gifted motivational speaker/teacher. Neva and her husband make their home in California.

Prologue

A hush fell across the crowd gathered in Summerwind's outdoor amphitheater for the Class of 1957's graduation exercises. The newest, and youngest, pastor of the community had opened the ceremony with a stirring invocation. Finally, the last of the more than three hundred graduates had received their diplomas, and the class stood in the traditional silence as the carillon in the church four blocks away played the alma mater in their honor.

The graduates, full of promise and hope, were eager to get the momentous ceremony over with and on with their lives. Many were looking forward to college; others were heading out into the work force. Rows of mortar boards bowed reverently in the dim light. As the last chime of the music faded away into the evening sky, the excited graduates laughed and yelled as they tossed their mortar boards high into the air.

The young people filed off the platform into the arms of waiting families and friends. Retta McCarron was greeted warmly by her older sister, Glenna, who had graduated two years earlier from this same school, and Glenna's twin brother, Paddy. Aunts, uncles, cousins, and both her parents had all attended here. Her younger sister, Joanna, would be following the family tradition in another three years.

Retta searched the crowd for her father's face. They had finally come to an agreement. Retta would take a year of business school, and then Sean McCarron would let her help him manage the family orange-growing business. What else could he do? He had no son, except his beloved Paddy, crippled by polio, and turning over the family business to his nephews was out of the question. His brother was already considering selling his part of the family farm to an investor from the East. Sean didn't want his part of the family legacy to fall into the hands of strangers. For Sean, growing oranges was more than just a way to make a living—it was his life. And it was Retta's too.

As tough as things were financially, if nothing went wrong, if there were no unexpected surprises, he and Retta would be able to preserve their cherished way of life inside the privet hedge surrounding the grove—for another generation, at least.

One

"How could he?" Retta cried, slamming her floppy-brimmed leather hat hard against her thigh. Bursting with anger, she threw a rock high into the dense branches of a nearby orange tree. "How could he?" Her tone turned from anger to anguish, and the tears that earlier had only threatened to escape now ran unchecked down her cheeks.

"I can't believe it!" she shouted to the trees all around her. "I thought he'd change his mind."

Even though she had been told on more than one occasion this was coming, the nineteen-year-old had refused to accept it, hoping against hope that something would prevent it from happening. She had no one to blame but herself for her disappointment. But the sale of her uncle's half of the family orange grove had taken her by such surprise. More than once she had overheard conversations between her father and his brother as they discussed the possible—even probable—outcome of her uncle's decision. *Uncle Pat*, she thought, wincing at the memory of his pained face at her outburst earlier today. *Why couldn't you hold out for just a little longer?*

Retta wandered down the long row between the squat, round trees. The citrus leaves, rich and deep, shiny green, hung in severe contrast to the dusty brown dirt beneath them. From her earliest childhood, the grove had been her sanctuary; its silence had often comforted her. Retta found she could leave all her troubles far behind by simply walking to its center. But not today—today was different. The grove *was* the trouble.

On this Sunday afternoon the grove gave her none of the comfort she needed. The center line of the old family estate was clearly marked with chalk dust, dividing the orchard in half. The property line had never been marked with chalk before. There had simply been an invisible division of honor and understanding—but that was before Patrick McCarron sold his half of the family orchard to a stranger.

With the toe of her leather boot, Retta stabbed angrily at the line in the dirt. Letting the anger she so carefully hid from the others swell, she released it in unchecked sobs as she fell to the ground and beat at the chalk line, trying furiously to erase it from the earth. Finally, hands throbbing, she sat and stared at it. Painfully, the reality sank in. Though she might be able to remove the chalky boundary from the earth, her uncle's decision was final. "A done deal," he had said earlier. "It's over."

———————

"She'll be all right, Pat." Sean McCarron tried to comfort his older brother. "She doesn't understand, that's all. She'll come around, just you wait and see. She's got a good head on her shoulders, that one."

"As I see it, I didn't have a choice, Sean. Maybe she'll understand that one day. I'd give anything to have the place stay the same. But I've got my troubles, too. Ranchin' is a good life, and it's paid us a fair livin'—but there's been no room for extras. Now if my boys had the same hankerin' for the place as Retta does, maybe I'd have found another way. But they've no interest in oranges."

"What're they interested in, then?" Sean asked.

"Not much of anythin' I can see." Pat's shoulders sagged. "I've not done them any favors, lettin' them run the way I've done. But without their ma . . ." His voice cracked and he turned his face away from his brother.

Sean tipped the old wooden chair back on the two back legs and hung his hands from his pockets by the thumbs. Looking over the porch rail out toward the grove where Retta had disappeared more than an hour earlier, his heart was torn between his brother and his daughter. "You did the best you—or anyone else, for that matter—could do. It's not easy raisin' kids these days. Even with a wife's help, it's not easy." Sean motioned toward the second story of the Queen Anne style house where he and his family lived. "Glenna," he said, referring to his first-born daughter, "will give us fits yet."

Leaning on the porch rail, Pat turned slightly and rested his foot between two posts. "She's nearly grown, Sean. What she needs is a good husband to settle her down."

"Like us, huh, Pat?"

The older brother smiled slightly. "Like us, that's for sure." Patrick's gaze drifted back toward the grove. "We were something, weren't we?"

"We thought so," Sean laughed. "We sure thought so."

"How many girls you kiss there?" Sean nodded toward the dense citrus trees.

"Only Maisie," Pat said softly.

"No kiddin'?"

"Just her. I didn't want any other girl. As far back as I can remember, it was only her."

"She was in my tenth-grade class."

"That's when she first moved here."

"Long time ago," Sean said. "A very long time ago."

"Seems like yesterday," Patrick said. "When was it?"

"That was '32." Sean let his chair lean forward until all four legs rested on the wooden floor.

"That's right, '32. Her father took quite a beating in the '29 crash. Barely had enough to scrape by and make a new start."

"Drove a vegetable truck, didn't he?" Sean asked.

"For a while at first, anyway. Finally found a way to open a stand on the highway. Eventually he built up enough business to open the store."

"Hard-working man. Remember how we all tried to get jobs there?"

"All wanting to see if we could manage to get close to Maisie." Patrick laughed.

Sean realized how long it had been since he had heard his brother laugh. He leaned forward and tried to prolong it. "But she had eyes for only one boy. You had that one all to yourself from the very beginning." Sean tried to see Pat's face. "She loved you, Pat. 'Twas no use for any of us to try to make time with her."

"I miss her, Sean."

"I'm sure you do."

"She never was strong again after the twins. Those boys came kickin' and screamin' and they never let up. A fussy baby is one thing, but two—it's more than a body can take sometimes."

Sean thought of his own twins. Consuela had known she was carrying twins, but it didn't seem to matter to her. She worked alongside the brothers in the grove until she couldn't bend over any longer. Sean had had to insist she stay behind and take it a little easier the last two months before Paddy and Glenna were born. Maisie, on the other hand, was on bed rest by doctor's orders most of the time. The two brothers couldn't have picked women any more different from each other, and the two women couldn't have been better friends.

"Connie misses her too," Sean said, breaking the moment of silence.

"Still?"

"Never had a sister, you know. Only brothers. Maisie was good company for her." Sean stood, stretched, and came to stand beside his brother. "What'll the boys do now?"

"Can't say," Pat said flatly. "They've got it in their heads they'll get the money."

"I figured as much."

"Not so," Pat said, a determination edging his voice.

"Oh?"

"Gonna pay off the bills, first."

"That still a problem?"

"I had to borrow against the place to pay Maisie's medical bills." Pat looked toward the early evening sky. "Then the freeze of '51 set us both back. Donny's tonsils cost an arm and a leg that year, too. Maisie's funeral in '53. And then I had to replace the roof on the old house. Even five years later, I never can quite get ahead. Don't want to die before I pay off my debts, Sean."

"Any danger of that?"

"No, not really. Just the idea of it bothers a man sometimes."

"What are you going to do now?"

"I don't know. Thought I'd like to see Ireland. Remember the tales Grandpa used to tell of the homeland?"

"I never paid much attention, I guess," Sean said nonchalantly.

"I used to listen to that old man spin his stories, and even as a boy I promised myself I'd see the old family place someday."

"I thought *this* was the old family place."

"It is, isn't it?"

"To our kids, it is."

"I didn't have any choice, Sean."

"I know that, Pat. I'm not blaming you. It's just kind of sad, that's all. Something that's been all our lives, coming to an end."

"Not an end," Patrick said. "Just a change."

"Can't stop that, I guess."

"Nope. No one can. Change is comin' and we'd better all get used to it."

"Or at least ready for it." Sean scanned the sky. "Gonna be a sunset."

"Some things never change," Patrick said.

"Where you gonna live?" Sean dreaded asking the question.

"Gonna stay on the place for a few months anyway. The new owner asked me to stay. Said there's not goin' to be a big change in things for a while. Maybe even a year or two. I'll just stay on until he tells me to leave."

"What about the boys?"

"They can stay if they want. I'll be givin' them a few thousand dollars—not much, but enough to get a start. Then it's up to them. There's still a crop hangin' out there." Patrick motioned toward the grove. "It's ours if we want it. Could get a couple seasons to market before anythin' changes too much."

"When did you say the boy was coming?"

"This week sometime. Wants to look over the place. You know his old man bought the place cash money without even layin' eyes on it."

"What's there to see? Twenty acres of oranges isn't much to look at. Not like he was buying a house or anything."

"He bought the location. That's what land speculators do. Just what you can see on a map and somethin' called projected population growth trends."

"So he sends his boy to look at it after the fact," Sean said.

"My guess is he wants him to get the hang of land investin's."

"Teaching him the family business?"

"Maybe so. More power to him, I'd say," Pat said. "Maybe if my boys had been more interested in the family business, I'd have made a different decision."

"Like Retta?" Sean caught a glimpse of his daughter coming out of the grove.

"Will she ever forgive me?"

"Does it matter?"

"Sure does. She's the only one who thinks anythin' of this place, Sean."

"I know. That's why I'm not sellin'."

"Made you a good offer, didn't he?"

"Mighty good."

"What'd Connie say?"

"She says there's more important things than money." Sean nodded toward the figure approaching the porch.

"She's right," Patrick said as he braced himself to face his niece.

Two

Retta could hear Sean's and Patrick's voices coming from the front porch. Knowing she'd have to face them sooner or later, she straightened her back and walked slowly toward them.

Without a word she approached her uncle, nodded toward her father, then suddenly plunged herself into the circle of her uncle's arms. Tearfully, she snuggled her face in his suntanned neck.

"Uncle Pat," she cried. "I'm sorry. I had no right to—"

"You had every right, baby." His tone told her that he hated what his decision was doing to his beloved niece. He loved her almost more than he loved his own two children. "I'm sorry, too."

"I just hate to see it all change," she said softly.

"It'll be a while yet, honey," Sean offered from the sidelines.

"I'll not be leaving yet. Maybe not for a year or two," Pat said.

"I know." She wiped her nose on her shirt sleeve. "But it won't be the same."

"Nothing ever stays the same, Retta," Sean said. "You know that."

"Our side will," Retta said with determination.

"For now, yes. But someday it will have to change. We can't help that. The town is movin' this way."

"There ought to be some way to stop it." Retta glanced at the crimson display in the clouds overhead.

"Not any more than you can stop that sunset up there," Pat said. "Change is comin', baby. You might as well get used to the idea."

"I'll never get used to it."

Balancing a tray in her hands, Consuela kicked open the screen door with her foot. "How about some iced tea?" She glanced at the tense faces. "I made some special, fresh today. And here's some sandwiches made with the beef left over from lunch." She winked at Sean. "Let's eat."

"Connie," Sean said to his wife, "you sure know how to feed us. Right, Pat?"

"You can say that again," Pat agreed.

"Mama, I'm not hungry," Retta said.

"You'll eat, young woman," Consuela ordered. "Tomorrow's a big day and you'll need your strength."

"What's so big about tomorrow?" Retta asked.

"It's Monday," Consuela said.

"Oh." Retta shrugged and reached for a sandwich.

"Did I hear you say the Conrad boy is coming this week?" Consuela asked.

Retta's sandwich suddenly seemed dry and a lump formed in her throat.

"This week sometime," Pat said between bites. "That's all I know for sure."

Sean looked at his daughter and back at his brother. "We'll do our best to make him feel welcome. Connie here will fix him an authentic Mexican dinner. How about it, sweetheart?"

"Si." Consuela's eyes sparkled. She loved to cook her native recipes. "I wonder, shall we invite Jim and Linda, too?"

"Jim and Linda?" Pat looked puzzled.

"The pastor and his wife from River Place Community," Sean explained. "Connie has been going there on Sundays. Jim's taken a real liking to Paddy, and stops by to play chess with him once or twice a week."

"I just thought the Conrad boy might enjoy meeting someone more his own age," Connie explained.

"The girls will be here," Sean said. "I don't know if we have to force the pastor on him right off."

"I wasn't going to force anything," Consuela countered. "I won't even mention the church."

"Let's not plan a party in his honor, all right, Mama?" Retta said, her voice edged with irritation.

"Watch your tone, Retta," Sean warned. "Your mama's just

trying to make things easier for everyone."

"But I don't think—"

"She's the hostess of this house. If she thinks Jim and Linda should come, then they'll come. Jim's been wonderful to Paddy. Now that's the end of it." Sean shoved another sandwich into his mouth, ending the discussion.

"I'll plan for the end of the week, then. He'll be here by Friday, don't you think?" Consuela addressed the question to Pat.

"I'm not sure he's staying, but we could at least extend the invitation."

"Invitation to who?" Joanna asked, merrily swinging her crinoline-poufed skirts and her long ponytail as she crossed the porch and reached for a sandwich. "Is there going to be a party?"

"No," Retta said flatly. "There's not going to be a party."

"It's a dinner, Joanna," Sean said. "Mr. Conrad's son is coming to inspect Uncle Pat's property sometime this week. I want us all to make an effort to be friendly."

"Is he cute?" Joanna asked.

Retta rolled her eyes toward the porch ceiling and let out a groan. "Is that all you think about?"

"She's sixteen, Retta," Consuela said. "Remember what that feels like?"

"You sound like an old lady, Retta," Joanna said. "Almost twenty and you act like you're thirty-five. How old is Mr. Conrad's son, anyway?"

"Haven't the faintest idea, honey," Pat answered. "Graduated from college last year, I understand."

"Whoa!" Joanna said. "A college man. Maybe he'd like to meet Glenna."

"Why, Jo-Jo," Retta said sarcastically, "you know Glenna isn't interested in meeting anyone who would buy an orange grove. She's only interested in selling."

"She wants to live in town," Joanna said, defending her oldest sister.

"Then let her. She's got a job." Retta was perfectly aware of Glenna's feelings and the pressure she had tried to exert on their father to sell out along with Uncle Pat.

"Girls," Consuela scolded, "that's enough. Your sister has a right to her opinions, just as the two of you do. Joanna, go check on your brother. See if he wants anything. Ask him if he wants to come out and join us."

Obeying her mother, Joanna went into the house, slamming the screen door behind her. Sean took a long drink of iced tea, wiped his mustache dry with his sleeve, and cleared his throat. "I'd like you to be civil when Mr. Conrad comes," he said to Retta.

"Daddy," Retta said quietly, "don't expect too much."

"I'll expect you to be polite. After all, he's here for his father. He's not to blame for this." Retta saw him look at the frown that momentarily crowded his brother's face. "No one is."

"Look, Retta," Pat said, moving to put his arm around her shoulders. "I have lived here all my life, just like you. Mama and Papa planted those very trees." He motioned toward the grove. "I remember picking the new little oranges when they were no bigger than marbles because the branches couldn't support mature fruit. I can still see my father, tired and black from smudging, trying his best to keep his little trees from freezing. You think I want to leave this place?"

Retta's eyes filled with tears and her voice would have stuck in her throat had she tried to speak. She remained quiet and Pat continued.

"The trees back there"—he nodded toward the rear of the house—"need replacing. That takes money. Some of them are older than me. Sixty years is about all you can get out of an orange tree. We'll have a good crop this year. It'll put food on the table, but there won't be enough for replacing any trees. I just don't have the money to put into the place like I should. I wish I did, but I don't. And even if I did, I don't have anyone like you that wants to keep farmin'. Bobby and Donny, well, they don't have a feel for the farm like you do. When your daddy here and I are gone, then what? You can't handle it all alone. Someday you'll get married and have babies to tend to. Who'll do the farmin' then?"

"I'm not going to—" Retta decided against finishing her sentence. "I'm going in," she said, starting toward the door.

Sean's voice stopped her as she reached for the handle.

"I mean it, daughter," he said firmly. "I'll expect you to be polite when Mr. Conrad comes."

"Yes, Daddy," she said without turning around. "I know you do."

———

On Thursday, Retta drove the old pickup into the yard and saw the convertible parked in the circle drive under the eucalyptus trees. Immediately she knew—Mr. Conrad had arrived.

Slowly, she steered the pickup toward the shed at the back of the house and sat motionless for a moment, trying to find a way to avoid going in. Glancing at the brown paper bag on the seat, she knew she had no choice. Paddy needed his medicine as soon as she could get home, and the ice cream her mother had asked her to pick up for dinner would soon begin to melt. She would have to go into the house. Hoping to enter undetected, she slipped in the back door and avoided the front hall.

"Oh, there you are," Consuela said cheerfully. "I was hoping you'd get back before Mr. Conrad left. They're in the den. Go on in. Your daddy's been asking for you."

"But, Mama, I'm not dressed properly," Retta protested, looking for an excuse.

"Nonsense," Consuela scolded. "He's not looking for a date, Retta. He's a very nice young man. You look fine. You look just like a farmer. Isn't that what you want him to see, anyway?"

"Oh, Retta," Joanna said sweeping into the room dramatically. "He's so dreamy. Wait 'til you see him. He's really cool."

"Go on," Consuela said, gently shoving Retta toward the kitchen door.

Retta glanced at her reflection in the mirror above the buffet in the dining room. That morning she had pulled her hair neatly back into a ponytail, then woven it into a thick braid that fell to the middle of her back. A few wavy strands had escaped during the morning as she worked in the grove clipping back dead branches. She tucked the stray strands behind her ears and dusted imaginary dirt from her jeans. Tying the tail of her shirt into a knot at her waist, she pulled her leather gloves from her back pocket and left them on a nearby table in the hall as she walked toward the den door. Pausing for a deep breath, Retta finally entered the room where the men sat talking amiably.

"You made it back just in time." Sean stood and crossed the room to stand beside his daughter. "I want you to meet Alan Conrad. Alan, this is my daughter Retta."

"How do you do?" Alan said, coming toward her with his hand extended.

"Hello." Retta felt immediately uncomfortable thrusting her work-roughened hand into the clean, soft hand waiting for hers.

"We've just been explaining the orange business to Alan," Pat said from his place on the sofa near the center of the room.

"Why?" Retta asked, removing her hand from Alan's and stepping away from his appreciative gaze.

"Because he asked," Sean said, giving her a warning look.

"I don't understand why he'd be interested in the orange business," she said.

"Because, Miss McCarron, I have just bought the orange grove next to yours."

Retta felt a blush creeping up her neck toward her ears. "I thought you bought the land, not the business."

"Is there a difference?" he asked.

"Quite," she said stiffly, averting his eyes.

"I see," he said. "Then why don't you explain it to me?"

"I'll leave that to my father and Uncle Pat." Retta looked at her father, then quickly away when she saw the shadow in his eyes. "I'm sure they can tell you that much better than I can." She moved toward the door.

Retta had no way of knowing that Alan watched her angry retreat with more than just a little interest. Her cotton shirt and jeans, while practical for working around the grove, did nothing to conceal the fact that she was quite an attractive young woman. Her Levi's, which were tucked neatly into her high leather boots, accentuated her long legs. As she passed by a window, the soft light brought out the reddish highlight in the long dark braid that fell down her slender back.

"I have work to do," she said. "I'll see you at dinner later this week."

"Dinner?" Alan asked innocently.

"My mother plans to invite you for dinner." Retta was immediately sorry for mentioning it. Perhaps the men had forgotten. She was angry at herself for bringing it up.

"That sounds wonderful. Did she say when?" Alan seemed almost too eager to accept.

"How about tomorrow night?" Retta said when she realized Sean and Pat were not going to come to her rescue.

"Friday night, that's perfect. Thank you."

"It's my mother's invitation," she said, unwilling to leave a false impression.

"Then I'll thank her tomorrow night."

"Fine." Retta fairly spit the word out between clenched teeth. "Tomorrow night."

"Tomorrow night," Alan repeated.

Brushing by her mother, who was coming into the room with a pitcher of fresh-squeezed lemonade and tall glasses balanced expertly on a tray, Retta hurried toward the stairway. She bounded up the stairs, entered her room, and closed the door soundly behind her. Throwing her body across the bed, she buried her face in a pillow and let out a loud, angry groan. *How could I be such a fool?* she silently scolded herself. *I had to go and open my big mouth. I'm worse than Joanna!*

"How'd it go?" Consuela asked Sean as she poured lemonade for the three men.

"Fine." Sean took a long drink and winked at his wife.

"Your daughter invited me for dinner," Alan said. "I hope she wasn't talking out of turn."

"She did what?"

"Retta invited us all for dinner tomorrow night. That okay with you, Connie?" Pat asked.

"Perfectly okay." Consuela smiled at Sean and wondered how Retta managed to get caught in such a delightful web. "I hope you like Mexican food."

"Free-holies and beans?" Alan asked.

"Frijoles," Consuela corrected, "and some of my favorite dishes."

"Can't wait," Alan said, rubbing his hands together.

————

Upstairs, Retta got up from her bed and moved to stand in front of the full-length mirror. "Get hold of yourself, Retta McCarron," she said in a loud whisper. "Alan Conrad has just bought out half the family farm. Don't let him get to you!"

Without thinking, she opened her closet door and began searching for something to wear. Catching herself, she threw the dress she was holding onto the bed, walked quickly from the room, and headed toward the stairway. She needed to be outside.

Like so many times before, Retta sought solace from the grove. *How long will this be a safe place for me?* she wondered as she meandered between the trees.

Three

Consuela spent all day Friday in her kitchen preparing an authentic Mexican feast. From midmorning on, the entire house was filled with tantalizing aromas. Nothing pleased her more than cooking, from scratch, the dishes filled with the secrets passed on to her by her own mother. None of her three daughters had showed much interest in cooking, although Retta offered to help out from time to time. Consuela was convinced that Retta was being more thoughtful than interested. But no matter, Sean was fond of her cooking and that's what really mattered. For an Irishman, he certainly loved Mexican food.

"What's this?" Sean said at lunchtime, lifting a lid on a pot of simmering beans.

"Irishman!" Consuela scolded. "Keep your dirty hands away from my stove."

"Dirty hands, is it now?" Sean teased. "I'll show you my dirty hands!" He reached for his wife and pulled her, wooden spoon and all, away from the stove and into his arms. Pinning her arms to her sides, he held her tight until she stopped trying to squirm from his grasp. "And what of my lips, my darlin'?" he whispered softly. "Gimme one of those kisses I love so much."

"Sean McCarron, you'll make yourself much less a pest if you know what's good for you," Consuela warned.

"I know what's good for me," Sean said. "I have her right here in my arms."

"Kiss him, will you, Connie?" Pat said from the doorway. "Then feed us both so we can get back to work."

Consuela placed a firm but quick kiss on Sean's lips, then scooted out of his arms and back toward the stove just in time to keep Pat from lifting the same lid Sean had only moments before. "Stay out of things, will you? The both of you!"

"Can't help if a man can't resist the smells comin' from this kitchen, Connie," Pat said. "You can smell it from the far corner of the grove."

Consuela motioned toward the table and both men sat while she served them their lunch. She set a plate of cold cuts and homemade bread in front of them. Hot soup made from homegrown vegetables and generous chunks of chicken would satisfy the hungriest farmer on a bright October day.

"Where's Retta?" Consuela asked.

"She was right behind us. She's hardly said a word all morning," Sean told his wife.

"Except when she's pruning. Whatever's botherin' her, she sure takes it out on the trees," Pat added.

"She's mad at herself," Consuela said.

"How's that?" Sean asked as he reached for a piece of bread.

"She's mad at herself. For asking young Mr. Conrad to dinner. She didn't want him to come in the first place. My guess is, she thought you had already invited him. By then she was caught. Couldn't back out then, could she?"

"Not without looking rude," Sean said.

"Well, she's got it bad. She's takin' it out on every dead branch she can find. Not so good for her, but good for the grove, I'd say."

Just then, the three of them heard Retta's boots on the back porch. Pat reached for a slice of bread and wrapped it around a slice of bologna, but before he could stick it in his mouth, Consuela stopped him. "Sean will say a blessing, Pat."

"Connie," Sean protested, "it's only lunch."

"And you're not thankful for it, Irishman?" she retorted. "Retta, sit yourself down here. We're ready to eat."

As soon as Retta sat in her chair, Sean bowed his head and mumbled a few words of thanks. Sean, Pat, and Consuela picked up their conversation and tried to include Retta, but she remained silent and moody.

"You feeling all right, daughter?" Sean asked.

"I'm fine," she said, her words clipped.

"Maybe she's got a bit of a tummy ache," Pat said.

"How's that?" Consuela looked at her daughter and reached to lay a hand on her forehead, checking for fever.

"Eatin' one's words can cause a mighty bellyache," Pat laughed.

"Almost as bad as havin' to swallow one's pride," Sean added.

"That's enough," Consuela warned the two brothers. "Let her be."

Retta picked up her plate and grabbed her full glass of lemonade. "I'll be up in my room," she said. "You two will have to do without me this afternoon."

"Need some time to pretty up there, Retta?" Sean teased.

Retta's brown eyes flashed her father a severe warning as she pushed the kitchen's swinging door open with her backside.

"I'm warning the two of you," Consuela said, her own black-brown eyes blazing. "Leave her alone. This isn't easy for Retta. She'll come around, but not as long as the two of you keep nagging her."

"Just tryin' to snap her out of it," Sean said.

"Leave her be. She'll work her way through this." Consuela had confidence that Retta's common sense would take over, given a little time.

Pat grinned. "Or maybe Alan Conrad will . . ."

"Will what?" Consuela leaned forward, her expression clearly indicating that Pat better finish his sentence.

"Well, it's just that he's been askin' questions all morning."

"About what?" Consuela persisted.

"Her," Pat said, nodding toward the closed kitchen door. "Seems he's a bit smitten by her. She is a beauty, Connie."

"All our girls are pretty," Sean said.

"Yeah, but he's lookin' at that one."

"And she's looking at him, if you ask me," Consuela said.

"Not on your life," Sean scoffed.

"What you two know about women wouldn't fill a thimble," Consuela said. "Why do you think she's so mad? She was hoping for someone she could be angry with. But no—Alan Conrad turned out to be a good-looking young man with polite manners and proper respect. He's not at all what she hoped for." Consuela looked smug. "He's more."

"No kidding," Sean said and gave off a low whistle. "Maybe I'd better keep an eye on that young man."

Up in her room, Retta kicked off her boots and slowly loosened the braid that hung down her back. Flopping down across the bed, she dropped her head, letting her long hair tumble down toward the fluffy white oval rug at the side of her bed. Gently, she began to run a hairbrush from the nape of her neck toward the top of her head and down the length of her hair. She brushed it for several minutes until her scalp tingled. Eventually, she gathered her hair in her hands and twisted it into a knot on the top of her head. Finally, she walked down the hallway to run a bath. She couldn't remember the last time she had taken a leisurely bath in the middle of the afternoon. But today the idea of being immersed in warm water appealed to her.

She couldn't fight Uncle Pat's decision. She couldn't help the way she felt about it, but she could stop thinking about it. She willed herself to think of nothing at all.

When the water cooled, she got out of the tub, wrapped herself in a heavy chenille bathrobe, and walked quietly back to her room. Pulling down the covers on her bed, she slipped between the sheets and buried her face in a pillow and let the tears she had been fighting back all morning flow unabated. *It's a done deal.* She could still hear Uncle Pat's words. *I might as well try to get used to it. Daddy wants me to be polite. I guess I might as well be.*

After all, Alan Conrad would be gone soon. Investors from the East usually disappeared once they saw what they had bought. All they were interested in was buying at a low price and hanging on until the real estate values increased. The only interest the Conrads had was to make a handsome profit off of Uncle Pat's property. At least they had asked him to stay on and work the farm until they sold it off to someone else. Some land investors just let the oranges shrivel up right on the trees. Thankfully, she wouldn't have to watch that happen. Uncle Pat would see to that, and she would be there to help him harvest the grove.

Without warning, Retta fell into a deep sleep. She didn't even move until Glenna came storming up the stairway and slammed the door to her own room down the hall. Glenna was always mad about something these days. Retta stretched lazily and knew she had to get up. She should at least try to give her mother a hand with dinner. Glenna wouldn't—she knew that for sure—and Joanna was so clumsy it made Consuela nervous to have her around the hot stove and underfoot in the kitchen.

Wearing a dress seemed a bit too overdone, so Retta slipped into a pair of red wool slacks and a matching cable sweater. She pulled her hair back on one side and fastened it with a black barrette. A black onyx pin, matching earrings, and a pair of black patent leather t-strap flats completed her outfit. Running a red lipstick over her lips, she didn't even take time to appreciate her stunning appearance. She hurried downstairs to see what help her mother needed before their dinner guests arrived.

"Go and see to Paddy, will you, honey?" Consuela said when Retta offered to help with dinner. "He wants to have everything set up when Jim comes."

Jim Henry made a regular weekly visit to play chess with Paddy. The young minister had become a family friend, and it was easy to forget he was a pastor. Paddy and he had become especially good friends, and their competition on the chessboard was keen. Sometimes they sat in silence for several minutes. Other times their voices rose in loud groans as one or the other got the upper hand in the game. Frequently they could be heard laughing loudly, slapping their knees or pounding on the table good-naturedly.

Retta hadn't seen Paddy so happy in years. Stricken with polio as a young child, he had been left to suffer with a severely crippled leg. He could manage with crutches, but usually preferred his wheelchair. No one spoke of how disappointing his infirmity was to his father. But even without a word, Paddy could sense it. He would never be able to even help, let alone take over the grove from Sean. At times he sat on the porch watching Retta in the grove. He yearned to be doing what she did. He didn't resent her for it, and only recently had admitted his jealousy toward her, but only to Jim.

"How's it going?" Retta said, coming into the den where Paddy waited.

"Good," he said. "Jim taught me a new move last week. Now I have to figure out how to beat it."

"I don't know how you guys play that game. Seems too confusing to me. Pawns go anywhere, rooks go only certain places, bishops, who knows where, and that queen, how ugly can you get?" Retta squeezed her face into an expression of disgust.

Paddy laughed. "You have to have an interest, Retta. And you have to want to concentrate on the game."

"And," Jim's voice boomed from the doorway, "you have to have a worthy opponent. That's my job."

"Hi, Jim. Linda with you?"

"She's already headed for the kitchen. She's hoping to catch Connie in a good mood. She's out to weasel some of the secret family recipes, I think."

"Nothing would please Mama more," Retta said as she headed back toward the kitchen. "Goodness knows her daughters aren't that interested."

Just as she passed through the dining room, Retta heard Sean's booming voice welcome Alan Conrad at the front door. She knew he'd be showing him to the den and introducing him to Jim and Paddy. *I wonder if he plays chess*, she thought; then, with a shrug, *What do I care?*

Once the family was gathered around the big table in the dining room, Retta couldn't help but notice Glenna's sullen mood. Hardly civil to anyone, her sister ate silently and acted as if every attempt to draw her into the conversation was an intrusion. As soon as she had eaten, Glenna found an excuse to refill a bowl in the kitchen, but didn't come back to the table. A few minutes later Retta heard Glenna's car leave the yard. As disappointed as that made her parents, Retta sensed them both relax.

When the meal was finally over, the men sat back and rubbed their stomachs, complaining that too much of Consuela's cooking could make a man eat himself to death. Connie stood and began clearing the table. Joanna asked to be excused to go to the school dance, and Paddy challenged Jim to try to repeat his newest move on the chessboard.

"Is this a long-standing feud you two have going on?" Alan asked.

"It's building into one," Jim said good-naturedly.

"Mind if I look over your shoulders?" Alan hadn't played since he graduated months earlier. He missed the challenge of being captain of Harvard's chess team.

"No fair giving him advice," Paddy warned.

"I promise I'll keep my mouth entirely shut," Alan said to Jim and Paddy, but his attention was drawn to Retta. All during dinner, he had made himself look away from Retta in order not to stare. Glenna was attractive in her own right, though he thought her heavy use of makeup detracted from her looks. And Joanna was a delightful teenager. But Retta was the most striking young woman he had ever seen. Even the sophisticated girls back East couldn't come close to her beauty. Her soft brown eyes, framed by long, silky, black lashes, made his heart catch in his throat every time she glanced his way—which wasn't very often. Somehow he got the feeling that she didn't like him very much. She seemed very polite, even pleasant, but he sensed it wasn't for his sake. For some reason he hadn't made a good first impression. He wanted to correct whatever had gone wrong between them. Used to having women fawn over him, he was puzzled and challenged by her aloofness.

He noticed, even without looking at her directly, how gracefully Retta stood and how delicately she handled the dishes and silverware as she helped Consuela clear the table. She seemed as much at ease in the softness of the woolen sweater and slacks as she had in the jeans and cotton shirt she had worn yesterday. Released from the thick braid, her long, wavy hair's reddish tint was even more noticeable.

"I'll bring coffee into the den," Connie said.

"Can I help carry those to the kitchen?" Alan offered, extending his hands toward Retta.

"No," she said flatly. "I can do it."

Connie shot her a warning glance. Softening her tone, Retta added, "Thanks anyway."

In the kitchen, Consuela faced her daughter. "Whatever is eating you is not that young man's fault. Don't take out your sour attitude on him, you hear me?"

"Mama, I didn't do anything—"

"You listen to me, young lady. Alan Conrad is a guest in our home. Your daddy and I have always made sure that guests feel welcome in our home. Whatever your feelings are, you will treat him kindly. Is that understood?"

"Mama, what did I do?" Retta's eyes were filled with tears.

"You said it yourself—nothing. You haven't gone out of your way one inch to make Alan feel welcome. What are you afraid of? That he might be a nice boy? That you won't be able to be mad at him? You made up your mind about Alan Conrad before he ever got here. I didn't expect this—not of you, Retta. I'm very disappointed at your behavior." Consuela turned from facing Retta and plunged her hands deep into hot, sudsy dishwater, mumbling to herself in Spanish.

Tears stinging her eyes, Retta turned from her mother and busied herself with putting things away in the cupboard.

"M'hija, baby girl," Connie said softly, drying her hands and moving to stand near her daughter. "Why do you fight so hard against things you cannot change?"

"Mama . . ." Retta turned to find comfort in Consuela's outstretched arms. "I can't help it, Mama. I can't get used to the idea that someone else owns part of our farm."

"You don't understand. This is hard on everyone, m'hija, not just you. Don't you think your uncle Pat has agonized over this decision? How do you think he feels?"

"I know, Mama. But now there's that line drawn through the grove. I never thought of it being divided before. Oh, I always knew that Daddy and Uncle Pat owned it together, but I thought of it being a partnership."

"How did you think it was divided, then?"

"Not divided, but each being half-owner of it all. Why did they have to draw that line?"

"How do you think Mr. Conrad would know where his

property line is? That line of chalk was to show him how much he was getting."

"It's just so hard for me to think that you can draw a line in the dirt and say that dirt over there is yours, but this dirt over here is ours. Last week there wasn't a line at all. The whole grove belonged to all of us."

"No, *m'hija*, it didn't. The line didn't divide the property— your grandpa did. In his will, he divided it between his sons. Half for Pat and half for your daddy. The division has always been there, Retta, but they worked the entire farm together. They chose to ignore the line and keep the business as it always was. But that has to change now, your uncle Pat—"

"I know," Retta interrupted her mother's explanation. "I've heard it all before. I can't change it, and I can't make myself like it."

"You'll have to find a way to accept it, *m'hija*."

"Have you?"

"Yes, baby girl, I have. I didn't like it at first, but my mama taught me that there are some things you just can't change. I've lived on this farm all my life, too. My papa worked this farm with his own hands and gave his life for it, too. My family lived in Uncle Pat's house even before I was born. When he married Maisie, my family had to find another place to live. When he and your daddy got old enough to farm the place themselves, they didn't need my papa anymore. We all grew up as close as you kids and Donny and Bobby. But then one day, my family had to find another way to make a living. It wasn't easy, but until her dying day, I never heard my mama complain. It wasn't fair, I know that, but it wasn't anyone's fault, either."

"But Papa José had his own business," Retta said between tears.

"Not at first," Connie said, returning to the dishes. "At first it was very difficult. All he knew was orange growing. He lived on this farm from the time he was a young man. Worked it, sweated over it, prayed for it, harvested it right along with your grandparents. But he never owned a single orange. It took your daddy and Uncle Pat to help him make the change and see that what he knew about oranges would help other growers. Your grandpa could spot the best oranges, and he could tell immediately when a grower had skimped on water or fertilizer. It was your uncle Pat who helped him learn to be an orange buyer. It wasn't long before growers started coming to him for advice. Finally he realized that what he knew about growing oranges was a gift. His knowledge became his business. He spent his last days happy and fulfilled, but those days of change were not easy."

Consuela put the last dish in the drainer and turned to face her daughter again. "Listen to me, Retta. There has been change on this farm before. You think everything has been the same for generations, but you're wrong. Change has always been happening. You just didn't know it before. You can't stop things from changing—and you really shouldn't even if you could. Change is how things grow—how people grow."

"It's too painful, Mama."

"Yes, *m'hija*, it's painful."

Alan stopped short of entering the kitchen. He quietly turned and set the empty coffeepot on the dining room table. Too polite to interrupt Retta and her mother, he decided he'd have to find another excuse to be near her. And he'd have to find a way to convince his father he needed to stay on in Summerwind awhile longer. But for now, he thought it best to call it a night.

Four

"You can always spot an Easterner," Sean said as Alan pulled out of the driveway in his convertible, leaving a cloud of dust behind.

"Top down, and here it is the middle of October." Pat smiled good-naturedly. "He isn't even wearing a sweater."

"Let Connie be around him a bit more. He'll come around," Sean said.

"He's not what I expected. I thought he'd be a bit more—well, I don't know. . . ."

"Snooty?"

"Yeah, maybe. But it seems that young boy's got a good head on him. Comes from a wealthy family, but doesn't seem as spoiled as you might expect."

"Where's he staying?"

"Down at the boardinghouse in town," Pat said. "That surprises me too. I thought he'd be stayin' at some fancy hotel."

"You'd think so, wouldn't you?"

Pat nodded. "But he said he's on an expense account."

"How long you figure he'll be staying?"

"As long as he can, would be my guess," Pat said. "You see the way he looked at Retta?"

"I saw," Sean said.

"Did she?"

"Don't think so." Sean stuck his hands deep in his pockets and turned to go back into the house. "Let's go see if Paddy has managed to beat that young preacher."

Alan glanced in his rearview mirror as he headed toward town. *Even that's beautiful,* he said to himself. *Everywhere you look, it's beautiful.* The dashboard clock registered eight forty-five, hardly late enough to go back to his small room at the boarding-room hotel. Circling around, he spotted what appeared to be a popular hangout. All the cars parked in the lot were decked out and polished to a high shine, indicating the establishment's young clientele.

Swerving easily into a parking slot, he left the Ford Fairlane hardtop convertible and went inside. The jukebox blared from the corner, and girls in full poodle skirts were twisting furiously to Chubby Checkers' newest dance craze with their dates. Finding a booth second from the corner, he slid casually across the Naugahyde seat and ordered a Coke and fries.

"What do you mean, he won't sell?" The voice was coming from the booth behind him. Alan didn't pay much attention until a young woman spoke in response.

"That's what I said. He won't budge. I've begged, pleaded, and even threatened to leave home, and he simply won't hear of it. We finally have a chance to leave that stupid farm and move into town and live like real people for a change. With the money he'd get, we could buy a nice house in the right part of town and even have a pool."

Without looking, Alan thought he recognized Glenna's voice. He had heard very little from her at dinner, but her whiny tone was hard to forget.

"It's Retta's fault," one of her male companions said. "She always gets her way. From the time we were little, she's been playing up to Dad and Uncle Sean."

"Little kissy face," the other young man said. "There ought to be some way to make her pay—you know, get even."

"Right," Glenna said sarcastically. "You guys know if we do anything we'll catch it for sure."

"What can they do to us now?" one of the boys said. "We're too old to spank."

"What're you going to do with the money?" Glenna asked, changing the subject.

"I'm getting out of this dump—I can tell you that. I'm heading for the beach just as soon as my old man pads my pocket."

"I thought I might take off and hitchhike around the country and do some sightseeing," the other boy said. "I've been thinking about Montana, or maybe even Colorado."

"You know how much he's going to give you?"

"If we play our cards right, we'll get most, if not all of it," one boy said with a sneer.

Alan's stomach tightened at the implications of their conversation. Obviously Glenna was talking with her cousins—Pat's two sons. He thought of his own father and how much respect he had for him.

Never once had Alan ever considered taking money from his father. Even the car he drove, while paid for by his dad, was earned with a 3.2 grade-point average at graduation. A 3.5 would have meant a caddie, but then, this little dream machine wasn't half bad. His father had been pleased with his grades and openly told him so. He had done his best—that's all that was required. His best meant a Ford Fairlane retractable hardtop. His father had written him a check and told him to get the best deal he could. Whatever he saved he could put in his pocket. Alan knew he could have pulled off the 3.5, but then those chess tournaments kept him from studying as much as he could have. Oh well, he traded the Cadillac for a Ford and the chance to be the Harvard chess champ. Well worth it, in his opinion. Now that he had met Retta he was glad he wasn't driving a Caddie. She would not have been impressed.

"Anyone sitting here?" Jim's pleasant voice interrupted Alan's thoughts.

"Hey, sit down. Where's Linda?" Alan motioned toward the empty seat.

"She's over there talking to some of the girls from our church."

"Oh, I forgot, you're a minister."

"Of sorts," Jim smiled. "I'm not very traditional. How many other 'men of the cloth' do you see hanging out here on Friday nights?"

"I see what you mean," Alan said. Suddenly he was aware that the conversation in the next booth had stopped. Jim glanced past him and nodded toward Glenna with a knowing look at Alan. "Hey, that was some dinner, wasn't it?"

"Consuela McCarron makes the best tamale pie in the county." Jim's mouth spread in a wide grin. "Wait until she makes enchiladas for you sometime. I tell you, even her Irish stew is laced with jalapeño peppers."

Alan barely looked up as Glenna and her two cousins left suddenly without a word.

"Those three are trouble," Jim said as he watched them go out the door. "Gigantic attitudes, headed for nothing but trouble."

"Who's in trouble?" Linda said as she slid in beside her husband.

"The McCarron twins and Glenna."

"The McCarron family has their hands full with that bunch, that's for sure. We'll have to pray harder, Jim. What a miracle that would be to see those three give their hearts to Christ."

Alan sat back, emptied his Coke, and held his glass high, signaling the waitress for another.

"Have you lived here long?" Alan asked the young couple.

"Since December of '56. Almost three years," Linda said. "This is our first church."

"How did you come to—I mean, what brought you here?"

"We came looking for a pastorate right out of Bible school. We heard about this little struggling community church and thought we might be able to build something here." Jim stuck two French fries into ketchup, then into his mouth. "I applied and was accepted. I have to work now and then to make ends meet. The church is still pretty small and can't always meet our salary."

Alan noticed how many teenagers greeted the young couple as they came by the table. "How do you know so many of these kids?" he asked.

"I worked here for a while," Jim said. "Thought I might as well go where my future congregation congregated." He laughed and Linda leaned into him affectionately.

"We have a real burden for young people," Linda said. "Many of them have been raised with so much affluence, they don't have any real values or direction. Each generation has its own challenges, I guess." She glanced admiringly at her husband. "The kids just flock around Jim. They even asked him to give their graduation invocation the last two years in a row. This year they have already asked him to deliver the baccalaureate sermon."

"How do you manage to get down on their level?" Alan asked. "I mean, being a minister and all."

"Guess I never got off their level," Jim said.

"He's unconventional," Linda said.

"Unconventional?" Alan asked.

"I'd rather shoot baskets with these boys than play golf with their fathers."

"I'd say that's unconventional, all right."

"How about you?" Jim asked. "How'd you get to Summerwind?"

"Down the highway out there." Alan smiled. "No, really. I'm working for my dad. He's investing in some real estate out here. He lives in upstate New York; in fact, my whole family does. He's what you'd call a financier. His father was a railroad man."

"You mean like an engineer or conductor?" Linda asked.

"No, he was a railroad builder. I think my ancestors were some of the few wealthy immigrants that came to America. They came with money and determined to make more of it. Anyway, my father came into a large inheritance, and he's pretty much spent his life managing it and making more money."

"How does that involve you?" Jim asked, curious to know where Alan fit in.

"He sent me to Harvard, but in exchange I had to agree to work for him for four years or go on to graduate school."

"He didn't just hand you your education?"

"He hasn't just handed me anything," Alan said with a smile. "We don't just have a family business, but a legacy. My father decided very early that his son would either be prepared to manage the family money, or he'd turn it over to someone who could. My main job now is to prove I'm ready for the responsibility when the time comes."

"Are you an only child, Alan?" Linda asked.

"I am now. I had an older sister, but she died of pneumonia—a complication of polio."

"How sad," Linda said softly.

"Even the rich aren't spared when it comes to sickness," Jim said.

"You got that right," Alan agreed.

"So let's see," Jim said. "You're an only child. Harvard graduate and working for your father. Right so far?"

"So far, you're absolutely correct."

"And just what is it you do for him?"

"I'm out here looking over the real estate investments he made through a broker. Land in California is a hot item back East right now. Everyone says the growth out here is only just beginning. I'm here to learn about the culture, the economic situation, and to make some recommendations as to how we proceed from here."

"And how's it going so far?"

"So far so good, but then I've only been here for a couple of weeks." Alan sat back and threw his arm casually over the back of the booth. "I've already been out west of River Hills looking over the land out there. We're holding title to several hundred acres of what has been ranch land. We'll probably begin building houses out there, developing communities, looking for other investors to build shopping areas and the like."

"You think people will move out there? Where will they work?"

"We're guessing that within ten to twenty years more people will be commuting to Los Angeles than the present highway system can handle. We'll be promoting that idea for a while before we actually begin building houses."

"You'll be getting right into the thick of California politics, then," Jim said.

"Not me," Alan said. "I'm not one for the dog-eat-dog world. My dad will probably find someone who he can support politically and—"

"Invest in his career," Jim finished Alan's sentence.

"Something like that."

"How will he know who to support?"

"That's part of my job," Alan said. "I'm supposed to keep my ears and eyes open. When I spot someone I think might be our man, my dad and his cronies will take it from there."

"A progressive, I suppose," Jim said.

"I'm afraid so," Alan said. "Why did all of this sound better before I got here?"

"How long will you be here?"

"I owe my father four years," Alan said. "I've got lots of time."

"Maybe by then you'll be the politician," Jim teased.

"Afraid not," Alan said. "Besides, I'm kind of interested in something quite different."

"What's that?" Linda asked.

"Farming."

"Farming?" Jim almost choked on his Coke.

"Orange growing really fascinates me. Who would have thought it? Certainly not me—walking the ivy-covered halls of Harvard, I certainly wasn't thinking about hanging away my three-piece suit and donning coveralls to work in some orange grove. But I find it challenging. I never knew it took so much work. You know, when you see a bowl of juicy oranges sitting on the kitchen counter, you don't think too much of how they got there."

"Why oranges? Why not corn or grapes?" Jim asked.

"They don't grow corn or grapes in Summerwind, do they?" Alan smiled.

"No, they don't. And they don't grow girls as pretty as Retta McCarron anywhere else, either," Jim said.

"Well. . ." Alan hesitated and played with the paper wrapper from his straw.

"Don't tell me you didn't notice her," Jim said.

"She doesn't like me very much," Alan said.

"She doesn't know you," Linda offered.

"She doesn't want to, either," Alan said. "I'm afraid that if I get to know her, it's going to be an uphill battle all the way."

"You backing away from a little challenge, Al?"

"Nope. Just planning a strategy. I think my first step should be to give her time and a little space."

"A little space?" Linda asked.

"Just enough so that she knows I'm around, but not so that she feels crowded. I've decided to learn the orange growing business. I'm thinking I'll ask Pat McCarron to teach me."

"I think I like you, Alan Conrad," Jim said, sticking out his hand.

"Thank you, sir," Alan said warmly. "The feelings are mutual."

Alan picked up Jim and Linda's check along with his, and as they left the restaurant together, Jim challenged Alan to shoot baskets at the high school the next afternoon. "You're on. Say, I'd like you to show me that chess move you pulled on poor Paddy," Alan said.

"Not on your life," Jim said. "That's my secret weapon. I will take you on sometime, though, and see if you can catch on."

Five

"He seems like such a nice boy, doesn't he?" Consuela asked Sean after they said good-night to Pat.

"I think we're all a little pleasantly surprised. I think Jim liked him, too." Sean wandered to the other side of the den and looked at the chessboard in its semipermanent place in the bay window. He picked up one of the pieces and held it thoughtfully. "I should learn how to play this confounded game. Paddy seems to like it so much. Maybe. . ."

"You'd have to sit still once in a while if you were to take up chess," Connie said. "You think you could manage that?"

"Sounds better every day." Sean replaced the piece on the board and turned to face his wife. "I've been a little tired lately."

"I've noticed," she said. Consuela didn't miss anything when it came to Sean.

"I'm glad Pat's decision is final. Every day I thought he might change his mind. Almost afraid he would."

"That's a funny thing to say," Connie said. "I thought you didn't want him to sell."

"It's not what I want that's been the most painful part of this whole thing."

"I know, my sweet husband." Connie came to stand close to Sean. "It's Retta, isn't it?"

"I would have bought Pat out if I could have."

"I know." Consuela had known it almost before Sean did. "And you would have done it for all the right, yet wrong, reasons."

"She's had her heart set on working the grove since she was barely big enough to climb a ladder. Her whole life is in the grove."

"You still think not selling was the best choice?"

"For now, yes." Sean lowered his large body onto the sofa and pulled Consuela down beside him. She began to remove the pins that held her silver-streaked black hair in a neat bun, letting it flow softly down her back the way her husband liked it.

"Citrus is in her blood, Sean. She gets it from both sides. Her grandpas were the best growing team in the Los Angeles basin. She comes by it naturally." Consuela snuggled next to her husband.

"I guess she does at that," Sean said, putting his arm around her shoulder.

"When the other kids were playing with bikes and kites, she was in the grove making sure the irrigation ditches were clear. Whenever I couldn't find her, I knew to look under that tree out there in the center of the grove. She crawled under the branches many times and fell asleep in the dirt."

"You know my father trimmed the low branches away to make that place for her, don't you?" Sean asked.

"And you kept it trimmed, didn't you?"

"Yeah, I guess I did. She was born for the business, wasn't she, Connie?"

"Almost born in it—I went into labor out there picking Valencias."

"You're quite the woman, you know that?" Sean nuzzled his face into Consuela's dark, thick hair.

"I wonder," Connie said quietly, "if Pat has really thought about what it will be like not to live on the farm?"

"I don't know. I've wondered that myself. Says he wants to do a bit of travelin'."

"Travel is only fun if you have someplace to come home to."

"This has always been home to him, Connie."

"I think it should always be, don't you, Sean?"

"What are you saying, girl?"

"I am saying that we've talked about finishing off that loft area in the carriage house before. Maybe it's time we got started. He'll need a place to call home, Sean. Can you honestly think it should be anywhere except here with us?"

———

Upstairs in her room, Retta brushed her long hair with slow, repeated strokes. Letting her mind drift back over the evening, she sensed an edginess in herself she couldn't describe. It wasn't like her to be so short the way she had been with Alan Conrad. She didn't like the words of rebuke her mother had spoken to her while they did dishes. Somehow she had to find a way to face the inevitable. How would she manage to accept the changes she found so painful and threatening?

It was true, none of this was Alan's fault. While he was part of the change, he certainly didn't bring it. His father hadn't forced her uncle to sell—Uncle Pat had gone looking for a buyer. She had no real reason to resent Alan. She didn't see him as the invited guest Consuela declared him to be. He seemed more like an intruder. Retta had noticed the way he had looked at her during the evening. Not that he was obvious the way other men had been, but still, there was the uninvited eye contact she found so uncomfortable. Why should she feel shy around this man? She worked with men every day of her life. Even the seasonal workers who ogled her while she worked didn't cause her this much discomfort. Nor were Alan's glances the same. She knew how to handle men's unwanted advances, but it was different with Alan. He hadn't made any advances—and Retta wasn't so sure that the slight interest he had shown was totally unwanted.

"Stop it!" she said aloud to her image in the mirror. "Stop it right this minute!"

But stop what? The interest she also felt toward him? Her unplanned thoughts about him? The pleasant feelings she got when he smiled in her direction? The butterflies she felt in her stomach at that very moment?

She knew that her well-planned strategies for handling men would not work this time. She wasn't prepared for the changes on the farm that Mama said were bound to come. But she felt even less prepared to deal with the likes of Alan Conrad.

Oh, God, she moaned inwardly, *what am I going to do?*

———

Back at the boardinghouse, Alan paced around his small room. He had to think of something to tell his father. Something so convincing that he'd approve of his staying in Summerwind—maybe even indefinitely. He could study the political atmosphere from here. He'd read the *Los Angeles Times* daily. Besides, it would be helpful to know how the people on this end of the proposed freeway system felt about it and the change it would bring to their lives. Surely Pat McCarron had some opinions on the matter—and of course, Sean. Maybe even Retta.

Without invitation, she crowded into his every thought. So distant and so unreachable. Why did she dislike him so much? He'd been rather popular with the girls back home—or at least with their mothers, who were trying to make a favorable match for their up-and-coming debutante daughters. He wasn't used to being kept at arm's length. Usually he was trying to escape some invisible net. Now he wished he had paid closer attention—now he wanted to know how to spread one of his own.

With a great deal of effort, he brought his thoughts back to his father. A phone call wouldn't work. He'd have to write a long and convincing letter—one that was strong and logical. One thing his father responded to was decisiveness. He'd go have a talk with Pat McCarron in the morning. Maybe a conversation with him would shed some light on Alan's idea. At least he might be able to pick up some of the right words to use. After all, the man had been an orange grower as long as Alan, Sr. had been in finance.

And, just maybe he'd have a chance encounter with Retta.

It was no use. Alan couldn't get the young, dark-headed woman out of his thoughts. Lying down on his bed, he gave up trying.

———

"Good morning," Alan called to Pat, who was working out near the back privet hedge.

"Well, mornin'," Pat responded cheerfully. "What a mornin'! Ever see such a beautiful day?"

"You know, Mr. McCarron, I don't think I ever have."

"What brings you out here, young man?"

"I have a few questions, sir. I was wondering if I'd be a bother if I just kind of followed you around while you work and picked your brain a little."

"Well, there's not much to spare up there." Pat laughed and pointed to his temple. "But what I've got I'd be glad to share."

"It's just that the orange business fascinates me. All my life I've just gone to a bowl on the table and helped myself. I never gave any thought to where they came from or how they got to that bowl. Am I making any sense?"

"You're curious, you say?"

"Not exactly. I'm more than curious. I'm interested. While I was sitting in the classroom, you've been out here growing oranges. Somehow, out here in the grove, that classroom seems pretty far away and even a bit dull."

"Well, there's not much excitement in citrus, Mr. Conrad. Believe me, it can be pretty dull at times."

"Alan. Please call me Alan."

"Alan." Pat squinted against the bright sunlight and stuck his hand out toward the clean-cut young man. "Then my friends call me Pat."

"Yes, sir. Pat." Alan grinned wide and Pat slapped him on the shoulder as they shook hands.

"So, Alan," Pat said. "You'd like to know about growin' oranges, would you?"

"No, sir," Alan corrected. "I don't want to learn about growing them. I want to learn *how* to grow them."

"I see." Pat took off his hat and wiped his forehead with his sleeve. "You know, there's no better way than to get right in the grove and get in touch with the trees—they're the real orange producers."

"I'd like that," Alan said.

"You got any different clothes than those slacks?" Pat laughed and poked good-naturedly at Alan's chest. "We don't usually work in a tie, either."

"Guess I should get some work pants, huh?"

"Go down to J.C. Penney's. In the basement where the work clothes are."

"What's going on out here?" asked Consuela, coming to bring Pat a midmorning cold drink.

"Hired myself a hand," Pat said. "Needs some work clothes."

"I'm going to town," Connie offered. "Want to tag along? I'll steer you in the right direction."

"That'd be great!" Alan's eyes sparkled with excitement.

As he turned to follow Connie from the grove, Pat shouted after him, "And, put that top up on that fancy car of yours. Parked out here, it'll get full of dust. Won't look new for long if you don't take care of it."

"Yes, sir." Alan turned and saluted. "I'll take care of it."

"And, Connie." Pat continued to bark orders. "Get him some shears and gloves. Then send him back out here. We've got lots of branches to trim."

Consuela answered her brother-in-law with a broad smile and a wave. Alan couldn't help wondering if Retta's smile were as disarming as her mother's.

"And one more thing," Pat yelled just before they rounded the corner by the shed. "Get him a big jar of Vaseline, and a box of Band-Aids."

"What do I need those for?" Alan asked Connie.

She glanced at his soft, white hands and laughed. "Just standard equipment," she said. "You'll see."

Six

Retta was enraged when she found out that Pat had agreed to teach Alan how to trim the trees. "We don't need his help," she said loudly. "We can manage this quite well, the three of us."

"It's not a matter of us needin' his help, Retta," Pat said calmly. "He wants to learn. I'd think you'd be more than happy to help teach him what he wants to know. Shouldn't he learn? After all, he's the new grove owner."

"He's not a grove owner," she insisted, almost in tears. "He's a real estate speculator. He's not interested in growing oranges. He's only finding something to keep him busy while his land appreciates in value. He said you could have the crop—now what's he going to do, go back on his word?"

"I think you're makin' too much of this," Sean said at last. "Let the boy alone. He wants to learn somethin' new. What's so wrong with that?"

"He's shown more interest in one day than my own boys have in their entire lives," Pat said quietly before he quickly turned and left Retta and Sean standing in the sorting shed.

Retta put both hands on her hips and shifted her weight from one foot to the other.

"Let it alone, Retta," Sean warned. "There's not been much to bring a little light into Pat's life. Can't you see how he's taken to this boy?"

"I don't understand it at all. Alan Conrad is a nuisance. He buys the farm like any other land grabber, and you two welcome him like a long lost relative or something."

"You jealous, daughter?" Sean asked.

"Of course not," Retta retorted, reddening suddenly.

"That's good," Sean said. "You had me worried there for a minute."

Even Retta had to admire the zest with which Alan tackled the pruning. Before long, his khaki pants and matching shirt were covered with dust.

"Like this," Pat said, grabbing a limb firmly in his left hand. "You just pretend the tree has feelings, and the quicker you get that dead branch off, the better. Cut swift and it hurts less, see?" Pat lopped off a small dead sprig and flung it into the lane between the trees. "We'll come back later to do the cleanup. Prunin' isn't neat. Just get the cuttin' done, and we'll worry about the mess later."

Finding his new leather gloves stiff and awkward, Alan abandoned them and handled the dry limbs with his bare hands. His shears were sharp, and once he mastered Pat's technique, he moved quickly, pruning one tree after another.

"I had no idea these trees grew so thick. From a distance you get the idea they're hollow under the branches."

"Not unless you cut them that way," Pat said as he stopped to wipe his brow.

"Why do you bother with this?" Alan asked. "Why not wait until winter when the leaves fall and—"

Retta could barely stifle a giggle.

"The leaves don't fall, son," Pat said patiently. "Our growing season is all year long. We have to train these trees to grow the way we want them. See that old tree over there? It's almost sixty years old. No tellin' what she'd be like if we hadn't kept her under control all these years."

"I can't get used to the idea of a climate that doesn't have a winter season," Alan commented as he worked alongside Pat.

"Oh, we have winter. Not like you're used to, of course. But we have our own brand of winter. I remember once when I was just a boy, and then again in '51, we had such a freeze we lost most of our summer crop. The Valencias hadn't even blossomed yet, but the trees were so shocked by the cold that they didn't produce much that year."

Retta finished her stand of four trees and moved on to the next. Listening from a safe distance to Alan's questions, she was amused by Uncle Pat's answers and the stories each question triggered. She hadn't heard him talk this much in a long time. She had to admit, Alan's curiosity seemed to breathe new enthusiasm into Pat for the grove. It seemed so ironic—now that the grove no longer belonged to him, he seemed to care for it even more.

"Better put on those gloves, son," Pat said.

"I'm fine. They're too stiff—they slow me down."

"Ridin' in your pocket won't break 'em in. Best do that on the job."

Retta pulled off her own gloves and looked at her calloused hands. Working barehanded was out of the question, even for her. Alan would pay the price for working without his gloves. Pat gently reminded him several times, and each time Alan answered that he was doing fine without them.

She smiled and pictured the large jar of Vaseline sitting on the kitchen counter. By four-fifteen, Retta knew her mother would stick the jar in a pan of water to heat on the stove. Alan had no way of knowing—if you didn't wear gloves in the grove during the day, you wore bandages over a thick coating of Vaseline at night. She almost pitied Alan for the pain she knew he had coming. But he had been warned.

———

By the end of the week, Alan was changing the Band-Aids on his hands several times a day. They came off inside his gloves, and the rough leather interior rubbed without mercy against the blisters and cuts. At the end of each workday, he welcomed Connie's warm Vaseline treatment. He even went out and bought a soft pair of white cotton jersey gloves just to drive home.

Every night the McCarrons invited Alan to stay and eat supper with them, but each night he was so tired, all he wanted was to go back to his room, soak in a hot bath, take three aspirin, and fall into bed exhausted. He hadn't ever experienced so much pain. His hands throbbed, his back ached, and his legs were sore from climbing up and down the wooden ladders in the grove. One day he was bitten on the back of one of his hands by a spider that had crawled down into his glove. His neck burned from the autumn sun. He had blisters on his feet from his new leather work boots, and his bloodshot eyes itched from the dust.

On Friday evening, he lay in the darkness of his room, barely able to find a comfortable position. He had finally convinced the landlady to give him two extra pillows. He was flat on his back with the pillows on both sides to prop up his sore, bandaged hands and an ice bag on his forehead. He was almost asleep when he heard someone knock lightly on his door.

"Yes?"

"Conrad, you in there? It's me, Jim Henry."

Alan started to get up, then remembered he hadn't been able to manage locking his door. "Come on in, Jim. The door's open."

"Alan?" said Jim as he walked into the dark room.

"Turn on the light over on the dresser, will you? The overhead is kind of bright."

"What happened to you?" Jim said when he saw Alan's bandaged hands.

"The citrus business," Alan said. "That's what happened."

"I heard you were messing around out at the McCarron place."

"I don't think what we've been doing all week could be called messing around." Alan's voice held more than a tinge of warning.

"I see." Jim covered his mouth with his hand to smother his grin.

"You ever prune orange trees?"

"Oh, yeah. But I had enough sense to wear my gloves. I can see that you—"

"I wore my gloves," Alan said flatly. "My new leather gloves." He tried to raise himself up on one elbow, but a spasm in his back flattened him again. "Ow," he moaned. "For short trees, they sure do take a lot of stretching and reaching."

"You sure you don't need to see a doctor?" Jim asked.

"I need something, but I don't think it's a doctor."

"What then?"

"I need a new body."

"What? When you've just about got this one broke in?"

"You sound like Pat."

"Yeah, I bet I do at that." Jim laughed, found a chair, and slid it up beside Alan's bed. "Well, I've come on a mission."

"A mission of mercy, I hope," Alan said.

"I've come to invite you to my church on Sunday."

"No kidding?"

"How can you turn me down? You stood me up for basketball last week."

"Oh, Jim. I forgot all about it. I was working in the grove."

"I gathered that by the injuries."

"How about it? Ten-thirty on Sunday. I have to warn you, though. My church is a bit different."

"It's not one of those strange California types, is it?" Alan asked.

"No, nothing like that," Jim laughed. "A bit on the informal side. I hope you don't mind that."

"No, not a bit. My parents attend church. I go whenever I'm home, but I haven't been for a while."

"Good, then it's time you did." Jim stood and walked to the door. "I'm on my way to a game with Paddy. Care to come along?"

Alan's only response was a low moan.

"I thought as much. Maybe next week."

"Jim, before you go, could I ask you a question about Paddy?"

"Sure," Jim said, returning to his chair as Alan succeeded in propping himself on one elbow.

"He seems like such a bright fellow. I've talked to him several times, just in passing. Does he just sit there all the time?"

"Most of the time. He's really come a long way since I first met him. Feels pretty useless, I guess. I don't know the whole story. Sean loves him, but hasn't been able to hide his disappointment at Paddy's inability to do things—you know—"

"Like work in the grove?"

"That's my guess."

"He's really very smart. I bet he'd get a kick out of the *Journal*. What do you think?"

"The *Journal*?"

"You know, the *Wall Street Journal.*"

"Summerwind isn't what you'd call a *Wall Street Journal* town, Al. What a strange idea."

"But I think—"

"You know, you might be right. He might just take an interest in something like that."

"One of my dad's companies is listed on the Dow. Maybe I could, you know, sort of bring it up—"

"In casual conversation, I suppose." Jim didn't have the heart to tell Alan that people here didn't watch the Dow's rises and falls.

"I'll think of a way," Alan said. "Did he finish school?"

"I think so. He's mentioned having a home tutor. Yes, I think he said he finished the same year Glenna graduated."

"Why doesn't he go to college?"

"I don't think it's occurred to him—or to Sean, for that matter. All they've ever known is physical work. They're smart people, but education has always taken a backseat to hard work."

"I figured that much," Alan said, shifting to try to get comfortable.

"You're a smart fella there, Conrad." Jim paused before opening the door. "Retta's been to business college, though."

"No kidding?"

"Her father wouldn't let her work in the business until she finished a year in some sort of higher education. She took a basic business or bookkeeping course. Sean thought she would either meet someone and get married, or be happy keeping the books for the family business. She does that and works in the grove, too. She held him to his promise."

"Too bad Paddy can't take care of the books," Alan said.

"And have Retta working outside and Paddy keeping the books? Now that would be quite an adjustment for Sean to make, wouldn't it?"

"You know how much the accountants that work for my father make?"

"I have no idea."

"More than an orange grower."

"You don't say," Jim said. "Listen, Al, you take it easy, okay?"

"I'm planning to do that very thing. I'll probably stay right here until Sunday. Hope I can tie a tie," he said, lifting his bandaged hands.

"Don't even bother," Jim laughed. "This is California, remember?"

Alan laughed. "I knew I liked it here."

"And the citrus business, you like that, too?"

"Love it, can't you tell?"

Seven

Alan couldn't help but contrast the humble school gymnasium with the elegant church his parents attended. Jim and Linda led their small congregation in a familiar hymn and a few choruses with only their clear voices and their guitars to accompany them. The Conrads would have listened to the strains of a large concert pipe organ and a hundred-voice robed choir. Their minister's voice would have reverberated through massive marble arches. Jim's straightforward manner and easy tone came through a portable PA system. Alan's parents would have heard a great speech from a highly educated man standing behind an enormous, polished pulpit. Jim delivered his message seated on a stool with his notes propped on a music stand. Alan had to conclude, however, that the genuine impact of Jim's casual demeanor and simple message went beyond anything he could have imagined. Jim's message probably had more application and certainly more effect—at least on him—than anything he had ever heard in his parents' church.

For the first time in his entire life, Alan caught a glimpse of God that went beyond religion to relationship, beyond lip-service to lifestyle. These people were here because they loved coming here, not because it was the right place to be on Sunday morning—or the right place to be seen. He sensed the people attending this unlikely service were here without any sense of obligation, drawn by an overwhelming atmosphere of belonging.

After the service Consuela came over to him, her broad, striking smile extending to him approval and welcome. Immediately, she began introducing him to many of the others. He met Ben and Mattie, who reminded him of a Norman Rockwell version of grandparents. Then there were Kate and Jerry

Hill, who acted more like newlyweds than a couple with six or seven children. And of course, Holden and Karissa Kelly and their charming baby, Hope. A middle-aged general contractor named Mark seemed quite interested in the fact that he had purchased Pat McCarron's orange grove.

Consuela insisted he come home for dinner and ordered him to bring—not wear—his work boots and gloves. He agreed and happily went to collect them before driving out to the McCarron place.

"Come on," Paddy insisted after dinner, "let's see how good you are at chess."

Retta, silent all during the meal, excused herself and headed up to her room. Sorry to see her go, Alan couldn't help but watch her ascend the stairway. Joanna was playing tennis at three, and Glenna agreed to drive her to the high school courts. Sean and Connie insisted on doing the kitchen work together, although Alan guessed Connie would do the actual work and Sean would simply keep her company.

Alan soon became engrossed in the game with Paddy. Two hours later, Alan had to admit that Paddy, surprisingly, was a worthy opponent.

"Hey," Paddy said when Alan countered one of his favorite moves, "you're pretty good at this. I thought I'd beat you with that one."

"Well," Alan looked around to make sure no one could hear what he was about to say, "I need to make a confession. But I must insist you swear to secrecy."

"I swear." Paddy held up his right hand.

"I was captain of the chess team my last year in college."

"No kidding?"

"I'm afraid my grades suffered because of it." Alan looked embarrassed.

"Could you give me some pointers? I mean, Jim's been on a winning streak lately. I'd sure like to trounce him, just once."

"How about not telling him I'm coaching you?" Alan loved a good-natured conspiracy. "Let's keep it between you and me. He sure pulled one on you last week, didn't he? How'd that go, anyway? There's got to be a way to outsmart that move."

Paddy and Alan began to plan a defensive strategy against what Jim referred to as his "secret weapon." The next time they met, they would see if they could figure out an offensive strategy that would keep Jim from being able to play it in the first place.

Within an hour Sean and Connie had finished cleaning up in the kitchen and settled on the den sofa. Sean picked up the paper, and Connie lay contentedly with her feet in his lap. The only disturbance to the tranquillity was an occasional outburst from one or both of the chess players.

"You still here?" Retta said abruptly when she entered the room just before five.

"Retta!" Connie responded immediately to her daughter's rudeness.

"I was just—" Alan started to get up.

"You were nothing," Sean said. "Finish your game." The stern look he flashed at Retta made her blush with embarrassment.

"We're done here for today. Right, Paddy?" Alan said. Noticing the disappointed expression on Paddy's face, he added, "Really, I need to get back."

"To what, may I ask?" Connie's voice still held an angry edge. "Your luxury accommodations at the hotel?"

"I must admit, it's not much to brag about." Alan smiled. "But you see, I'm on a fairly strict budget. My boss keeps me on a pretty short leash." Alan rose to leave.

"I'll walk you to your car," Sean said.

The glance between Sean and Connie reminded Alan of the unspoken way his parents often communicated. He guessed that once he was safely out of earshot, Connie would have a few choice things to say to Retta about her attitude. *At least her parents like me*, he thought.

"Ever done any carpentry work, son?" Sean asked, leaning against Alan's car.

"Not much," Alan said. "My dad and I reroofed our summer place ourselves. We also paneled a basement room once. I mainly followed directions. Smashed my thumb, but other than that—well, the paneling is still standing."

"I'd like to do a bit of remodeling up in the carriage house and could use some help." Sean pointed in the direction of the building out at the edge of the yard. "Come on, I'll show you what I mean."

Sean pulled down the retractable stairway and brushed a few spider webs out of his way as he climbed to the upper floor.

"What do you want to put up here?" Alan asked.

"My brother," Sean said simply.

"Pat?" Alan asked, surprise showing on his face.

"He's going to need someplace to call home. He makes noises about becoming a world traveler, but I think he'd appreciate a place to come back to, don't you?"

"But there's the house over—"

"Over on your property, Al. How long do you think he'll be livin' there?"

Alan hadn't thought of displacing Pat. On the contrary, he wanted him to live there as long as possible. Yet he could tell that Pat was a proud man, as was Sean. They didn't take handouts from anyone, and Alan knew to offer the house would be suggesting they do just that.

"There's plenty of room up here, isn't there?"

"The building itself is as sound as a dollar. I'd get the wiring and plumbing done, of course. But I'd like to handle the rest myself. It would make it a whole lot easier if I had a go-fer."

Alan laughed at Sean's choice of words. "A go-fer? You mean someone to do all the hard work—carrying, climbing and—"

"Fetchin' stuff. Like I said, a go-fer. Somebody to go for this and go for that."

"What about the grove? The pruning?"

"Well, son, what you have been doing out there isn't really pruning. You've been just cleaning the trees. Pruning comes later. We have water coming in a week or so, and Pat always insists the cleaning be done before the November irrigation takes place. We usually start it and then get a crew to come in to finish up. Pat and Retta will stay in the grove and oversee the crew. I'd like to get this underway so that we're mainly working inside before the rains hit."

"When's that?"

"Middle of December, most of January. We'll check the roof first thing, then proceed from there. You interested in the job? I'll pay you a laborer's wage."

"But I don't need—"

"You don't need to make a livin'?"

"I never thought of it that way," Alan admitted.

"Maybe it's time you did." Sean walked away and started pacing off the floor. "Five, six—I figure close to eighteen, maybe twenty feet this way." He turned, moved some boxes around, and paced off the opposite direction. "Seven, eight, nine—close to ten yards this way. Thirty feet would be big enough to make two rooms up here."

Alan let Sean's admonition sink in. He might be right at that.

"You'll need a bathroom," Alan said. "Any ideas where to put that?"

"Let's take a look around outside." Sean led the way down the stairway and Alan followed.

The outside of the carriage house revealed an addition to one side that was almost hidden in the trees. The high-pitched roof line hadn't been extended to the addition, and the lean-to roof, Sean pointed out, could be removed, the walls re-inforced, and a second floor added without much trouble. Although the project seemed overwhelming to Alan, Sean seemed to think it to be a fairly simple one.

"We'll get some framers in here once we have the roof taken off. I think we'll end up with a nice homey place up there. Three rooms and a bath."

"What you two up to?" Pat asked, coming out of the grove. "Planning a little remodeling?"

"Thought we could put an apartment up there," Sean said, pointing to the second level.

"For our young friend here?" Pat laughed. "Why not just sweep out the place and throw an old mattress on the floor? This young fella don't need nothing fancy. Right, Al?"

"Well, it's not for him."

"No?" Pat asked.

"No, I thought we might take in a boarder," Sean said without looking at his brother.

"No kiddin'?" Pat said. "Got anyone in mind?"

"Thought we'd look for an older gent—someone quiet and stable. Maybe somebody who'd just need a place to come back to once in a while. Know anybody like that?" Sean asked.

"Might," Pat said. "How much you say the place would be goin' for?"

"Can't say, right off," Sean said. "Connie would be in charge of that department."

"The landlady, huh?"

"Yeah, she's the boss."

"Well, if I do think of someone—"

"Have them talk to her." Sean nodded toward the house.

"I might know somebody," Pat said, rubbing his unshaven chin.

"Thought you might." It was settled. Sean's face broke into a broad grin. Pat extended his hand to his brother. Sean grabbed his brother's hand and with the other slapped Pat soundly on the shoulder.

"A window out this side would be nice," Pat commented as he wandered around to the side.

"You watch," Sean said to Alan. "Now we're gonna get all kinds of advice."

"But the trick is," Alan said, "knowing who to listen to."

"Good head you got there, Conrad. Good head." Sean gave Alan an affectionate but firm pat on the back.

———

The irrigation crew arrived early Monday morning and Retta and Pat headed into the grove with the men. Sean put a hammer in Alan's hand and showed him where the ladder was stored. "Get that roof off," was his only instruction before he went into the house to join Consuela in the kitchen for coffee and a planning session.

"You put him to work?" she asked.

"Yep." Sean leaned toward the window to watch Alan carry the ladder to the side of the carriage house. "Where're you goin'?" he asked as Connie headed toward the back door.

"To give him these," she said, holding up Alan's work gloves.

"What'd you do to them?" he asked.

"Never you mind," she said. "You could have told him to treat them before he got those blisters, you know."

"Thought a blister might be good for him," Sean said as the back screen door slammed behind her.

"How'd you do that?" Alan examined the soft, supple leather gloves Connie handed to him.

"It's a special oil. I'm doing your boots, too. No wonder your feet are sore."

"I thought it was just because I'm still a little soft," Alan said almost sheepishly.

"Well, that too," she smiled. "But you'll toughen up. Got any Levi's? That roofing will eat those khakis through before the day is out. Go on now, go change and get yourself right back here."

Retta stepped back out of sight and listened to her mother talking to Alan. She couldn't help but smile. They liked him. *And,* she had to admit, *so do I.*

"You'll mother-hen anyone who gets too close," Sean said to his wife when she came back into the house.

"Never you mind about that," she warned. "Let's tend to business, shall we?"

"Cluck, cluck," Sean teased. "Little mother hen. Come on over here."

Connie moved willingly to sit on Sean's lap, welcoming his strong arms as they encircled her, pulling her close.

"Thought you two were working," Paddy said, wheeling himself into the kitchen.

"We are," Sean said. "But we're gettin' our smoochin' out of the way first. Your mama here requires a lot of attention."

Eight

As she had done most mornings of her married life, Consuela thrust her hands into the sudsy water to wash the breakfast dishes. In spite of her busy routine, pleasant thoughts of Sean filled her mind. This morning, her thoughts drifted back to her childhood. As long as she could remember, she had loved Sean McCarron. Even when they were children, he had often watched out for her, protecting her.

When he started junior high, leaving her behind in elementary school, she had ached for his company as she walked home alone for the very first time. For two years, she walked home alone, knowing that when she started seventh grade, they would once again walk home together under the eucalyptus trees. She remembered the dull ache in her heart when she discovered that he was far too busy with other interests and after-school activities to spend time with her.

It was different, however, the year she entered high school and he started his senior year. A warm feeling spread over her as she recalled that day in the grove when she had gone to take her father a cold drink and Sean had surprised her by blocking her path.

"Hi, Connie," he had said simply. "Where're you goin'?"

Without a word, she had lifted the thermos bottle in answer to his question.

"He's out there," Sean had said, nodding toward where her father was working. "Can I talk to you on your way back?"

Connie remembered how she had hurried on shaky legs to take her father his refreshment and how her mouth had become dry in anticipation of meeting Sean. He was waiting just where she had left him only moments before. She could still feel the warm grip of his broad hand as he took hers and walked slowly with her back toward the small house at the edge of the grove. She would never forget a single detail of that day, including how she suddenly became speechless with someone she had known so well all her life.

"You want to go to the homecoming dance?" Sean had asked.

"Yes," she had answered, barely audibly.

"Would you go with me?"

"Yes."

Sean's face had fairly lighted with joy, and he had exhaled a long sigh of relief. "I was afraid you'd say no."

Without answering, she had flashed him a wide smile. Connie would never forget the awkward silence that fell between them as they walked along together, Sean staring at his feet, his curly red-bronze hair gleaming in the sun. Suddenly, Sean had tightened his grip on her hand and pulled her close to him. Quickly, he had touched his lips to hers like a gentle whisper, released her hand, and disappeared once again into the grove.

From that moment, Sean and Connie both had known that someday they would marry. Neither dated anyone else, nor cared to. Something else happened that day that she'd never forget. After supper, before the family left the table, her papa announced that she was never to go to the grove alone. Too many snakes, he had said. It was a simple statement, but he and Connie's mama had exchanged glances and she had nodded in agreement. Consuela never again entered the grove alone.

She smiled at her parents' insight. Sean asked her to marry him the night she graduated from high school. The wedding was six months later, and after a short honeymoon she moved into the big farmhouse with Sean and his parents. She easily became a treasured member of the family and doted on his parents until they died. Her life couldn't have been more wonderful.

But then, she recalled, just a few years ago, Sean's faith had begun to waver. She thought he had handled the disappointment of Paddy's illness and lingering disability very well. Glenna's misbehavior had distressed him, and he finally admitted he had to leave her up to Connie because he was afraid his anger at her would flash and he might lose control. But it was the tense situation at church that finally pushed Sean too far.

The disappointment and hurt coming out of a board meeting had sent Sean walking in the grove many nights until well after midnight. He never discussed the meetings with Consuela. Other board members' wives seemed to know all the details. When she mentioned this to Sean, he angrily told her that what was discussed in those meetings was strictly confidential. Other men may share with their wives, but he wasn't going to violate the pledge he had made. Once the meeting was over, the board would speak with one voice. Who disagreed in the meetings was unimportant once a decision was reached.

Shortly afterward, the winter freeze of '51 kept Sean home from church for several weeks as he tried every known method to save their trees and keep their crop from succumbing to the bitter cold. Afterward, he never returned to church. After a year, Connie became discouraged going alone, and her attendance became irregular. Finally, she gave up going as well.

Connie first met Mattie Sloan at a community harvest festival. Mattie was the most vivacious and contented woman she had ever met, and Connie was immediately drawn to the older woman, intrigued to know the secret of her inner happiness. Within a few months, Mattie had unselfishly shared her faith, encouraging Connie to renew her commitment to Christ. It wasn't long afterward that Mattie announced the beginning of a new church. Several people had been meeting informally each Sunday evening for Bible study and prayer. Mattie was so excited about this new "fellowship" that Connie couldn't resist her invitation to attend the very first Sunday. She had been faithful to attend each week since, though Sean flatly refused to have anything to do with it.

Connie knew her energies would be wasted if she openly confronted Sean's stubborn stand. So once again she took Mattie's advice to simply pray and trust God to bring about a change in Sean's heart. For two years Connie had made it a daily practice to pray for her husband whenever she touched anything that belonged to him in the normal routine of her day.

When she picked up the dishes from the table, she prayed that God would find a way to nourish his bitter soul. As she made their bed, she asked God to bring Sean to a place of rest in Him. Picking up his clothes, she prayed that God would clothe him in garments of righteousness. Sending his shirts through the wringer and into the rinse water, Connie asked God to wash Sean's mind and heal all the deep wounds in his heart. Mending meant prayers for a restoration of Sean's walk with the Lord.

Consuela chose to face the harsh realities of her spiritual loneliness with faith. Whenever she felt the acute sense of loss, or was threatened with heavy feelings within, she simply took a deep breath, praying for God's presence to fill her, then exhaled all the doubts and fears that made her shudder inwardly. *No matter what*, she had decided, *I will trust God*.

Many times she had found solitude in the small attic above the second floor where she kept the family mementos. Kneeling in front of her mother-in-law's cedar chest, more than once she had yielded to the tears that blinded her eyes and choked her voice. Weeping aloud, rocking back and forth, Connie frequently stained the pages of her Bible with her tears. But when she came down the stairs, no one could ever guess the wild grief that had ripped through her just moments before. She might ascend the stairway quiet, withdrawn, and worried, but she was always peaceful and optimistic when she came back down. God was in charge; day after day she depended on Him for the strength to keep on believing that one simple fact.

Her morning reverie was suddenly interrupted by a voice. Startled, she turned to face Jim Henry.

"I knocked. I guess you didn't hear me," he said. Noticing her eyes were darkened with pain, he came quickly to stand beside her. "Everything all right?"

"I just—" Her voice broke. "It's Sean," she said, wiping her eyes on a corner of her apron. "I pray so hard for him, Jim. Why isn't God hearing me?"

"He's hearing you, Connie. He just isn't answering—yet." Jim stood beside her and together they looked out the window over the kitchen sink toward the orange grove. "He's not on our time schedule, we need to remember that. Don't you give up, you hear me? God's not about to give up on Sean Mc-Carron. No sir, He'll have the last word in this situation—just you wait and see."

"Thanks, Jim," Connie said. "But you didn't come all the way out here to dry my tears, now, did you?"

"No, I came looking for work."

"Work?" Connie said, surprised.

"You know I have to supplement my income from time to time. I heard that Sean was hiring a grove crew. You think he could use me?"

"You can ask him," she said. "But he's pretty much left the farm work up to Pat and Retta. He's involved in remodeling the carriage house right now. He's even got Alan working."

"I'll go see if he needs any more help. In the meantime, let's love him to Jesus, shall we?"

"If I loved him any more, I'd have to repent of idolatry." She smiled and broke into a gentle laugh. "I'm sure glad you came when you did, Jim. Thanks."

———

"Hey, McCarron," Jim called up to Sean.

"Right here," Sean answered from the roof.

"I hear you're taking on hands," Jim said.

"Maybe. You lookin' for work?"

"For a few weeks, anyway."

"Can you do more than pound a pulpit, preacher boy?" Sean teased.

"I can learn," Jim countered.

"Well, Santana's crew is workin' the grove, but I could use a carpenter."

"Yeah, that's what I heard." Jim smiled at the implication of Sean's admission.

"You a carpenter?"

"Of sorts," Jim said. "But maybe I'd do 'til the right one comes along. What d'ya say?"

"Well, come on up here, then, and give this young man a hand. We're takin' off the roof. But he needs someone to show him the difference between removin' and destroyin'." Sean tossed Jim a crowbar.

Jim caught it in his left hand while retrieving his work gloves from his back pocket with his right. Giving Alan a wink, he said, "This bully hard to work for?"

"Nah," Alan said. "More bark than bite, if you ask me."

"I don't know," Jim teased. "He's a mighty tough man."

"You two gonna sit around jawin', or you gonna earn your pay?" Sean's smile contradicted his words. "I must be crazy. Hirin' an Ivy Leaguer and a preacher to build a house. I may rue the day, but let's get to it."

From the porch, Paddy waved to Jim and Alan. Silently, Paddy ached with inner pain. If only he could be a part of those working near his father. Life's bitterness left a sour taste in his mouth. Sitting in lonely silence, he struggled to swallow the lump that lingered in his tight throat.

Paddy's loneliness may have escaped Sean's notice, but not Alan's. He looked from the older man to the deformed figure of Sean's only son sitting on the porch and a determination began to form within his mind and heart. He didn't know exactly how he'd change the situation, but Alan decided Paddy had been left out of the mainstream of activity long enough.

———

Retta worked alongside the men in the field, ignoring their raking gazes and dismissing their suggestive remarks. While she never got used to it, she expected it and was determined not to show her uneasiness. From a distance, she could see Alan working alongside her father. They seemed to enjoy taunting each other—a fact she found disturbing at first, but pleasing the more she thought about it. Alan wasn't like anyone she had ever met before. Feelings of interest were stirring sensations deep within her heart that she had vowed she would never entertain.

Determined she would never go looking for romance like so many of her friends had done, Retta had to admit she never considered it might come looking for her. The thought of Alan quickened her pulse, but the sight of Paddy sitting helplessly on the porch brought the reality of her responsibility back into sharp focus. With vengeance, she turned her attention and her clippers mercilessly back to the trees she was working on.

———

Connie swept the last of the crumbs from her kitchen floor and caught sight of Paddy sitting on the porch watching the men on the roof. Untying her apron and throwing on a smock, she took a deep breath, opened the door, and went to his side.

"How about those clippings?" she asked. "If we're going to have any decent poinsettias for Christmas, we'd better tend to them."

Paddy pulled his eyes and thoughts from the men on the roof and forced himself to smile at his mother.

"You haven't seen them lately, have you? They're the best we've ever done."

Connie pushed his wheelchair to the sunny side of the house, where more than fifty pots of the traditional Christmas plants were bushing thickly in response to the special gift Paddy had for growing things.

"Why so many, Paddy?" Connie asked.

"I thought we might want to give some to the church," he said quietly.

Tears immediately sprang to her eyes. "The church?"

"I thought I might . . . I mean, I want to go with you some-time, Mom. Would it be too much trouble for me to go?"

"Oh, Paddy," Connie said, bending to hug her son. "Of course not. I just thought—" Connie stopped, not knowing really what she thought. Glenna had flatly refused to go, and Retta always found excuses to stay home to help Sean and Pat. Connie had never even considered what Paddy might want. "You're never too much trouble, Paddy. Don't you ever think otherwise."

Nine

When the roof was completely disassembled, Sean carefully supervised the laying of the planks forming the subfloor for the second story. He put Alan to work pounding the heavy nails into the planks while Jim helped him reinforce the walls beneath to support the added weight. Fortunately, the foundation was deep enough to handle the extra load.

Jim and Sean finished before Alan did. Sean took Connie and drove to town to inquire about a plumber, and Jim took the afternoon to work on his Sunday sermon. Alan worked on, alone. Pausing for a moment in the warm afternoon November sun, he glanced toward the house, where Paddy sat reading in his wheelchair on the porch.

"Hey, Paddy," Alan called. "Get yourself over here and give me a hand!"

"Would if I could!" Paddy called back. "Not much good with a hammer, I'm afraid."

"How do you know? Ever try it?"

"Chess and house plants are more my speed," Paddy said. Secretly he wished for nothing better than to climb that ladder and be a part of the carriage house project. He couldn't help but notice with a certain amount of envy how working together drew the men closer to each other.

Alan looked around at the floor he had already finished nailing into place. He glanced at the ladder, then climbed down and located a second one stored in the lower level. Within a few minutes, he had the ladders tied securely together, side by side.

"Hey, I could use some help up there," he called, walking over to where Paddy sat on the porch.

"You crazy?" Paddy looked excited and nervous at what he thought Alan was hinting at.

"You lazy?" Alan said.

"Of course not," Paddy said a little forcefully.

"Well, I figure it this way. If you use your good leg and lean on me, we can make the climb together. How about it? You willing to give it a try?"

"You bet!" Paddy couldn't believe Alan actually wanted to help him climb to the upper floor. "I've never been on a roof before."

"It's no longer a roof," Alan said. "It's the new floor to the second story."

"I don't care what it is—just get me up there," Paddy said, excited.

Awkward at first, the two young men soon found a way for Paddy to lean on Alan while he slowly advanced up a rung, then waited for Alan to step up beside him. Reaching the top, Paddy trembled while Alan explained how he was to lean on the adjoining slanting roof and wait until Alan could get around on the other side for support. Once they were both safely on top, Paddy crawled a safe distance from the edge and collapsed on the new wood flooring.

"Now that I've gotten up here," he said, "how am I going to get down?"

"Jump." Alan's face relaxed into a wide grin. "Hey, now that you're here, you might as well lend a hand." He shoved Sean's hammer toward Paddy and picked up his own. "These are three-penny sinkers, whatever that means." Alan held up a large nail for Paddy's inspection. "We're putting them in, two to every crossbeam, like this." Alan pointed to the floor where the nails were already pounded in place. "Think you can handle that?"

"Probably," Paddy said, smiling triumphantly. He picked up the heavy hammer, and Alan showed him how to hold it nearer the end of the handle.

"Let the weight of the hammer do most of the work," Alan said. "Holding it up near the head will wear you out fast." Soon the two had worked out a system and were rhythmically pounding at the boards until Alan had to go below for more lumber. With Alan handing it up and over the edge, Paddy was able to guide it into place, even from a sitting position.

"Paddy!" Consuela's voice brought the heads of the two young men up from their task. "Pad-dy!"

"Here, Mom. I'm up here!" Paddy answered with excitement.

"How in heaven's name did you—" Her question was cut short when she spotted the ladders tied together. "Sean!" she screamed, and her husband came bounding out of the house and down the side porch stairs. With swift long strides, he crossed the yard and came to stand beside her.

"Have you lost your mind, Conrad? Do you know what could happen to him if he lost his balance and fell? Hold still, Paddy," he said firmly. "I'll have you down in a minute."

"He's all right, Mr. McCarron," Alan reassured the frightened father. "He's been helping me with the flooring. And doing a good job."

"You don't understand, do you, Conrad?" Sean climbed the ladders and came over the edge. His eyes were blazing with anger and his cheeks were bright red.

"Take it easy, Dad." Paddy tried to move closer to his father.

"I said hold still, Paddy!" Sean shouted at his son.

"*I* said to take it easy," Paddy shouted back. "You're the one who's about to lose your balance. I'm sitting down. Come on, Dad." His voice pleaded for Sean's understanding and permission to be like everyone else.

"You're coming off this roof right now, Patrick McCarron," Sean said decisively. "And," he added, directing his comment to Alan, "I'll deal with you later."

"I'm not finished up here," Paddy said firmly, refusing to move.

"Oh, yes you are," Sean argued.

"What's goin' on?" Pat's voice brought Connie's attention momentarily away from the commotion above.

"Alan's put Paddy on the roof," she said almost in tears. "Dear God, what if he fell? *Oh mi Dios, ayúdanos, por favor!*"

"How'd he get up there?" Retta asked as she joined the group.

"Alan," Pat said simply, trying not to break out into a full laugh.

"This is not funny," Connie said.

"Yeah, it is," Pat said just before breaking into a hearty belly laugh.

Retta looked from her mother to her uncle and up to the three on the floor above.

"Stop it," Connie said, turning her fury on her brother-in-law.

"Can't," Pat said between gales of laughter.

Connie swung her fist at him, and Pat caught her hand midair. Spinning around, she tried to kick at him, but he jumped easily out of her reach. She threw herself headlong at Pat, and he simply folded his strong arms around her and held her tight, all the while laughing uproariously.

"I can't believe you can laugh at this. He could get hurt up there!"

"So could young Conrad," Pat said, trying to catch his breath. "But you don't see his mama throwin' a fit out here in the dirt, do you?" Pat let go of Connie when he saw Sean attempt to pull Paddy toward the ladders. "Wait up there, Sean. Lemme give you a hand."

Bounding up the ladder, Pat took Sean's arm. "Let's give this a bit o' thought, shall we? The way you're goin', you'll both be on the ground before you know it."

In response to his brother's voice, Sean let go of Paddy's arm and straightened himself to a standing position. "What d'ya propose, Pat? He'll have to be carried down."

"Will he, now?" Pat said, winking at his nephew. "Maybe we just ought to let the boys tell us how they were plannin' to get down."

Paddy and Alan stared blankly at each other. Finally, Paddy broke the silence. "Well, I thought . . . I guess we . . . Yeah, Alan, how'd you plan to get me down, anyway?"

Afraid to even glance at Sean, Alan looked to Pat for support. Eyes twinkling, Pat simply shrugged his shoulders.

"I wasn't," Alan said with a shy smile. "We're not done yet. By next week, there ought to be a hole cut in that part of the roof and we'd be able to get down the stairs inside. That ladder there," he said pointing toward the side, "is only an *up* ladder."

"You think this is some kinda joke, do you, Conrad?" Sean roared. "You didn't think this through very well."

"Now, Sean," Pat interrupted in a tone meant to calm his younger brother. "I don't think Alan did this all alone—did you, son?" The last of his question was directed at Alan, but he was looking straight at Paddy.

"I did have some help," Alan said.

"I think, Sean," Pat said confidently, "that we ought to go below and just let the boys get out of this mess themselves."

"I'm not leavin' him up here!" Sean insisted.

"You goin' to carry him down alone?" Pat asked.

"Come on, Paddy," Sean ordered, "let's get you down from here."

"I don't think so," Paddy said softly.

"Paddy!" Connie ordered from below. "You do what your father says."

"Stay out of this, Mama," Retta said as she moved to her mother's side. "Let them handle this themselves."

"I can do it, Dad," Paddy said. "I'll be down for supper. We've only got a few more boards to lay and we'll be finished. You're standing in my way."

"Good idea," Pat said, giving Sean a gentle shove toward the ladder. "He's up here now. Might as well let him finish the job."

"I don't—" Sean started to refuse, but stopped when he saw his brother's raised eyebrows.

"I think you'd best come down and we'll discuss our ideas for gettin' him down if they can't manage it on their own."

Sean grudgingly moved toward the ladders.

"Don't leave him up there!" Connie ordered, her hands on her hips.

"Retta," Pat said, "take your mama into the house. Go on, Connie. We'll call you if we need you."

"Come on, Mama," Retta urged.

"I'm fine, Mom," Paddy said. "I'll finish up here and be down for supper." But to Alan he whispered, "Won't I?"

"It might be safer to stay up here," Alan said quietly. "I'm sorry, Paddy. I had no idea—"

"Don't blame yourself, Al." Paddy felt bad that Alan had

been caught in the middle of such an unpleasant family scene. "I'm as much to blame as you. More, maybe. I should have known how something like this would affect them. I just didn't think about that."

"Do we know how we're going to get you down?" Alan asked almost in a whisper.

"The same way we came up, I guess," Paddy answered. "What choice do we have? If we can't do it, we prove we made a mistake. We have to do it, even if we break our necks trying."

"Well," Alan said smiling, "if you go, I go. I sure don't want to face your parents by myself."

"I'll give you exactly half an hour to get those last boards on. Then you get yourselves down here!" Sean shouted from below as he paced back and forth.

"You make me nervous, pacing like that, Dad," Paddy said. "It's not easy doing this with you watching every move we make."

"I make you nervous?" Sean nearly screamed. "I make *you* nervous?"

Pat walked away and disappeared into a nearby tool shed. A few minutes later he reappeared carrying a thick rope and a good-sized pulley.

"I hardly think this a hanging offense, Uncle Pat," Paddy called out.

"Well, in your grandpa's day," Pat replied with a broad smile, "they hung a man for stealin' a mule. No tellin' what they'd do to somebody who made off with a man's boy."

Pat curled his tongue over his upper lip and climbed the ladder. Walking to the far side of the newly laid floor, he swung himself easily onto the branch of a nearby tree, where he secured the pulley from an almost invisible metal eye sticking through one of the thicker branches overhead.

"Uncle Pat," Paddy exclaimed. "What a wonderful idea! I had completely forgotten about that!"

"About what?" Alan looked totally confused.

"I had a rope swing in that tree when I was a kid. I can't believe that old thing is still up there."

Alan shaded his eyes from the late afternoon sun and looked closer at the branch. A long bolt was fastened through the middle of one of the thickest branches, with an eye protruding through the bottom side. He watched as Pat securely fastened the rope, then tested the strength of the rigging. Next Pat tied a fat knot in one end of the rope and held the other end tightly in his hands. With a swift motion, he gave a slight jump and, wrapping his legs tightly together, sat on the knot. With ease, the old man lowered himself smoothly to the ground below.

"Be right back," Pat called, once again disappearing into the tool shed on the other side of the yard.

"That man's a genius," Alan said to Paddy.

"He built a swing for me and my cousins here when we were just little kids. We used to swing each other so high our mothers would make us stop."

"How'd it work? The only swings I've ever seen were in city playgrounds."

"We'd stand on the knot, barefoot. You kind of learned to hold on with your feet. There was about five or six feet of rope below the knot—that's what we used to swing each other. Once when Retta was little we got her to catch the rope. Donny was on the rope and swinging really high. Pulled her completely off the ground." Paddy laughed at the childhood memory. "That's when Mom made Dad cut the thing down. Then, when they built this add-on to the carriage house, we couldn't swing again. Good thing we didn't think of getting up here then—we'd have jumped from the roof just to see how far we could swing out, Tarzan style. Mom would've had a fit and probably had the tree cut down."

Soon Pat returned carrying a short length of board with a hole drilled in the middle. Sean watched with interest as Pat untied the knot, shoved the rope through the hole, and retied the knot tightly once again.

"Now, try that," Pat called up to the boys. "Conrad, you help him onto the seat and we'll lower him from here when you're ready."

"Ready!" Paddy said, hanging on to the rope with both hands. Without any visible sign of fear, he scooted himself over the edge and dangled for a few moments as Sean and Pat slowly lowered him to the ground.

"Get his chair," Pat ordered Sean. "I'll hold him here."

Sean scurried toward the wheelchair, abandoned at the base of the ladders, and brought it around just in time to slip it under his son as he descended.

"Hey, can I try that?" Alan asked.

"Why not?" Paddy said, shrugging his shoulders.

"Why not, indeed?" Pat said. "Haul it back up," he said to Alan. "Swing yourself out away from the building a bit and lower yourself with your arms."

"Hey!" Alan said with enthusiasm when his feet touched the ground. "This is great!"

"I should knock some sense into you." Sean's eyes bulged with anger, and both his huge hands were clenched in tight fists as he approached Alan.

"Simmer down!" Pat ordered. "No harm done."

"No harm done!" Sean wasn't to be deterred so easily.

"Look, Mr. McCarron, I had no idea you'd feel this way. . . . I just thought—"

"No, you didn't. You didn't think at all. What a lame-brained trick to pull. I no more pull out of my driveway and you get my son up there where who knows what could've happened to him!"

"Dad!" Paddy said from his wheelchair. "Stop treating me like some sort of frail child. I wanted to be up there!"

"Stay out of it, Paddy," Sean ordered.

"That's what you want, isn't it, Dad?" Paddy shouted.

"What do you mean by that?" Sean turned to face his son.

"You want me out of everything." Paddy felt unwanted tears filling his eyes. "You can't stand the thought of me near you when you're working," he exclaimed. "I sit there day after day, watching from a *safe* distance while you do all the work. Jim and Alan come around and you show them what to do. But not me—isn't that right, Dad? You want me to stay out of it all right." Paddy couldn't suppress his anger any longer. "You want me to stay right over there," he yelled, pointing to the porch, "safely out of your way."

The impact of Paddy's outburst was evident on Sean's face. Drops of moisture clung to his damp forehead, and he blinked rapidly. In his determination not to endanger his son in any way, Sean had driven a silent wedge deep between them.

"Get my crutches, Alan. This dirt is no good for a wheel-chair."

Sean stood there, visibly amazed and shaken at his son's words. He watched helplessly as Paddy struggled to his feet and dragged his bad leg behind him through the dirt. After Paddy and Alan reached the porch, Sean turned and walked quickly around the corner of the carriage house to vent his emotions in private.

Pat waited by the empty wheelchair for his brother to return.

"Take that confounded thing down from there," Sean said, pointing to the rope rigging.

"Don't think so," Pat said clearly.

"What?" Sean spun to face his brother.

"We might be needin' it for a while yet. How else will Paddy manage?"

"I said take that thing down!" Sean said through clenched teeth.

"Take it down yourself, Sean McCarron." Pat put his finger squarely in the middle of Sean's chest. "But I tell you this. You do and you'll lose your son. He's told you that—if you heard him clearly. He's not a boy anymore, Sean." Pat put a restraining arm around Sean's shoulder. "You've got to let him choose for himself—to take his own risks. You've protected him far too long."

Sean shrugged off his brother's arm and turned to take ahold of the wheelchair. Folding it up, he lifted it to one shoulder and stomped toward the house.

Pat watched his brother disappear into his house, then turned and walked slowly toward his own home in the opposite corner of the grove. He'd have to fix his own supper tonight. They lived and worked together inside the privet hedge, but they didn't have to be in the same room. Not tonight, anyway.

"How about staying for dinner?" Paddy asked Alan after they were inside the den. "Then a game of chess."

"No, thanks," Alan said. "I think I'll head on back to my room. I'll grab a burger on the way. See you tomorrow."

Paddy struggled between his crutches, following Alan to the front door.

"I'm sorry, Paddy," Alan said, resting his hand on the door knob. "I didn't mean to get you in trouble with your folks."

"Don't be sorry," Paddy said with a smile. "I wanted to do it. And who knows, I might try it again. We got a lot more done than you could have done alone, didn't we?"

"We sure did," Alan admitted. "You're pretty good with a hammer."

"Not too bad on a rope, either, even if I do say so myself," Paddy declared triumphantly.

Alan smiled. "Not bad at all," he said.

Just as Alan opened the door and said good-night once again, Glenna came up the front walk. She passed Alan without so much as a word, leaving the cloying scent of her cologne in her wake.

"Hey, how'd you get so dirty?" she asked Paddy with a sneer.

"Working with Alan."

"Yeah, sure," she said sarcastically, brushing by her twin brother and heading toward the stairs. "Tell me another one before that one gets cold. Where is everybody?"

"How should I know?" Paddy answered gruffly.

"My, aren't we in a good mood?" she taunted.

"Drop it," Paddy warned.

Glenna paused midway on the stairway. "What's eating you?"

"I said to drop it."

"Okay by me," she said curtly and went on up to her room.

Paddy returned to the den and stood quietly for a moment beside the small table where he played chess. Impulsively, he bent slightly and with a single swoop scattered the game pieces across the floor. He turned to face the empty room and resolutely made a firm decision. He'd be back on the job first thing in the morning—even if he had to manage all by himself.

Ten

"It sure is quiet in here," Glenna observed as she sat down at the dinner table. She didn't miss the warning glance her mother shot her. "Sorry," Glenna said sheepishly, "just trying to make conversation."

"Pat coming?" Connie asked, as she set a bowl of food on the table and sat down.

"No," Sean snapped sternly.

"You sure?" she asked her husband.

"I said *no*," he shot back.

"What's eating everybody tonight?" Glenna asked.

"Never mind," Connie said.

Glenna looked at Retta, who was sitting across the table from her, and then to her twin brother at her side. Joanna was absent.

"Where's Jo?"

"She's at the library, I think," Connie said matter-of-factly. "She'll need a ride home later."

"I suppose that means me," Glenna said with disgust.

"I can go," Retta said quietly.

"You've worked hard all day," Sean said to his middle daughter. "Glenna can go."

"And I haven't?" Glenna challenged her father.

"I didn't say that," he said. "Retta has been out in the grove all day. I hardly think office work can compare with that. You'll go."

"Dad," Retta said quietly, "I don't mind going."

"No," he said flatly. "Glenna will go."

A long and uncomfortable silence fell over the family, broken only by the sounds of the utensils hitting against the dishes.

"What is going on here?" Glenna insisted, looking around at all the somber faces.

Connie found an excuse to refill a bowl in the kitchen. Paddy continued to eat, his silence communicating his refusal to tell his sister about the incident with Alan earlier that afternoon. Retta's eyes never lifted as she picked at the food on her plate.

"For heaven's sake, daughter," Sean said roughly. "Eat your dinner. Don't stab at it like that."

Glenna shot a surprised look in her father's direction. He never spoke angrily to Retta.

Retta put her fork on her plate and dropped her hands in her lap, her insides churning. She had never spoken up to her father before—even when she was convinced he was wrong. But this was going too far. Barely able to keep her silence, she fought for composure. Just then, her mother returned and sat down.

"Out with it," Sean said, slamming his fork against his plate. "You've got something to say—so say it!" His bright blue eyes flashed with anger as he glared at Retta.

Raising her cold gaze to meet her father's angry eyes, Retta took a deep breath. She noted his taut face and the muscle that flicked angrily because of his set jaw. This was not going to be easy. But someone had to speak up—not just for Paddy's sake, but for Alan's. Groping for the right words, she was aware that everyone was staring at her. Paddy's eyes pleaded with her to speak up; Consuela's piercing look warned her to be careful. Glenna's expression dared her to continue, and Sean's stare contained an open challenge.

"Are you interested in my opinion?" Retta asked. Her calm tone belied the knot in her stomach.

"I said say it, didn't I?" Sean didn't even try to conceal his anger.

"That's not what I asked," she said.

"Just say what you have to say and be done with it," Sean ordered.

"Are you interested or not?" Retta's voice rose slightly with irritation.

"Okay, I'm interested. Is that what I'm supposed to say?"

"Forget it," Retta said in defeat.

"Pardon me?" Sean's brows knit together in an affronted frown.

"Dad, do you think you're the only one with an opinion worth listening to?" Glenna said.

"You stay out of this," he warned, pointing at his eldest daughter.

"Somebody has to get to the—"

"I said, you stay out of it. This is none of your business, young lady."

"Like everything else around here," Glenna retorted as she stood suddenly. "I work outside—so I'm an outsider, is that it, Dad?"

"This has nothing to do with you," Sean insisted.

"Of course not," Glenna said angrily. "Like everything else that happens around here."

"And what do you mean by that remark?"

"You don't want to know, Sean McCarron," Glenna shot back.

"Glenna! You'll not speak to your father in that tone of voice," Consuela said, raising her voice to match Glenna's.

Glenna glanced toward the front hallway, grateful for the convenient ringing of the telephone. "I'll get it," she said, hurrying out of the room.

"Retta," Connie said firmly, "I believe your father has asked you for your opinion."

"No, he didn't," Retta said. "He has given me permission to speak and nothing more. It's not the same thing, Mother."

"It's Joanna," Glenna said from the hallway. "I'll go get her."

"Wait!" Retta called after her sister but looked directly at her father. "I'll go with you."

"We're not finished here, young lady." Sean's irritation was escalating.

"Yes, Dad. I think we are—at least I am." Retta stood, looked at her father, and turned to hurry after Glenna.

Watching helplessly as his daughters left in what he considered open defiance, he turned to his wife. "What in the world has gotten into everyone? Have our children all gone mad?"

"I'll be in my room," Paddy said quietly.

"Paddy," Consuela said pleadingly.

"Let him go, Connie," Sean said. "Let me have the rest of our dinner in peace."

"Sean McCarron," Connie said softly, her eyes brimming with tears. Standing, she quickly gathered the plates filled with food her children had left. "You can not only have your dinner in peace," she said, "you can have it alone." Turning on her heel, she headed for the kitchen.

Sean sat in stony silence, his temples throbbing with anger. Grabbing his steak knife, he furiously sawed at the innocent piece of beef on his plate. Stabbing a generous hunk of meat, he paused, then flung it—fork and all—against the opposite wall.

Consuela stood silently at the sink, her tears flowing freely down her face. Hearing a thud against the wall, she put her hand across her mouth to stifle her deep sobs. *Dear God*, she prayed silently, *help that man!*

"I'm not going to the library to get Joanna," Glenna said once she and Retta were out of the driveway.

"What?" Retta said, surprised.

"She's over at Jake's." Glenna's mouth spread into a thin-lipped smile.

"How'd she get there?"

"Friends, I guess. Anyway, she doesn't need a ride home. Howie's got his father's car. He'll bring her home later."

"Then, where are we going?"

"To Scottie's," Glenna said, referring to a bar in the middle of Summerwind's small downtown.

"Glenna," Retta said, "I don't want to go to Scottie's."

"You should have thought of that before you tagged along."

"Take me back home," Retta insisted.

"You really want to walk back into that?"

"No, but I certainly don't want to go to Scottie's. Drop me by Jake's and I'll hitch a ride with Howie and Jo-Jo."

"She'll be thrilled to see you," Glenna said sarcastically. "She's been trying to get him alone for weeks. I think he wants to ask her to go steady. And she wants to, too. In the worst way."

"She's too young to go steady," Retta said.

"You sound just like Dad."

"Well, she is."

"Listen, Retta, you may want to be an old maid, but the rest of us sure don't. You need to lighten up a little. Put on a dress now and then. Who knows, you might even catch yourself a boyfriend."

"No thanks," Retta said flatly.

"Hey," Glenna said. "What's going on at home, anyway?"

"You wouldn't believe it," Retta said.

"Great," Glenna complained. "Dad says it's none of my business, and you say I wouldn't believe it. I wish someone— just for once—would treat me like a member of the family!"

Retta took a long look at the frustrated expression on her sister's face. "All right," she said. "I'll tell you." In the few minutes it took to get to Jake's Burger Bar, Retta told Glenna about Paddy and Alan's escapade on the roof earlier that afternoon.

"Well, what do you know!" Glenna said when Retta finished. "Paddy said he had been working with Alan. I didn't believe him."

"I told you you wouldn't believe it."

Glenna threw her head back and let out an uproarious laugh. She tried to control herself when she saw Retta's angry expression but couldn't contain her amusement at the scene Retta had described. She laughed so hard tears coursed down her face. "I bet Dad about popped a vein!" she said finally, wiping her tears. "I wish I had been there to see it."

"It's not funny," Retta said, opening the car door.

"I think it is," Glenna said, breaking into laughter again.

"You saw the look on Dad's face." Retta closed the car door and leaned in the open window. "He didn't think it a bit amusing. I'm surprised he didn't fire Alan on the spot." Retta stood back and watched her sister pull the car away from the curb and out into traffic. Then she went in to find Joanna and Howie.

Spotting her sister coming toward her booth, Joanna asked, "What are you doin' here?"

"I came with Glenna. You think I could catch a ride home with you and Howie?"

Joanna's face fell with disappointment. Howie looked more than a little disturbed by the request. They looked at each other, then Howie spoke. "I was hoping to spend a few minutes with Jo-Jo alone."

"Fine," Retta said. "Drop me off and go somewhere, then."

"And how would you explain that to the folks?" Joanna asked.

"You don't have to worry," Retta said. "I probably wouldn't even see them. It's a little tense at the house right now."

"Really?" the youngest McCarron sister said.

"Really," Retta said rolling her eyes. "Just get me home; I'll walk up the drive. They won't even know how I got there."

"Got where?" a familiar voice interrupted.

Retta turned and found herself staring into Alan Conrad's deep blue eyes.

Joanna quickly introduced Howie to Alan and explained that Alan was working for her father, but said nothing about the sale of Uncle Pat's share of the orange grove.

"Home," said Retta without emotion.

"You just got here," Alan said.

"And I want to go home."

"Why so soon?" Alan inquired.

"Because," she said without looking at him directly.

"I can give you a lift," he offered.

"No thanks," she refused, instantly.

"Retta!" Joanna pleaded. "Howie and I have other plans. Can't you let him take you home?"

"I'd be glad to do it," Alan said, a smile teasing his lips.

"If it were any other time . . ." Howie shrugged his shoulders. "But like I said, tonight is kind of special."

Retta glanced from Howie to meet Joanna's pleading eyes.

"Okay," she said, heaving a deep sigh.

"Hey, it won't be that bad," Alan said with a laugh. "Come

on, do you have to go right now? I haven't had anything to eat and my burger's probably almost done." He motioned toward a booth a couple of places behind Joanna and Howie's. "I think they want to be alone, anyway."

"Thanks, Alan," Joanna said brightly. "You're just an absolute doll."

Sitting across from Alan, Retta suddenly felt hungry when his hamburger arrived.

"Let's cut this one in half—" he said.

"No, I couldn't do that," she interrupted.

"I wasn't going to give it to you," he said. "I was only suggesting we cut it in half and order another while we eat this." He signaled to the waitress without waiting for her to object.

"Now," he said, settling back after they had eaten both hamburgers, "what brings you out tonight? I've never seen you here before."

"You come here often?" she asked, avoiding his question.

"You might say that."

"Really? I'm surprised," she said.

"Not much else in town. I'm not really suited for the bar scene."

"I know what you mean. Me neither."

"You're not old enough," he said.

"Almost."

"You're barely twenty," he said. "Pat told me."

"Hey, you two." Jim's friendly voice broke into their conversation. "Look who's here," he said to his wife over his shoulder. "You mind a little company?"

Linda joined them and they ordered ice cream sundaes. Alan decided to have one too, but Retta refused, accepting only a refill of her Coke.

Retta noticed how easily they slipped into friendly conversation.

"Get that floor done?" Jim asked.

"Well, now, that floor," Alan said slowly. Casting a furtive glance at Retta, he wondered if this was a conversation he wanted to have in her presence.

"What? Something go wrong?" Jim asked, looking at Retta.

"Not exactly," Retta said, exchanging knowing looks with Alan.

"What's this all about?" Jim said with a slight laugh. "You guys know something you're not telling?"

"I'm not sure you'd want to hear about our afternoon," Alan said and let out a low whistle. "I almost lost my job. That should tell you enough."

"Not on your life," Jim probed.

Linda watched Retta's face for a moment before laying her hand on her husband's arm. "Maybe it's none of our concern, honey."

"I'm sorry," Jim said quickly. "I didn't mean to butt in or anything."

"You're not butting in, Jim," Alan said. "It's just a sore subject at the moment."

"I see," Jim said, raising his eyebrows. "Well, then, what's up for tomorrow? You need some help? I'm sure Sean wouldn't mind if I pitched in. We'd have it done in no time."

"It's done," Alan said, wishing he knew how to read Retta's mind.

"How's that?"

"It's done. I don't know what we'll do tomorrow." Alan didn't take his eyes from Retta's face. Noticing her discomfort, he tried to change the subject. "Maybe I'll go back out and work in the grove. Or," he paused, waiting for her to lift her gaze to his, "maybe I'll just take some time off."

"You can't take time off now," Jim said. "Sean wants to have that upper story framed and closed up before the holidays. That only gives us a few weeks. How are you at framing?"

"I don't know," Alan admitted. "I've never done it before."

"Well, you hadn't laid a subfloor before either, and look at what a whiz you were at that. I can't believe how you got that done all by yourself."

"He didn't," Retta said finally. "He had help."

"Oh?"

"Paddy," she said without explanation.

"Pardon me?" said Jim, his puzzled expression emphasizing his question.

"I said Paddy helped him."

"I didn't know Paddy could—"

"We didn't either," Retta said, staring at her Coke. As much as she wanted to, she couldn't bring herself to meet Alan's gaze.

"I don't understand," Jim said.

Linda cast a glance in his direction, hoping he'd drop the conversation or talk about something else. It was obvious that something had happened and that they were reluctant to talk about it. "Jim," she said, "I don't think this is any of our business."

"It's all right, Linda," Retta said. "You're bound to hear about it sooner or later. And I'd really like to hear Alan's version, myself."

Alan took a deep breath and began, slowly at first, to fill them in on what had happened.

"And you know what's so sad?" he said, concluding his account of the afternoon's adventure. "Paddy really liked being up there. You should've seen how he took hold of that hammer. It was like he'd been holding one all his life. He's really got a lot of strength in his upper body. Too bad Sean . . ."

"Sean?" Linda asked.

"He means it's too bad my father is being such a fool about this," Retta said.

"I don't think I'd call him a fool," Alan said.

"Well, what would you call him, then?" Retta said, her voiced edged with irritated anger.

"I'd call him protective," Alan said gently.

"What would Paddy call him?" Jim asked quietly. "Retta?" He directed his question at her. "How is Paddy? How did he handle this?"

"Quiet," Retta said. "He's hardly said a word since."

"He sure wasn't quiet earlier," Alan said.

"He wasn't?" Retta finally looked Alan straight in the eye.

"No, he wasn't," he said, shaking his head. "He really told your father off."

"He did?" Retta could barely believe what Alan was saying.

"Right after you took your mother inside, he let him have it with both barrels. If he had been standing, he might have thrown a punch. He was really mad."

"Paddy?" said Retta, her eyes wide in amazement.

"Yes, Retta, your brother. Your soft-spoken, uncomplaining, easygoing brother."

"Finally," Jim said knowingly.

"What do you mean by that?" Retta asked.

"He's been holding that in for a long time, Retta," Jim said.

"Paddy? I live with him. I've never noticed him holding anything in."

"You've never noticed because Paddy hasn't let anyone notice. But something like this was bound to happen sooner or later."

"Are you telling me you know my brother better than I do?" she challenged Jim.

"Not better, really." Jim searched for the right words when he saw the pain in her face. "Maybe just some things—some part of him, his feelings about certain things."

"That he hasn't even shared with his family," she scoffed.

"It's not that he doesn't want to." Jim reached for Retta's hand, but she quickly dropped it in her lap.

"Then why doesn't he?"

"He doesn't think he *can*," Jim said gently.

"He's told you that?"

"Not so much told me. But I've seen it. You look in his eyes, Retta. Maybe he'd like to tell you."

"Maybe I will," she said softly, purposely hiding the determination she felt to make sure he did. Turning to Alan she said, "I'd like to go home now, if you don't mind."

Eleven

Once they were in Alan's car, Retta felt both better and worse for being alone with him.

"You sure you want to go home right now?" he asked.

"Of course," she said.

"I just thought you might like to take a drive or something first." He caught a glimpse of her looking at him out of the corner of his eye. "You know, to sort out your thoughts, or something."

"I don't know. I'm just so confused." Immediately, she regretted telling him.

"About what?"

"About everything," she said, turning to look out her window.

"Mind if we go for a drive and talk about it?" he ventured.

"I don't care," she said. She knew that Alan was a large part of her confusion. She liked being with him, driving with nowhere specifically in mind. But she also knew she feared being with him. As gentle and kind as he was, Retta recognized him as a threat to the wall she had so carefully built around her heart.

"Tell me," he said after a few moments of silence, "how did you get interested in working in the grove? I mean, it's wonderful out there, being in the fresh air and all. But really, do women often work in the citrus business—I mean right out in the groves themselves?"

"Many do," she said. "My mother worked out there until she had to stay inside to take care of her babies."

"I didn't realize," he said quietly. "It's just so—"

"Unladylike?"

"No, I didn't mean that. At least not in your case." He glanced at her. "Did I offend you?"

"No," she said quietly.

"I meant that working in the grove hasn't . . ." He groped for the right words.

"I know what you mean," she said. More than once she had noticed how he had looked at her. He wasn't the first man to show masculine appreciation toward her. Even the cat calls she got occasionally from the hired hands made her aware of how surprising it was for men to find her working alongside them in the grove.

"What I'm trying to say, Retta, is that I find you, well—"

"Please don't, Alan."

"Listen, Retta. I don't know what I've done to make you not like me. Have I been rude to you? Have I said something to make you angry?"

"No," she said flatly.

Alan pulled the car to the side and shut off the motor. Orange trees lined both sides of the road, and only the moon streaming in the windshield softly illuminated the inside of the car.

"What are you doing?" she asked nervously.

"Listen, Retta," he said, turning in the seat to face her. "We need to have a talk. Maybe we need to clear the air or something."

She stared wordlessly out the front of the car, her heart pounding. She stubbornly refused to look at him.

"Retta," he said softly. "Retta, please look at me."

She loved the ease with which her name rolled off his tongue. Turning, she saw a twinkle of moonlight in his eyes as he looked at her.

"That's better," he said. He cleared his throat, and when he spoke his voice was calm, his gaze steady. "I can't for the life of me figure you out."

She dropped her eyes, afraid to look at him any longer.

"See? There you go again." His eyes wandered over her dark hair, caught up in the usual braided ponytail. "I try to get to know you, and you pull away. Am I such a bad guy? How would you know? Why won't you give yourself a chance to get to know me?"

She nervously traced imaginary lines on her jeans with one

hand and tucked a stray tendril behind her ear with the other.

"It's not you," she said quietly. "Not really."

"I'm listening," he said.

"I just don't date, that's all."

"A pretty girl like you? I find that hard to believe. I bet all the guys in town would give their right arm to take you out."

Retta blushed, shocked that he could speak so freely. "Not really. Not anymore."

"Not anymore? You mean you used to go out?"

"I used to date," she said. "All during high school, anyway. Then I made this deal with my dad."

"What deal?"

"I wanted to work in the grove—you know, in the family business. But he said I had to go to college first. I talked him into business college. I think he thought I'd meet someone, fall in love, and change my mind."

"So you stopped dating to prove him wrong?" Her slight shrug was barely perceptible in the darkness. "Have I guessed right?"

"Almost," she said. "I didn't think it was to prove him wrong, necessarily."

"But you were afraid he might be right."

"I guess."

"What happens now?"

"Now?" she asked.

"Retta," he said in a low voice. "I find you the most attractive girl I've ever met in my entire life. I talked my father into letting me stay in Summerwind just so I would have an excuse to be near you. I want to know you better—a lot better."

Clearly surprised at what he was saying, Retta found the closeness of the dark car suddenly confining. Even though the evening was chilly and she had neglected to grab her sweater in her hurry to catch up with Glenna, she rolled down the window, hoping for a bit of fresh air.

"And you're not about to give me the time of day. Am I right?" he said.

She met his accusing eyes without flinching. "I'm not interested in any relationship right now, Alan," she said.

"That was a quick answer," he said. "Too quick."

"What do you mean by that?"

"It sounds rehearsed. You've said it before, haven't you?"

"I don't know what—" she said, but as she turned and their eyes met, her voice broke off in midsentence. Even in the darkness, she could feel the penetrating honesty coming from deep within his hauntingly blue eyes. "Don't look at me like that."

"Like what?" he said. "It's dark in here, how do you know how I'm looking at you?"

I can feel it, she wanted to scream. *I can feel it now just like I can whenever you look at me.*

He leaned toward her and lowered his voice. "How do you know I am looking at you at all? Much less *how* I'm looking at you?" He stared at her in the darkness and waited in silence for her response.

In her heart, Retta had always feared this moment would come. She had been so careful not to lead boys on. She had been even more so with Alan Conrad. Yet here she was, sitting on a darkened street in his car. The strange surge of emotion she felt frightened and defeated her. She willed her heart to keep still, but it ignored the command and pounded within her.

"Take me home, Alan," she whispered hoarsely. "Please."

If she were to keep her wall of defense against him, she had to get out of this car. She glanced out the front, then out the back of the car, fighting back a wave of panic that was beginning to engulf her.

"Please, take me home." She was barely able to lift her voice above a whisper. "Or," she said, "I'll walk home." It took all the strength she had to maintain her fragile control.

"I'll take you home," he said sarcastically. "I'm not one for keeping a lady against her will. But tell me one thing, Retta McCarron. Tell me honestly," he said.

"If I can," she responded, promising nothing.

"Tell me you don't feel any attraction for me."

"No," she whispered, "I am not attracted to you."

His hoarse whisper broke the uncomfortable silence that fell, then lengthened between them. "You're lying."

She swallowed hard, then lifted the dark lashes that lay

heavily on her cheeks and boldly met his gaze.

"You're lying," he repeated. His voice was calm, even soothing, yet all the while oddly disconcerting.

He reached across the back of the seat and gently touched the braid that hung halfway down her back.

She stiffened, met his eyes with hers, then quickly looked away, pretending not to understand what she saw there.

"What are you afraid of?" he asked quietly.

"Nothing," she lied. Taking a deep breath, she tried to relax.

Starting the car, he paused before putting it in gear. "Now that I've told you, I suppose you'll find a way to avoid me."

"Do I have to?"

"Not on my account," he said. "Like I said, I'm not into forcing my way into anyone's life. You've made it perfectly clear. You're not interested. That makes it easier, I guess. I thought I saw some interest in your eyes. But, as you've said, I guess I was mistaken."

"I guess," she said.

But you're not sure, are you? the question echoed through her mind and heart. Retta McCarron knew she was lying, not only to him—but to herself.

Pulling away from the curb, they drove the rest of the way to the McCarron place in silence. It was she who broke the silence this time.

"Alan?" She wanted his insight on the afternoon's events.

"Hmm?" he said, pulling the car to a stop and shutting off the engine. Though barely inside the driveway, he shut off the car lights.

"Did Paddy really enjoy helping you this afternoon?"

"He really did," Alan said. He crossed his arms across the top of the steering wheel and leaned his forehead on them. "He really did, Retta. I'm not just saying that to excuse my part of the whole fiasco. I can't imagine being cooped up like that. He must get tired of just sitting there. Staying out of everyone's way isn't my idea of being very productive. What amazes me is how he stays so cheerful. It would drive me crazy."

"I've thought about that, too," she said. "But whenever I've suggested he help us out, Dad comes apart at the seams."

"Do you know why he's so set against Paddy having as normal a life as possible? There's just so much I can't understand."

"Dad will let him help me sort when the crop is picked. That's about all he'll allow."

"Imagine how that makes Paddy feel," Alan said thoughtfully.

"I don't think that has ever crossed Dad's mind," Retta said.

"Until today." Alan turned and looked at her in the darkness.

"Today?" she asked.

"I think today was a significant day in the life of Paddy McCarron."

"How do you know?"

"I was there, remember?"

"How can I forget?"

"Paddy said some pretty strong things to your father."

"Paddy?"

"Why are you so surprised at that?"

"Paddy never crosses him—*never*," she said.

"Before today." Alan looked from her face toward the fully lighted house. "I just pray that he heard him."

"Dad can be so stubborn sometimes," Retta said.

"Is that where you get it?"

"I'm not stubborn," she said forcefully.

"You're not?" he asked, looking directly into her eyes. "Then, Retta McCarron, I'm asking you again—is there not even a slim chance. . . ?" He let his voice trail off.

"Alan," she said softly. "Please, don't."

"You're weakening," he teased.

Suddenly she felt anxious to escape the closeness of the car—and his disturbing presence.

"Will you think about it, at least?" he asked.

"Maybe," she said smiling, hoping to lighten up the situation for both their sakes. Opening the car door, she turned to get out. Then over her shoulder she said, "And then again, maybe I won't."

Alan grabbed her long braid, pulling her back toward him. When she felt her head touch his chest, her heart threatened to explode.

"You are so stubborn." His voice was husky and thick. "Please . . . think about it."

"Okay, okay!" she promised, laughing to cover her nervousness. "I'll think about it."

With her spoken promise, he released his hold on her braid and she sprang from the car. Walking in front of his car, she motioned to him in the dark. Turning on the headlights, he saw her holding up both her hands, fingers crossed.

"King's X," she called cheerfully before turning and running away from him and up the driveway to the house.

Twelve

At Scottie's Bar and Grill, Glenna found Donny and Bobby in their usual booth. The regulars called to her as she crossed the dark, smoke-filled room and slid in to sit beside her cousins.

"What took you so long?" Bobby said between gulps of his beer. "We almost gave up on you."

"Had to drop Retta by Jake's," she said.

"Isn't she getting a little old to hang out there?" Donny asked.

"Retta doesn't hang out any place except home. Tonight was an exception. We sort of had a tense situation at home. Everyone who could escape did. Poor Paddy. Oh, well, he probably went to his room."

"What's going on?" the twin brothers asked in unison.

Glenna recounted the story of Paddy's afternoon and how he openly defied his father.

"I bet Uncle Sean was fit to be tied," Donny said.

"I wondered when Paddy would finally get up the nerve and stand up to your old man," Bobby said.

"You know what gets me," Glenna said slowly. "That Alan Conrad. The way my dad looks at him you'd think he was a gift sent from heaven or something. And the way *he* looks at Retta—makes me sick."

"Or jealous?" Bobby teased.

"Get real," she said sarcastically.

"You have to admit," said Donny, "there's something about a rich boy from the East that makes girls drool."

"Hey, what's he got that we haven't got?" Bobby wondered aloud.

"Money, for one thing," Glenna said, then added with a laugh, "and decent clothes."

Bobby and Donny had only marginally cleaned up since leaving work. Bobby had simply removed the coveralls he wore at the garage and donned a clean pair of jeans and a white T-shirt. Donny had come straight from his job of driving a gravel truck in the jeans and shirt he had worn all day.

"You saying we don't dress good?" Bobby said in mock ignorance.

"I'm saying you guys should consider taking a shower before you come out into public."

"This isn't public," Bobby said, laughing.

"No, this is Scottie's!" Donny joined in.

"No place like home, right?" Glenna said.

Donny left the booth to put a few quarters in the large jukebox in the corner. When he returned, he had a serious look on his face. "We need to get rid of that Ivy-League brat, that's for sure." He sat heavily back on the booth bench beside Glenna. "If we don't, he'll ruin everything."

"We were counting on having someone buy the ranch and plunk down the cash, and then we were going to split." Bobby drained his glass and raised it to signal the bartender for another.

"And you think Uncle Pat will just give you the money, right?" Glenna said.

"It'll be ours someday, anyway. Why shouldn't he?"

"Because he still has to live somehow," she said. "That's why."

"There should be plenty for that," Bobby said. He winked at the waitress delivering his drink.

"I don't get it," she said. "How does Alan Conrad interfere with your plans?"

"The old man's not as easy to persuade," Donny said. "He's almost taken a new interest in the place, now that Conrad's here."

"I wonder . . ." Bobby said.

"Oh, oh," Glenna warned. "Better look out, Bobby's thinking again."

"Lay off," Donny said. "He comes up with a good idea once in a while—well maybe once, anyway."

"Knock it off, you two," Bobby said. "Listen, maybe Conrad

can help us all get what we want. Maybe we've been going about this all wrong. Suppose he could be encouraged to pull more stunts like he did today. If Uncle Sean could be persuaded to see him as a threat to the family—you know, like getting Paddy to stand up to him—maybe Uncle Sean wouldn't be so interested in living next door."

"You know," Donny said, "you might have a good idea there." He smiled and relaxed against the back of the seat. "If Sean McCarron thought the man was chasing one—or more—of his lovely daughters, encouraging his precious son to defy him . . . You know, guys, it might just work."

The three put their heads together and began discussing ways to get Alan even more deeply involved in the McCarron family. If they could let him in far enough, then begin making him look like an intruder instead of a welcome guest, they might not only persuade Pat to divide the income from the sale of his property—but Sean to sell out as well.

"One thing bothers me," Glenna said. "What do you mean by 'one or more of his daughters'?"

Bobby and Donny exchanged wry grins. "Why, little cousin, I think you know exactly what we mean." The two brothers gave her knowing looks.

"Me?" she said incredulously.

"Who else? Jo-Jo?"

"No, of course not. She's too young. Besides, all she thinks of is Howie."

"Afraid you can't do it?" Bobby teased.

"Of course not," Glenna said, frowning.

"Well, then," Donny said. "It's time to turn on the old charm, cuz. That is, if you haven't lost your touch."

"Just watch this," Glenna said looking around the room. Spotting a man she'd never seen before, she nodded in his direction. "Just watch this. Five bucks says he'll be asking me to dance within ten minutes."

"Ten if you can do it in five," Bobby reached into his wallet and put a bill on the table.

"Twenty," Donny said with a smile, "if he asks to take you home."

"You're on," Glenna said. Getting up from her seat, she

sauntered toward the ladies' room, pausing at the doorway and flashing the unsuspecting stranger a shy, seductive smile.

————

"You're gettin' home mighty late for a school night, young lady," Sean said from the den as Joanna came in.

"Sorry, Daddy," she said sweetly, coming quickly into the room where he was sitting in semidarkness. "Where is everybody? They leave you up all by yourself? My goodness, you must be lonesome sitting here all by yourself. I would have come home earlier had I known." She flashed her father the practiced smile she reserved just for him for those times she needed to talk her way out of a tight spot. "I know it's late, but it couldn't be helped. I'll watch more carefully, next time. Will you forgive me, just this once?"

"It's not a matter of forgiveness." Sean could feel his anger toward her melting. "Tomorrow's a school day. You need your rest."

"You're right, Daddy," she said and came to sit beside him. Leaning into him, she said, "I'm so lucky."

"How so?"

"To have a Daddy that worries about me so much." Her voice was tinged with a higher, childlike pitch.

"Well," Sean said. "I do worry about all my girls."

"That's why we all love you so much," she smiled. Snuggling closer to her father, she continued her ploy. "You know we all love you, don't you, Daddy?"

"Your mother would ground you for coming home this late. You know that, don't you?" he said.

"Where is Mama, anyway?" Joanna asked, changing the subject.

"Upstairs. She went to bed early." Sean knew that though his wife had gone upstairs earlier than usual, there was little chance she was in bed asleep.

"Is she all right? She's not sick or anything."

"I don't think so," Sean said. "She seemed a bit edgy tonight," he lied. "I think she just needed some rest. She'll be okay tomorrow. But you, young lady—"

"I better go on up, too." Joanna sprang to her feet. Reaching the door, she turned and rewarded Sean's tolerance with a broad, white smile. "Thanks, Daddy, you're so cool."

"Go on with you," he said gruffly. But inside he was grateful that at least one member of his household wasn't angry with him tonight.

Retta had come in quietly an hour before. Without a word she had gone straight to her room. He hadn't called out to her, not wanting to risk any more of her displeasure tonight. She hadn't really confronted him—at least not to the degree that he knew she could. *And who knows*, he admitted to himself, *maybe with good cause.*

Glenna wasn't home yet, but then, she was almost twenty-three. Unlike Joanna, Glenna would be offended if she thought he waited up for her. Slowly, Sean rose to his feet and stretched, arching his back. He looked toward the stairway. "Might as well face her," he said into the darkened empty room. "Won't get any rest until I do."

Approaching the stairway, he heard Joanna's voice in the hallway above. "Yes, it's me, Mama. No, I came in a while ago. I've been sitting downstairs with Daddy."

Coming up the stairway, he shot his youngest daughter a warning. "Jo-Jo," he whispered loudly. He could hear his wife's voice from within their bedroom, but he couldn't make out the words.

"You can ask him yourself," she said, then turned to face Sean and threw him a kiss before entering her room and shutting the door quietly behind her.

From inside his downstairs bedroom, Paddy heard his father climb the stairs. For hours he had lain in the dark, ready to pretend sleep if necessary to avoid talking to him. Once he was sure Sean was upstairs and his parents' bedroom door was shut, he sat up and turned on the light. Reaching underneath his bed, he pulled out an encyclopedia. Finding the page he had marked earlier, he began to read with fascination. A pulley may work, but a block and tackle, now that would be much easier. With a block and tackle he just might be able to manage getting up there by himself. Getting the block and tackle rigged would be impossible alone. For that he'd have to convince Uncle Pat. Paddy took a deep breath and decided he'd have to have all his facts right and use all the power of persuasion he could possibly muster.

————

"All right, I'll do it," Glenna said as she pocketed Donny's twenty-dollar bill. "As you can see, it shouldn't be too difficult."

"Not for you," Bobby said. "You certainly can turn the charm on when you want to."

"But," Donny said, "she had us here to bail her out if necessary. When you go after Conrad, you'll be on your own, understand?"

"No problem," she said with smug confidence. "Should be as easy as taking candy from a baby."

"I don't know," Bobby said. "Have you ever tried to take a guy away from Retta before?"

"She's never had a guy I've been interested in before. Besides, I have more mercy than that."

"Mercy!" Donny said, laughing. "Is that what you call what you used on that chump over there?"

"No," Bobby said. "That was what you call no mercy." He winked at his cousin.

Saying she needed to head for home, Glenna left her cousins sitting at their table and walked toward the door. Bobby nodded in the direction of the man at the bar who had been dancing with her a few minutes before. Donny turned just in time to see him down his drink, snub out his cigarette, and start toward the door behind Glenna. Together, the twin brothers crossed the room and got between the man and the door.

"Come on, friend," Bobby said.

"We'd like to buy you a drink," Donny finished his brother's sentence.

"No thanks," the man said. "I want to have a word with the little lady there."

"Not tonight," the brothers said in unison. Coming on opposite sides, they took the man's arms and led him back to the bar.

"Three beers," Bobby said to the barkeep. "Then three more."

————

Up in her room, Retta was still awake when she heard Glenna come in. She tuned out the familiar sounds her sister made getting ready for bed and returned to her own thoughts—thoughts filled with Alan Conrad.

She had no way of knowing that Glenna's thoughts were filled with him too.

Thirteen

All through the night, Retta tossed and turned, unable to push the confusing thoughts and threatening fears out of her mind and rest. She had to admit, at least to herself, that her attraction for Alan was growing. At the same time, her resentment toward the sale of Uncle Pat's share of the family orange grove remained as strong as ever.

She let her mind drift back to the evening before. She hadn't been alone with Alan or had a real conversation with him before. The tightness in her stomach returned whenever she remembered the way he had looked at her. Her pulse quickened as she thought about how he had leaned toward her and accused her of lying about the attraction between them.

Somehow, admitting she was attracted to Alan threatened her love for family traditions and the security she found in the family-owned business. Yet she knew that hanging on to her love for tradition threatened any chance she might have for a relationship with Alan.

Nothing would please her father more than if she found a nice young man and settled down. But was Alan that man? And could she hope to have a normal life with any man? Who would keep the family business going once her parents were unable to do it alone, if not her?

She thought of each person, reviewing what she already knew—no one else would do it. Not Glenna, who wanted to sell out and move to a "nicer" part of town. Not Paddy, whose bout with polio at the age of eight ended his father's dreams that he would take over the business and keep it functioning the same as it had for three generations. Not Joanna, the flighty teenager whose life centered around her growing collection of 45s and dancing slowly to the smooth sounds of Pat Boone with Howie, the grocer's son. And certainly not Donny and Bobby, who had to be practically threatened to get them to work the grove in summers past. Uncle Pat had finally given up and hired outsiders to do the work his sons were too lazy to do.

Since Aunt Maisie's long illness, and after her death, Uncle Pat hadn't shown much interest in the business. Though he worked just as hard as Sean, Retta knew his joy in life was almost completely gone. It was only his keen sense of responsibility toward paying his debts and toward his partnership with his brother that kept him going. Retta understood that— she shared that same keen sense of responsibility.

Pat and Sean McCarron had only one hope of passing down the family heritage: Retta. She had known it since junior high school. It was her love for the family and its long-standing heritage that made her responsibility tolerable, especially on those days when it all seemed so difficult and unrewarding.

Somehow, Alan Conrad's presence made it easier and harder at the same time. The newfound excitement she felt because of him was at war with her deep sense of responsibility. Both tugged at her heart with equal power. She dreaded the day when she would have to choose between them.

———

Alan lay on the bed in his small room and decided to read the special delivery letter from his father in the morning. Tonight he had more pressing matters on his mind. Tonight his mind was filled with thoughts of Retta McCarron.

He closed his eyes tightly and took a deep breath as he recalled how she had glanced at him in the darkness of the car. He could still see her nervously tracing imaginary lines on her jeans with her finger. He remembered how gracefully she had reached up to tuck a wavy tendril of her long, red-brown hair behind her ear. He could still feel the rich, soft thickness of her braided ponytail in the palm of his hand.

In the four years he had been at Harvard, he had never met anyone like her. Her goals didn't include him, he knew that. But that was before—before tonight. What luck that she came to Jake's tonight. What luck that Joanna and Howie had other plans and couldn't give her a ride home. And what luck that he had been there, too, just at the right time.

"Yup," he said to no one. "I'm one lucky guy." By the time he switched off the lamp on the bedside table, he had managed to put the letter from his father completely out of his mind.

Closing his eyes, a thought interrupted the images of Retta's face filling his mind. *Luck has nothing to do with it—nothing at all.*

Opening his eyes wide, Alan laughed right out loud. "That sounds like something Jim Henry would say," he said into the darkness. Luck or providence? What did he care? Retta McCarron was warming up to him. Morning couldn't come too soon for Alan Conrad.

When Alan awoke, it took him a moment to remember why he had such a sense of inner triumph. He checked his watch: six A.M. Jumping out of bed, he grabbed a fresh pair of Levi's and decided he'd go out to the McCarrons' and see if he could manage an invitation to breakfast. Ignoring the letter from his father still waiting on the table, he grabbed his jacket on the way out. He still couldn't get over mornings cool enough to require a jacket, and afternoons so warm a man could strip off his shirt and work bare-chested in the bright sunshine. Not even the low-lying morning fog could dampen his high spirits. By ten the mist would be gone. It was going to be a wonderful day.

Sean McCarron was sitting alone in the kitchen drinking his first cup of coffee when Alan drove in. Connie was still in bed, having tossed and turned most of the night. Sean hadn't slept at all. At five, he had slipped quietly from his bed and made his way noiselessly down the stairs to the den. At six he went into the kitchen and put the coffeepot on the burner to perk while he read the morning paper. Only when he heard the sound of the gravel beneath Alan's tires did he look up.

Before Alan could knock, Sean motioned him to come in.

"Coffee, over there," Sean pointed to the stove. "Cups, there," he said, nodding toward the cupboard. "Help yourself."

"Thanks," Alan said quietly. "Sure is quiet in here."

"Everybody else is still sleepin'."

Alan sipped his black coffee, noting how strong and bitter it was, not at all like Consuela's. The silence between the two men was punctuated by the sound of Sean turning the pages of the paper. Finishing the front section, he shoved it toward Alan while he started on the back section.

"Looks like the plans for the freeway are coming along," Alan commented, trying to make a stab at light conversation.

"Looks like it," Sean said curtly.

"They say they hope to have this section finished by '65," Alan tried again.

"That's what they say."

"Think they will?"

"Will what?"

"Have it finished by '65."

"Who knows?"

"Bradford thinks he does," Alan said.

"Davis Bradford is full of . . . hot air," Sean said without looking away from his paper.

"Sounds like he's fairly confident to me," Alan said.

"Cocky is more like it." Sean tossed his paper on the table, stood, and retrieved the coffeepot from its place on the back burner. "Like a refill?"

"No thanks," Alan said.

"It's too strong, isn't it?"

"Maybe a little."

"Not too good in the kitchen," Sean admitted.

Alan folded the newspaper in his hands in half, creasing it carefully, then folded it several more times before tucking one side neatly into the other.

Alan watched Sean out of the corner of his eye, not knowing how to approach him and say what was on his mind. Both were distracted by the sounds of Glenna hurrying down the stairs. They sat in silence, waiting for her to enter the kitchen. Alan didn't know how he felt about the oldest McCarron daughter—more distrust than dislike, he guessed, although he really had no reason for either. His reaction to her was a gut level one, not a carefully formed opinion.

"Good morning, Daddy," she said cheerfully, coming to kiss him on the cheek. She flashed a smile in Alan's direction. "And good morning to you, Mr. Conrad."

"You seem happy this morning," Sean said.

"I am," she said. "Happy to see you—*both* of you."

"And to what do we owe this unexpected friendliness?" Sean looked puzzled.

"Now, Daddy," she teased, mussing his hair as she passed his chair. "Don't be such a grump on such a lovely day."

"It's foggy," Sean announced. "The weatherman says it may last into the afternoon."

"Who cares?" she asked melodramatically. "It's all in your mind anyway."

"Well, since you're in such a good mood, how 'bout scramblin' us some eggs? Your mama is sleepin' in this morning."

"Oh, Daddy," she said, looking at her watch, "I'd love to, but I have to be off to work. Don't want to be late. I can pick up some ribs—or how about Chinese?—on the way home. How's that sound?"

"Your mama wouldn't hear of it," Sean said. "She says if you're goin' to eat at home, you eat home-cooked. If you go out to eat, you eat restaurant-cooked."

"I'll call her later, just to make sure." Glenna kissed her father again and waved from the doorway to Alan. "See you again, soon I hope. Will you be here for dinner? We missed you last night."

"I doubt it," Alan said.

"Oh, what a pity. Daddy," she cooed, "see if you can convince him to stay, will you?"

"We'll see," Sean said, holding up his newspaper again.

Glenna smiled at Alan—the same shy, seductive smile she had used successfully in the bar the previous night.

Alan wasn't exactly inexperienced when it came to flirtatious women. He wasn't flattered by them, either. Glenna wanted something, and it was obvious she wanted it from him.

As the kitchen door swung shut behind her, Sean lowered his paper again. Staring at the movement of the door, he shook his head. "She's up to something," he said.

Before he could raise his paper again, he spotted the neatly folded section lying on the table in front of Alan. "Where'd you learn to do that?" he asked.

"I used to deliver papers," Alan said nonchalantly.

"No kiddin'?"

"I wanted a new pair of skis. Dad made me pay half. I worked my tail off for those skis."

"Didn't you resent him for that?"

"Sure, every morning at four-thirty." Alan laughed and fingered the folded paper.

"Do you still resent him?"

"No," Alan shrugged off the idea that he should harbor any resentment toward his father for this or any other reason.

"How long did it last?"

"The resentment?" Alan asked.

Sean nodded.

"Only until I took my first run down that hill one cold winter's day in Vermont." Alan smiled widely. "My dad said I'd appreciate those skis more if I had an investment in them. He was right. The next year I bought new boots. Paid for them myself that time."

"How long did you work the route?"

"Until tenth grade, then I got a part-time job at the supermarket. Still had to get up at four-thirty in the morning, though. I broke down cardboard boxes, burned them in a huge furnace in the back. When that was done I had to make sure all the check stands had a full supply of bags. Caught the city bus and made it to school just barely before the second bell. Only had two tardies all through high school. If I'd have gotten one more, my mom said I'd have to quit my job. You know how moms are."

Sean glanced toward the ceiling. "I know." He stirred uncomfortably in his chair.

"Sean?" Alan had never dared use the man's first name before now, but what he had to say to him had to be said man to man.

Sean looked directly into Alan's eyes without speaking.

"I owe you a tremendous apology. I intruded into family business yesterday. I can't tell you how sorry I am."

"I don't know what to say, Alan," Sean said in a low voice.

"It won't happen again, sir. I can assure you. It was not my intention to endanger Paddy in any way. You were right. I didn't think it through very well."

"Well, son," Sean said hoarsely, then cleared his throat. "No harm done, right?"

"I hope not, sir." Alan held out his hand toward Sean McCarron. After a brief awkward moment, the older man took Alan's hand and they shook on their reconciliation.

"We'll not speak of it again," Sean said.

"Not if you say so," Alan smiled.

"He did enjoy it, though," Sean said thoughtfully.

"That he did, Mr. McCarron."

Connie came into the kitchen then, wrapped in a white terry-cloth robe and looking tired. Alan noticed the dark circles under her eyes and wondered if he should leave.

"Sean!" she said fretfully.

"Come here, Consuela," he said.

"Sean," she said, coming closer to her husband. She raised a trembling hand to her mouth and moved quickly to the circle of his waiting arm. "Sean, Paddy's not in his room."

"He's in the den, darlin'," Sean said.

"No, he's not. I looked."

"Maybe he's out lookin' at those poinsettias he's growin'."

"I checked," she said tearfully. "He's not there either."

"He can't be far, honey," Sean said, giving his wife a warm squeeze. "I'll have a look. But first—" He pulled his wife down on his lap.

"Please, Sean," she said. "I'm worried."

"I'll have a look around," Alan offered, glad for an excuse to leave the room.

"Don't forget to check the tool shed. Sometimes he likes to tinker around out there," Sean said. "I'll get my coat and be with you in a minute."

As soon as the door slammed after Alan, Sean turned to his wife. "Listen, Connie," he said. "I've been givin' this a lot of thought. Let's not go runnin' after Paddy like he can't think or take care of himself anymore."

"But he's so—"

"Maybe he's stronger than we give him credit for," Sean said.

"It's just that—"

"Connie, look. He said some pretty straightforward things to me yesterday. Gave me somethin' to think about. I've been up all night thinkin' about what he said. Alan's out there lookin' now. He couldn't have gotten far. Let's have a look in his room. Come on now." He gently led his wife toward Paddy's room.

Opening the door, Sean couldn't remember when he was in his son's room last. He was shocked at the dense jungle of healthy plants that covered every inch of flat surface. Shelves made from boards and cement blocks were stacked along the walls, with books underneath and trailing green plants on the top. A well-tended fish aquarium bubbled quietly from the corner of the room.

Walking around the side of Paddy's bed, Sean spotted the corner of a book sticking out from underneath the bed. Stooping, he picked up the encyclopedia and noticed a page turned back, and opened it. His attention was drawn to where Paddy had underlined a paragraph and circled a picture.

Sean's mouth fell open as he realized what Paddy was planning. "Oh, my stars!" he exclaimed. Brushing roughly by his wife, he headed for the back door, leaving his jacket hanging on the hook near the door.

"Paddy," Sean murmured. "I'll wring your neck for this."

Sean quickly crossed the yard and circled around the side of the carriage house, not knowing exactly what to expect, but bracing himself for the worst. No one was there, and the rope was dangling right where Pat had told him to leave it the day before, so Sean headed for the tool shed.

As he approached he could hear voices raising and lowering in an argument.

"It will work, I tell you," Paddy said.

"I'm not getting involved this time, Paddy." Alan's voice was firm.

"You've got to help me," Paddy begged. "I know I can do it. All you have to do is climb the tree. You saw Uncle Pat do it. You can do it."

"I'm not going along with this," Alan said. "Your father would kill us both."

"Well, like you said, if one goes, we both go." Paddy tried to tease Alan into agreeing to help him carry out his plan.

Sean paused outside the tool shed and held up his hand, attempting to stop Consuela from approaching.

"What's going on?" she whispered in response to Sean's signal to be quiet.

"I'm not sure. Paddy's cookin' up some sort of plan. He's trying to get Alan to help him," he whispered in return.

"Don't try to get me involved, Paddy McCarron. Ask your father to help you."

"My father! You saw him yesterday. He'd have a fit if he knew anything about this. No. If you won't help, I'll get one of my cousins to do it. They'd do it just to spite my dad."

"What have they got against your father?"

"It's a long story," Paddy said, waving his hand in a gesture of dismissal. "But I know they'd do it."

"Do whatever you'd like—just leave me out of it!" Alan, adamant in his decision, turned on his heel and left Paddy alone in the shed. He was only a few steps from the shed when he realized that Sean and Connie had heard the entire conversation.

Sean kissed his wife slightly on the lips and shoved her gently toward the house. "I'm going to have a talk with our son, Connie. Man to man. It doesn't include you, sweetheart. Go on back to the house and cook us a big breakfast. I think we'll all be hungry as bears before long."

Connie reluctantly yielded to her husband and slowly crossed the yard to the house. When she opened the back door, she looked over her shoulder and saw Sean wave to her to go on in.

"Well, good mornin', son," Sean said to Paddy from the doorway of the shed. "You're up and at 'em kinda early this mornin'."

"Dad," Paddy said simply.

"You know, son, I've been thinkin' about what you said yesterday. I've been kinda stubborn when it comes to you, haven't I?"

"No, Dad. Not *kind of* stubborn. You've been immovable."

"I realize that," Sean said. He had hoped that Paddy wouldn't be as hard on him today as he had been yesterday. "Well, I've been wrong. All this time tryin' to protect you from gettin' hurt." Sean paused and paced back and forth in the shed. "I didn't know I was hurtin' you in other ways as bad, maybe even worse."

Paddy shifted his weight from his good leg to lean more directly on his crutches. He waited wordlessly for his father to continue.

"Y'know, I think there's a better way to get you up there, if you still want to help out." Sean walked toward the back of the shed and took down a rusty-looking contraption of pulleys and chain. "Your grandpa and me used this to pull the engine out of the old Model T years back. Guess if it was strong enough to hold that heavy engine, it ought to hold you. Might be you could even get to manage it all on your own."

Paddy's face paled with shock. Gathering his composure, he grinned slightly off to one side of his mouth. "You know, Dad," he admitted, "I tried to make it up with just the pulley myself this morning."

"Paddy!" Sean's heart gripped with the fear of what could have happened to his son.

"It didn't work. I couldn't even make it halfway. I knew then that the idea I had about the block and tackle would be my only hope. Tried to get Alan to help me, but he wouldn't."

"I see," Sean said. "Well, no matter. What's a soft Easterner know about this sort of thing, anyway?"

"He's not so soft," Paddy said.

"I'm seein' that myself, son."

"When can we get started?" Paddy's eagerness lit up his entire face.

"Right after breakfast, I'd say. Pat's the tree climber. Let's talk to him about this. That okay by you?"

"Fine by me."

Fourteen

Alan climbed the stairway to the upper floor of the boardinghouse. Every muscle in his body ached, and his hands still hurt from the unaccustomed exposure to manual labor. But his heart was light and happy.

Sean McCarron's sudden, though cautious, turnaround concerning Paddy was nothing short of a miracle to Alan. The change seemed to please everyone, especially Retta. Connie was more reserved in her enthusiasm. It was understandable, since she, along with Sean, had sought only to protect Paddy from further injury and pain.

Alan had been chosen to test the block and tackle that would enable Paddy to access the building project on the second floor of the carriage house. Several times he had gone up and back down again, hanging by his hands and sitting on the small wooden seat. It was finally decided that Paddy could only use the contraption with assistance. Alan recalled how agreeable Paddy was and how eagerly he promised not to try it on his own—at least for the time being. But, along with everyone else, Alan knew that once Paddy became adept at pulling himself up the rope, he'd try it on his own. Everyone knew it, but no one said it. Best not to push Sean too far. It was hard to tell how fragile his breakthrough was at this point.

Alan opened the door to his room and caught sight of the special delivery letter from his father that had arrived the day before. He picked up the letter and settled himself in the only chair in the sparsely furnished room.

Dear Alan,
    Your mother and I have been concerned that we haven't heard from you in a few days. We trust you are doing

all right and that the business activities haven't kept you from making some new friends. We also trust that making new friends hasn't kept you from your assigned business activities.

I have some items we need to discuss. Sooner, rather than later. Please call me collect at the office. Tell Nancy to put you through. I'll convey that message to her as well.

Your mother sends her love and insists that we must know what the place is like where you're staying, and how we can reach you by phone. If you are planning to stay in one location, your mother thinks it best if you had a nice apartment. I have reminded her that you're living on a limited business account. I would suggest that you do the same.

Let me hear from you within twenty-four hours of receiving this letter. The matters I have to discuss with you are fairly important—though not, at this time, urgent.

We both send our best regards, and of course your mother sends her love.

Dad

Twenty-four hours. Alan glanced at his watch. Six-thirty—nine-thirty in New York. Thursday night was the night the family played canasta at the club. His parents wouldn't get home much before midnight. The call would have to wait until morning.

Alan folded the letter and tucked it back in its envelope. He wanted to talk to them at home. He knew he'd need his mother's backing of the ideas spinning around in his head. He'd have to set his clock for five-thirty to call his parents when he knew they'd both be at breakfast.

Later that evening, he met Jim Henry at the high school gymnasium and decided to find a time when they could talk. Jim had a clear, keen mind as well as insight into the human heart and emotions. Alan was more than eager to tap into any advice Jim might be willing to give.

After shooting baskets, Jim suggested they meet at Jake's for sodas. Alan decided to stop by his place first and take a quick shower.

Coming out of the boardinghouse barely half an hour later,

Alan was surprised to see Glenna waiting by his car.

"Heard you're going to Jake's," she said with a friendly smile.

"How'd you hear that?" Alan still didn't trust her and found he was liking her less all the time.

"Ran into Jim Henry," she said. "Thought you'd maybe like a little more . . . what shall we say? Mature company."

"More mature than Jim?"

"I don't know Jim very well," she said, a slight pout forming on her full, soft lips. "I just think Jake's is a little, well, juvenile. Don't you?"

"I hadn't thought about it that much."

"How about a drink at Scottie's?"

"No thanks, Jim's expecting me."

"Later, then. Say about nine-thirty or ten?"

"It's almost nine now." Even though Alan wasn't interested in Glenna, he was curious as to what she was up to. Even her father didn't trust her—he had made that clear earlier this morning. "I think I'll pass on this one," Alan said.

"Well, then, maybe some other time?" Glenna coaxed.

Alan slid behind the wheel of his convertible. "Scottie's isn't my kind of place, Glenna. Now if you want to stop by Jake's and join the group for a soda—"

"And Jake's isn't my kind of place, if you know what I mean." She leaned forward, putting both hands on the door of his car. "I prefer more adult entertainment," she said, lowering her lashes slightly.

"Well, to each his own. See you around," Alan said coolly, shoving his car into gear. "And I do mean around," he said to her image in his rearview mirror as he drove away.

———

Jim listened intently to Alan's ideas and sat back thoughtfully when he was sure Alan had finished. Occasionally, Jim waved at or greeted a teenager passing by their table, but his attention always returned to Alan.

"What do you think your father will say?" he finally asked.

"I've never asked him for anything like this before. I have no idea. He didn't buy McCarron's to grow oranges. He bought it to either build houses on or wait until land values increased."

"Without even knowing him, I'd venture a guess he doesn't expect you to go into the orange business after investing in four years of Harvard tuition." Jim looked at his young friend thoughtfully. "You discuss this with Pat?"

"Not yet."

"How long's he got on the place?"

"Dad told him to stay as long as he wanted. That is, until other plans were made."

"Or the land sold to someone else?"

"That's a possibility."

"Now you want your father to hang on to the property and let you have your hand at being a farmer." Jim's comment was a summation of Alan's proposal.

"That says it in a nutshell," Alan said, grinning at Jim. "After all, he did send me here to evaluate and recommend the best usage for his land investments."

"Investments? You mean there is more property involved?"

"Oh yes," Alan said. "There's hundreds of acres out west of River Hills on Highway 60. There's a couple thousand, in fact."

"What did he want McCarron's twenty for? Seems like small potatoes to me," Jim said.

"To get a toehold in the area," Alan said. "From back East, it doesn't seem like people's lives are involved. All he's seen are maps, growth potential studies, and some speculative predictions. All my dad looks at is making his money make more money. He has no concept that families and individuals may be hurt or their whole lives turned upside down by the purchase of one small piece of property."

Jim raised one eyebrow and bit the inside of his cheek as he listened to Alan.

"You see, Jim," Alan continued, "when somebody lists their property with a realtor, and you offer them a price they're happy to accept, you don't anticipate you're buying half of a family history too."

"I see what you mean," Jim said. "But if he came to look at it himself—wouldn't that make a difference?"

"Maybe, maybe not. He was hoping Sean would sell too. Forty acres would be a lot better for building a new housing development than twenty. With the right planning, forty might even give you a little to donate back to the neighborhood for a small park or maybe a school. Public relations, you know."

"A planned neighborhood," Jim said.

"Right," Alan said, nodding. "It's happening all over New York. Suburban living is all the rage right now. Land investors have made millions."

"Your father, too?"

"Sure," Alan said with a shrug.

"What's he do with all that money, Al?"

"Makes more." Alan's tone was almost apologetic.

"It's that important to him?"

"He doesn't know how to do anything else," Alan said. "He honestly doesn't know how to do anything else. Seems kind of a waste, now that I'm three thousand miles away."

"Now that you've gotten in touch with the working world?"

"Yeah, maybe that's it. I really do like getting my hands dirty, Jim. I never thought I'd say that. I've been here only two weeks, but it seems like I've been here forever."

"You've got it then," Jim said.

"Got what?"

"California fever."

"Is it fatal?"

"No, not unless you go back East. Then you die a slow, agonizing death—unless, of course, you come back here. It's amazing how that works."

Jim studied the face of his young friend. Alan shifted uncomfortably, took a deep breath, and then relaxed against the back of the padded vinyl booth. "So," he said, "what's it going to be? How will you approach your father?"

"I'm not sure about that, just yet. But I'm going to. I've decided that for sure."

"Have you prayed about this, Al?"

In sudden surprise, Alan looked up from studying the ice in his glass. "I guess I hadn't thought about it. It's not really an emergency or anything. I can work this out on my own."

"Is that when you pray? Only in emergencies?"

"Hadn't thought about bothering God with the little details."

"I don't think He'd mind. Anyway, are you so sure this is such a little detail? I mean, compared to the thousands of acres of land, this twenty seems small. But it's not really land we're discussing here, is it?"

"I didn't think of it like that," Alan said. "No, it's not. It's my life."

"Is it?"

"I don't understand," Alan said.

"Is it *your* life? Have you ever given your heart to Christ, Al?"

"I remember once, in my catechism class, the teacher led us all in a prayer of repentance. It was right there in my book. I read it out loud with all the other kids. We accepted Jesus Christ as the Savior of the world and from then on I knew I'd go to heaven—or at least hoped I would if I kept my nose clean."

"Christ did come to be the Savior of the world, Alan. But not to save it as a collective group. You see, Christ came into the world to live as we live, to reach us one by one. He wins the world one heart at a time."

"I've always regarded myself as a Christian, Jim."

"Why?"

"I guess because I wasn't something else. I'm not Muslim or of the Jewish faith. I'm Christian."

"Christianity isn't just a religion, Alan. It's a rebirth of a sinful heart."

Alan listened intently as Jim explained further the plan of salvation by faith, of accepting Christ by letting Him come into your life, and letting Him call all the shots and influence all your decisions thereafter.

"Once you are born again," Jim explained, "you then live for Christ instead of yourself."

"But that day I prayed in class. Didn't that count?"

"Sure, it did. The way I see it, you've acknowledged Christ as Savior, but have you personally put Him in the position of being Lord of your life?"

"I don't think so."

"Do you want to?"

"It seems more that I need to, Jim. Honestly, wouldn't I be a fool not to? My Dad looks to all kinds of advisors, accountants, and lawyers before he makes a decision. And I could just look to God."

"Now, hold on a minute. I'm not saying you won't need to look to those kinds of counselors, Al, but adding the dimension of prayer means you'll be able to tell better if the advice they give is sound." Jim leaned forward to get closer to his young friend. He didn't want Alan to misunderstand what he was about to say next.

"Listen, Al. This is important. Letting Christ be Lord of your life doesn't mean that you'll have it easy all the time. In fact, sometimes it seems just the opposite. But it does mean that life has purpose and direction far beyond what you could ever imagine. Serving Christ is not an 'I'll scratch your back if you scratch mine' arrangement with God, but a relationship with Him that adds a depth and richness you can't imagine."

"You know," Alan said thoughtfully, "I think that's what I've been missing. Purpose and direction. I work for my father and I serve only his purpose. Sure, his money will all be mine someday. But it has little purpose. It's something you're given, but in the end it owns you. It seems so shallow to me sometimes." Alan played with the empty Coke glass sitting on the table in front of him. "I really do want something deeper, Jim. Some other purpose than I've experienced so far."

"Then," Jim said, "all you have to do is pray a simple prayer, in your very own words, telling God of your intentions to put His Son, Jesus, in place as Lord of your life."

"That's it?"

"That's it," Jim reassured. "You could do it right here."

"Here? Now?" Alan looked around at the teenaged crowd, laughing and dancing to the music blaring from the jukebox.

"God will meet you anywhere, anytime."

"It just seems it would be more appropriate in church."

"You don't have to go where you perceive Him to be, Alan. He comes to where we are. If He came to live among us by being born in a dirty cow stable, I'm sure He won't mind coming into a clean, although rather rowdy, hamburger hangout."

Jim smiled at Alan. "Let's look at it this way. If somebody you loved enough to die for was ready to accept a position in your household, would you care where you had to meet him to make a personal connection?"

"No, I wouldn't. I'd probably want to meet him anywhere, anytime."

"Go ahead then, right here. Just tell God you've decided to accept His offer of a lifetime job in His kingdom."

Alan self-consciously bowed his head slightly, hoping no one would notice, and simply stated his request. "God," he said, "I want to know you on a more personal basis. I accepted Christ as your Son a long time ago. Now I want to accept Him into my own life as well as my heart. Please, God, give me purpose—your purpose. Amen."

"Amen," Jim said in agreement. Beaming at Alan, he extended his hand and said, "Welcome to the family, brother."

Fifteen

Bounding up the stairs at the boardinghouse two at a time, Alan was anxious to get alone and pour out his heart to God in private. Jim had suggested that he talk over the situation with God before he called his parents.

Opening the door to his room, he was more than a little shocked to see Glenna sitting in his only easy chair.

"What are you doing here?" he said. "How did you get in?"

"I told the old busybody downstairs that I had a note from my father to deliver to you. She wanted me to give it to her, but I said I would slip it under your door myself—father's orders."

"Oh, and did you just slip yourself under the door, too?"

"No, silly," she said giggling. "I picked your lock. If you think that old keyhole is safe—well, think again. A bobby pin works every time."

"Then you've had practice." Alan's insides stirred with anger.

"Why are you so mean to me?" she cooed, swinging one long leg draped over the other. "What have I ever done to you?"

"Nothing. Let's keep it that way, shall we?"

Glenna hoped she was concealing her restless irritability. "Listen, Alan. We're really on the same side. Let's not be enemies anymore. Okay?"

"Why should we be?" Alan wondered but didn't ask what she meant by being on the same side.

"No reason, that's my point." She smiled shyly and dropped her long lashes to cover her smoldering eyes. "My family all likes you, and with a little encouragement, I could too. In fact, I like you better already."

"Fine," Alan said flatly, "you like me. Now let's leave it at that, shall we? I'm tired and want to go to bed."

She glanced at the small quilt-covered bed in the corner, then back at Alan. She hoped that his expression meant that he was weighing the unspoken question.

Alan knew immediately what she was suggesting and quickly opened the door to his room.

"It's time for you to leave," he said, flatly refusing to look at her.

"Is it?"

"It is," he repeated, lifting his eyes to hers.

Glenna saw the suggestion of annoyance hovering in his eyes and tried to decide if she should come on stronger or back off for the moment.

"Well, if you say so," she said, rising slowly from the chair. "I certainly don't want to get on your bad side." Trying to hide her irritation, she was pleased at how nonchalant she sounded.

Coming to stand very close to him, she lowered her voice to a purposeful whisper. "Let's see more of each other, okay?"

"I don't think so," he said with a distinct tone of disapproval.

"You might change your mind," she whispered.

"No, I . . ." he hesitated, determined to control his temper.

She seized the moment of hesitation. "See? You're changing your mind already." Leaning into him slightly, she felt him stiffen, as though she had struck him. Her lower lip trembled as she took a step back. Starting to blush, she knew she had gone too far. Alan Conrad wasn't like the men around Summerwind. He wasn't going to be so easy to wind around her little finger and manipulate. Even her father was easier to manage than this one.

"Look, Glenna," Alan said with a heavy tone of sarcasm in his voice. "You may be able to land most of the fish in this town with the bait you are using. But this one isn't biting. You got that straight?" Alan felt his hands shaking in anger. "Now," he said, whispering harshly, "get out of my room—and stay out."

"You say that now," she said. "But you'll see. I don't give up easily, Alan. I guess I'll just have to change my bait. Isn't that what all good fishermen do?" Without waiting for a reply, she turned and walked out of his room and down the hall toward the stairs.

Alan shut the door a bit more firmly than usual and turned the key in the lock, hoping she heard it and got the message. He took a deep breath, trying to recapture his original urge to pray. Slumping down in the chair Glenna had occupied a few minutes before, he leaned forward. Resting his elbows on his knees, he covered his face with his hands.

"Oh, God!" he said more in exclamation than in prayer. "She makes me furious!" Even though he didn't much feel like it, Alan knew that somehow he'd have to make himself discuss his ideas about the McCarron place with God. Glenna's visit could only sabotage his intentions if he gave in to his anger. He chose instead to put her into God's hands, along with everything else.

Kneeling beside his bed and pouring his heart out to God was foreign and awkward to Alan at first. But before long he forgot his surroundings and one by one told God his ideas, as if he were talking to a trusted friend. Eventually, a deep peace swept over him, and he suddenly realized how tired he was. Without even saying amen, Alan stripped off his clothes and climbed into bed.

"One more thing, God," he said after turning off the light. "It's Retta McCarron. I sure do like her. I hope that's all right with You."

When Alan reached his parents early the next morning, his mother's voice was filled with relief. "I have been so worried about you," she said.

"Mom, there's no reason to worry. All the time I was at school, I called home only once a month."

"I know," she said. "But that was a different environment. At least I knew you were safe there."

"This isn't the Wild West anymore."

"I know that," she said, laughing. "I miss you, that's all. What can I say? I'm your mother. I have a right to worry."

His father's voice, however, wasn't as gentle. "I thought I told you to call immediately."

"I saw the letter only last night. I've been . . . well, rather busy."

"I should hope so. How's it going out there?"

Alan filled him in on what he had learned about the locations of the different pieces of property and his thoughts about which might be better suited for early development. He purposely avoided mentioning the McCarron land, preferring to encourage his father's thoughts toward other possibilities.

"I've heard that there's more land east of River Hills that might prove to be interesting. I'd like you to drive over to that area today if possible and meet with the broker. See what's available there, and don't forget to ask about water and so forth."

"Today?"

"You have other pressing matters?"

"You're the boss," Alan said. "I'm at your disposal."

"Okay, then," his father said. "Get on over there and have a look. Stay around the area for a few days, read the local papers and see if you can pick up the general attitude toward new developers. It doesn't pay to be the first developer in an area if you offend the local population in the process. Find out what it would take to bring them around. No use making enemies right off the bat."

Alan fished around in his pockets for a slip of paper and wrote down the broker's name and number. He listened carefully to his father's instructions and promised to get back to him by the end of next week.

At the end of the conversation Alan's father said, "Wait a minute, your mother wants to talk to you again." Alan relaxed. The McCarron property didn't come up. For all his worrying, he would have more time to put together his ideas and make his case even stronger the next time he talked with his father.

"Alan," his mother said, "what's the place like where you're staying?"

"It's real comfortable, Mom," he said. "Almost homey."

"And clean?"

"Spotless," he said, closing his eyes to shut out the reality of the dust accumulating in the corner.

"And you have a good bed?"

"Never thought about it. I'm sleeping good, though."

"Well, that's good. You're getting plenty of rest. Eating good?"

"Yeah, the best ever," he said, remembering Consuela's Mexican cuisine. "Not quite up to your cooking," he added quickly.

"Alan," she said, "give me your phone number."

"Well, I don't really have a phone number. There's a phone here at the hotel, but I don't have one in my room."

"Well, then, get one," she ordered.

"It wouldn't do much good, Mom," he said. "I'm not here much. It would be better to wait until I call you."

"What's the number at the hotel, then? You never know, we may need to reach you sometime."

"I don't have it right here. I'll get it and send it to you when I write."

"When will that be?"

"Soon, Mom. I promise."

"Here, your father wants to say something else."

"Alan," his father's voice boomed over the wire. "How's the McCarron property look to you?"

Alan's heart dropped, skipped a beat, then flew up to his throat, threatening to choke him.

"Well, Dad," Alan said slowly, "I have some ideas about the McCarron place."

"I'm listening," the older man said.

"I'm not sure it's right for development. Somehow I just don't get the same feeling about it as I do the land you bought west of River Hills."

"Too small?"

"Maybe," Alan said, searching for just the right words.

"The brother interested in selling out yet?"

"Not yet," Alan said. "I'm not sure—"

"He'll sell." Alan Sr.'s voice held a note of confidence Alan Jr. found a bit annoying.

"I'm not so sure about that, Dad," Alan said, trying to sound more convincing than he felt.

"Well, then, let's dump it. I probably won't make anything on it this soon, but we won't lose much either."

"Not yet," Alan said quickly.

"No?" Alan Sr. sounded surprised at Alan's response.

"I just think we ought to hang on to it awhile longer. The grove's still producing, and Pat McCarron doesn't seem to mind working for the crop. It's not costing us anything to hold it awhile longer, is it?"

"No, I guess not. But we could put that money into something more immediately profitable if—"

"We don't know that for sure," Alan said to his father. "Isn't that pure speculation?"

"Sure, son. That's what the land business is all about."

"I know you can do whatever you think best, but really, Dad, I'd like you to hang on to this property for a while."

"That so?" Alan Sr. sounded pleased. "How long do you recommend we hold it, son?"

"I'm not sure," Alan said. "Maybe until I'm in a position to buy it from you myself."

"Well, now—"

"I really like this piece, Dad. I wouldn't mind living there myself."

"There's a house on it, isn't there?"

"Yeah, there sure is."

"Inhabitable?"

"Pat McCarron is living there."

"I see," Alan said, pausing. "And how long did we give him to occupy the property?"

"I'm not sure. I'd have to look at the contract. But we said he could have the crop for up to two years—longer if we haven't developed it yet."

"What's that got to do with the house?"

"Nothing the way you and I see it," Alan said. "But—"

"Not the way the farmer sees it, right?"

"I'm not sure. I can find out."

"You really want to live there?" Alan Sr. asked. "You thinking of settling out there on the West Coast?"

"I think it's a little early to make a definite decision. But it has crossed my mind."

"Okay, I'll hang on to the McCarron property a little longer. It certainly can't depreciate, the way real estate is climbing. Might be a good idea, in fact."

"And besides," Alan said to his father, "if I can live in the house, it will help my budget."

"Things a little tight, son?"

"No, not really. I sort of took a part-time job."

"What?" Alan Sr. exclaimed. "What kind of part-time job?"

"Carpenter work," Alan said.

"No fooling?" Alan's father sounded shocked. "Hey, that's a mighty smart idea. Get a feel for the labor work force. You never know, we may need them if we decide to develop that piece. If we could just get hold of the whole forty, we might have a better chance of buying out other adjoining acreage. Nice going there, Alan."

Realizing that all his ideas would only be interpreted with the perspective of pushing development, building houses, and making money, Alan decided not to push his father any further. He couldn't imagine his father's reaction if he admitted that he liked the idea of leaving the property mostly as it was. He'd have to leave that for later—hopefully much later.

Hanging up the phone, Alan realized he'd have to keep his father's business interests as his first priority. His part-time position with Sean McCarron had to take a backseat while he ran around the countryside looking for prospective land purchases. He didn't know which he dreaded most, leaving Summerwind or being away from Retta.

Sixteen

As Alan headed out of town, he let his thoughts drift back to the small community of Summerwind. Sean's reaction had surprised him. Alan thought he could actually detect a bit of disappointment in Sean's voice when he mentioned he would be gone for a while. Consuela tried to insist that Alan eat a large breakfast, but his meeting with the land broker was set for late morning, and he had to get going if he were going to make it on time.

Paddy seemed cheerful. The block and tackle idea needed some refining if it were to give him easy access to the upstairs building project. Pat had promised to help with that this morning. Sean had a crew of framers coming, and by the time Alan returned, the skeleton of the second story should be well in place.

Retta was already in the grove preparing for the November watering. Alan had looked forward to seeing the actual irrigation process, but he would miss it this month. His disappointment was relieved some when Sean said, "Oh, well. You'll be seein' it next month, then."

Glenna had tried to make eye contact with him in the kitchen before he left, but Alan managed to totally ignore her and keep his conversation light and friendly with the other members of the family, even offering Joanna a ride to school. She politely refused, however, saying she was expecting Howie to come for her any minute.

The one person he missed seeing was Retta, and Alan would have gone out to the grove to find her if it hadn't been for Glenna.

"I want to apologize for treating you the way I did last night," she had said, following him out to his car.

"The less said about that, the better," Alan replied, anxious to get away from her.

"I'm afraid you misunderstood—" she said.

"I don't think so." His response was short and curt.

"I don't want you going away mad at me," she said, lowering her eyes and forming her mouth into a pout.

"I'm not angry at you," he said. "I don't have any feelings toward you at all."

"I don't believe you," she said coolly, giving him a demure smile that looked a bit forced.

"There's only one thing I want from you, Glenna," he said before shifting the car into gear.

"Yes?"

"Space. Lots and lots of space."

Alan stepped on the accelerator and drove the length of the large circle driveway and out toward the street. Glancing over his shoulder, he saw her standing in the driveway waving as if they had just said a reluctant goodbye.

Maybe it was just as well he was leaving for a week or so. Maybe by then Glenna would have second thoughts about him and leave him alone.

———

When Alan returned two weeks later, his room had been rented out and he found himself with no place to stay. Before he looked further, he decided to pay a visit to the McCarron place.

"Hey, look who's here!" Pat walked toward him before he could even step out of his car. "How's it goin', stranger?"

"Not that bad," Alan said. "Not bad at all." Looking toward the carriage house, Alan let out a long, low whistle. "Look at that," he said, admiring the progress on the remodeling project. "You've been busy around here while I was gone, I can see that."

"Come on in, take a look," Pat invited.

"Where is everybody?" Alan asked.

"Paddy's being fitted for new leg braces," Pat said. "Sean and Connie took him to the clinic. Retta's around here somewhere. We're getting ready to pick the navels."

"Oh? When's that?"

"Soon—a week or two."

"How do you get ready? Don't you just go out one morning and start pulling them off the trees?"

"Hardly," Pat laughed. "But we'll get to that later. First, come on in and see what we've done here."

Pat proudly guided Alan's inspection of his prospective apartment and pointed out every wire, where it led, and what it was to service with power. "Gerry Hill did it," Pat explained. "We were lucky to get him. He came in evenings the first week; the Friday after Thanksgiving he put in twelve gruelin' hours. Finished up on Saturday. He's a friend of Jim Henry's."

"I think I met him at church," Alan said matter-of-factly.

"You went to Henry's church?"

"A few weeks back," Alan said. "Gerry Hill was there."

"Is that right?" Pat said, but without waiting for an answer he took Alan's arm and steered him toward another room. "Plumbing's all in, too. The bathroom's over there," he said, pointing to the black piping sticking through the floor. "There'll only be a shower. Saving space, you know."

"What's this?" Alan asked, pointing to a large opening over in one corner.

"That's going to be a sliding glass door. Decided to put a deck out there, after the work is done. There'll be stairs out there, too. In the meantime, that's where Paddy comes in. You know, that boy's showin' a real knack for all this. He hardly left Gerry Hill's side the entire time he was here. Sean thought he might be gettin' in Hill's way, but Hill insisted he was being a big help."

"You don't say," Alan smiled.

"Say," Pat said after the inspection was over, "you missed quite a shindig here on Thanksgiving."

"Sorry I missed that," Alan said, remembering his own quiet holiday spent in his small hotel room, then at the movies in the afternoon.

"Had quite a houseful. That Connie. She made the biggest turkey we ever had that I can remember."

Alan thought of the hot turkey sandwich he had ordered at

the twenty-four-hour restaurant out on the highway just west of River Hills.

"All the trimmings, too. That young preacher and his wife were here."

"Jim and Linda?"

"Nice kids." Pat stuck his hands in his pockets and leaned against an unfinished wall. "I think Sean could even be persuaded to go back to . . ." He paused for a moment. "Well, it's no business of mine."

"You mean go to church with Connie?" Alan asked.

"Like I said," Pat shrugged. "It's no business of mine."

"Or mine either," Alan said with a grin.

"It's sure good to have you back," Pat said, slapping him good-naturedly on the back. "You are back, aren't you?"

"For the time being," Alan said. "Until my dad sends me off somewhere else."

"Buyin' land, I guess," Pat said.

"Afraid so," Alan answered.

"Get what you wanted over by River Hills?"

"More than we'll ever need, if you ask me," Alan said.

"How so?"

"Hundreds and hundreds of acres—nothing but desolate land. Nothing green growing out there for miles. It's rolling, rocky land. Not good for much as I see it. But my dad, he sees it quite differently. But then he's sitting back there in an upstairs office with windows overlooking downtown Manhattan, not out here where the wind blows tumbleweeds as big as cars across miles of open land."

"What's he going to do with all that land?" asked Pat, scratching his head.

"Build on it, maybe, or hold it for a while and sell it for someone else to build on it."

"Build what?"

"Houses, I guess." Alan squatted and drew a rough diagram in a pile of sawdust with his finger. "Look, Pat. Here's L.A. and here's River Hills. The new freeway is supposed to go along the edge of Orange County and right out through here. The land we bought west of River Hills extends all the way from the edge of town, here," he said, indicating with his finger, "to here, just this side of the pass."

"That's a lot of dirt," Pat said, shaking his head.

"Then," Alan said, pointing to the other side of his drawing, "there's several thousand acres up for sale out here on the east side of River Hills. When the freeway is finished, it would only take a few more minutes to drive out to this area. That opens an entire new area for homes."

"Where are all those people going to work?" Pat asked.

"In the L.A. area."

"And drive all that way?" he said, shaking his head.

"They're driving all the way to Pomona right now," Alan said. "In twenty more minutes they'd be here," he said, pointing to his drawing again.

"You think they'll do it?"

"Investors like my father not only think so, they're betting on it."

"That's what it is, isn't it?"

"What?"

"A gamble."

"Yeah, a very calculated one, but it's still a gamble."

"Well," Pat said, rubbing his chin, "what isn't?"

Alan stood and looked out the opening reserved for a window and spotted Retta's black floppy leather hat moving through the grove. He watched her wordlessly for a moment before Pat interrupted his thoughts.

"You get moved back into the boardinghouse?"

"No, I think I'll stay someplace else this time."

"Something a little fancier, maybe?"

"No, not necessarily," Alan said. "Someplace that has a vacancy. They were all filled up."

"No kiddin'?" Pat turned away a moment, then back again. "You want to stay with me out there in the old house?"

"Thanks, but I hardly think there's room—"

"There's plenty of room. The boys have taken off—for a while, that is. I'm all alone out there for now. You're welcome to bunk out there with me. It's not like staying in a hotel, but it's clean—Connie makes sure of that."

"Connie cleans your house?"

"No, not herself. She hires a woman to come in every few

days and pick up the place—change the beds and so forth."

"You sure it wouldn't be an imposition?"

"Not at all. In fact, it would be nice to have someone around. I haven't been alone since—well, since Maisie passed on."

After Alan graciously accepted Pat's invitation, they drove around the block together in Alan's car and pulled into Pat's driveway. His house was quite a bit smaller than the Queen Anne that Sean's family occupied. But it was clean and the yard, while not landscaped, was neat, free of the debris found around many of the other houses tucked here and there in other orange groves.

"Could use a coat of paint, I guess," Pat said as they entered the front door. "Inside, too."

Alan noticed how clean the place was, but it was sparsely decorated and lacked the warmth of a woman's touch. He inwardly winced at what his mother would think of his living in such small, plain quarters.

"How did you come to live out here?" Alan asked. Thinking better of his question, he backed off. "Never mind, it's none of my business."

"And not at the big house?"

"This really isn't my business, Pat."

"I don't mind. I got married a couple of years before Sean. Our folks were living then, getting old, not as able as they once were. Maisie and I moved in here, had our boys. Then when Sean and Connie married, we had the choice of moving up to the big house and taking care of the folks or staying here." Pat sat heavily on his old mohair sofa. "By then this was home to us. After we had the boys, Maisie wasn't able to take care of a bigger place. We knew we'd never have any more kids. It was the right thing for Connie and Sean to stay there. Connie was strong and pitched right in taking care of Mother. Dad worked with us a few more years. Both lived at home until they died. Died at home. The way it should be." Pat looked around the small house, and Alan had trouble reading his expression.

"Anyway, this is your house now," Pat said. "The money's all been transferred. The escrow closed while you were gone.

Gave my boys their share, and they're off to make their way in the world."

"Where'd they go, if you don't mind my asking?"

"Bobby headed to the beach. Donny took off for the Rockies."

"Going into business, getting jobs?"

"Livin' high and mighty's my guess," Pat said sadly. "That won't last long. Didn't give 'em as much as they thought I would. Just enough to get a start, if they use their heads."

"And what are you going to do, Pat?"

"Once that apartment is done," he said, "I thought I'd move on over there. This house will be empty then."

"Going to stay and work with Sean, then," Alan surmised.

"I wanted to talk to you about that," Pat said, shifting to a more comfortable position. "I'd like to work through the navels," he said slowly. "Then, come January I'd like to go to Ireland. You know, my grandparents were immigrants. I'd like to see the homeplace and look up family, if there's any left."

"But what'll happen to the grove?" Alan felt the pit of his stomach tighten.

"That's your decision, son." Pat smiled out one corner of his mouth and leaned forward, resting his arms on his knees. "You bought yourself an orange grove. Guess you'll either farm it or rip it out and build houses. It's not up to me anymore."

"But I thought you agreed to stay on for a while."

"No, I didn't. Your father said I *could* stay. I didn't say I *would*."

"Well, now, that puts a whole different light on things, doesn't it?" Alan said, not really expecting an answer to the question.

"I guess it does at that," Pat said. "I can't help but wondering, though, what you'll end up doing."

"I wonder the same thing," Alan said, "the very same thing."

Seventeen

Within a week Alan was settled in Pat's house, and the surroundings seemed more comfortable and familiar. Even his mother was happier, since he could give her a phone number now. Living in a house that was kept up by a maid appealed to her more than a small, inexpensive boarding hotel. Alan didn't try to correct her, knowing her idea of a house and a maid was far different than the reality of this small, almost neglected building with a biweekly cleaning woman.

Pat and Alan soon began fixing breakfast together, much to the chagrin of Consuela, who insisted on supplying them with fresh-baked bread, cinnamon rolls, and a Mexican pastry she called *churros*. At a local hardware store, Alan picked up an electric orange juicer and an electric coffeepot. Each morning, he made it his ritual to pick oranges, juice them, and drink several glasses with breakfast. Pat watched with interest as Alan measured precisely the amount of coffee needed for the new percolator, and even had to admit Alan's coffee was much better than his own boiled version.

Alan found plenty to do at the McCarron place, helping out with the carriage house apartment or working in the grove. He loved this new life in California. For the first time in his life, he felt like he could be himself. The only thing bothering him was Retta's response to him since he had returned.

Noticing her polite, yet cool, reaction to him, he decided he would give her a little time. Then he would ask her directly what caused the change in her since the night he had driven her home from Jake's.

Alan found the small sorting shed and its system of belts and motors most intriguing. He watched with interest as Paddy showed him how each motor drove the belt system and mechanized the sorting of the oranges they sold directly from the grove to the customers.

One afternoon he helped Pat reinforce the small fruit stand at the edge of the driveway. Alan marveled at the idea of the locked money box that put customers on their honor when they purchased the oranges Paddy put there each morning.

Most of the oranges would be taken directly to the large packinghouse down by the railroad tracks. Suddenly, the first week of December, the place seemed to come alive with harvest preparation and activities.

"You ought to take a look down there," Pat said one night after dinner. "It's quite a system they have. Go see ol' Smitty Barnes. He's the packin' house manager. He's been around oranges all his life. He'll retire one of these days. Gettin' old like the rest of us, I guess."

Alan decided to ask Retta to show him the packinghouse one afternoon before the actual picking began—maybe even a Sunday afternoon, if she could be persuaded.

"Go on," Sean urged his daughter when Alan made the suggestion. "You know the back door's always open. Smitty hardly ever locks up the place this time of year."

Reluctantly, Retta left the dishes to her mother and went up to change into her jeans.

"Would you like to come along?" Alan invited Paddy.

"No, thanks," he said after exchanging glances with his mother. "You go. I've got to get those poinsettias ready for the church."

"You're sure?"

"You two go on. We'll all see enough of the packinghouse in a week or two," Consuela urged.

Once in the car, Retta fell into a silence that Alan found awkward. He kept asking questions, trying to make conversation, and she answered each with a short, even clipped, response.

When they finally entered the unlocked side door of the packinghouse and walked into the huge, almost empty warehouse-type area, Retta relaxed and even enjoyed explaining to Alan the procedure for washing, sorting, packing, and preparing the oranges for shipment.

"It's so clean," he said, glancing around the building.

"Smitty's a real tyrant about that," she said. "He used to save the large, oversized oranges for the kids walking by after school. Some navels can grow as big as grapefruit. They won't fit into the boxes, so rather than see them go to waste, he put them out into a bin in the alley. When he found some boys throwing them at the train, he stopped."

"Somebody's always got to spoil things," Alan said.

"Seems like that, doesn't it?" she said, looking directly into his eyes before turning and quickly walking away.

"It's so big and empty in here," Alan said. "Even my voice echoes."

"You wait until you see it in operation. This is really a small packinghouse compared to others. It gets quite crowded in here." She walked along a conveyer belt and ran her hand along the worn, rough surface of the belt. "It hasn't changed since I can remember."

"I guess when you find something that works well, why try to fix it?" he said.

"You saw the boxes stacked in the grove, didn't you?"

"Yeah," Alan said, following her around the room.

"Well, we load those boxes onto flatbed trucks and haul them over here. Once they're unloaded, Smitty takes it from there. Early in the morning he turns on the belt from up there," she said, pointing to an old-looking switch high over head on the side of a pole.

Alan glanced to where she was pointing and then looked closer at the wires leading to the switch.

"That wiring looks kind of old to me."

"Probably is," she said. "But as long as it carries current . . . like you said, why fix it if it works already?"

Alan nodded, impressed with the place.

"You really have to see it in full swing to get the whole picture," she said as they left the building. "In just a couple of weeks, it won't look quite this clean and neat."

When they got back in the car, Alan turned to her before starting the engine. "Retta," he said gently, "I get the idea you've been avoiding me."

"Not really," she said, dropping her long lashes and covering her dark eyes. "I've been busy."

"Everybody's busy," he said. "No, I think it's more than that."

"It's nothing."

"It's something to me."

"I'll try to do better, all right?" Her voice held a hint of sarcasm.

"I'm right, then. You have been keeping your distance." Alan waited for her response.

Retta turned away from him and looked out the window. "You asked me to think about it, remember?"

"I remember."

"Then let me do it," she said softly.

"You've had weeks," he said.

"Like I said, Alan, I've been a little busy."

"Okay, I won't pressure you."

"Thank you."

"You're welcome." Alan started the engine and turned the car toward home.

They drove the short distance to the McCarron place in silence. Stopping in the driveway in front of the house, Alan waited while she opened the door and got out.

"You coming in?" she asked.

"No, I don't think so."

"Paddy's expecting a chess match from you."

"Tell him we'll do it another time."

"You could tell him yourself," she said.

"Now who's pressuring who?"

Stepping back from the car, she turned and walked quickly around the house to the back door. Turning the car around in the driveway, he saw Glenna running down the front steps toward him, waving.

"Hi there!" she called cheerfully. "Where you going in such a hurry? I thought you were coming in."

"Not tonight," Alan said, staring straight out the windshield of his car.

"Got plans?" she asked.

"Not really." His words were clipped.

"Want to go to Scottie's?"

"No thanks."

"Too bad," she said, leaning against the door of his car. "I thought we might have some fun tonight. It's too quiet around here for me." She leaned slightly into the window, putting her face close to his. "I bet you would be a barrel of laughs if you'd only let yourself have a little fun now and then."

Turning his face toward hers, he dropped his voice to a raspy whisper. "Listen, Glenna. I've said it before, but maybe I didn't make myself clear. Back off. Get it? Stay clear of me."

"You don't scare me, Alan Conrad. Once I set my sights on something I want, I don't give up easily."

"You're wasting your time," he said angrily.

"I'll be the judge of that. Besides, it's my time, isn't it?"

Alan shoved his car in gear, gently pressed on the gas, and urged his car forward.

Stepping back a few steps, Glenna caught sight of Retta watching from the window in the den. "See you later," she called loudly after Alan. "I'll be at Scottie's."

Hurrying back into the house, Glenna ran past her mother and headed up the stairs.

"You going out?" Connie called after her daughter.

"Yeah, I'm meeting a friend at—in town," she said loudly enough for Retta to hear.

———

"I don't know what to do," Alan confided to Jim later. "I'm confused. I thought she was coming around before I left. Now that I'm back I get the freeze."

"Maybe she's confused right now," Linda suggested as she served the two young men steaming bowls of chili. "Perhaps you could give her a little more time."

"You think something could be bothering her?" Jim asked.

"That's my guess," Alan said. "But—"

"Maybe it has nothing to do with you." Jim dipped a large piece of French bread in his chili, then stuffed it into his mouth.

"Maybe," Linda offered, "it has to do with her family or the grove. That's it! Maybe she still doesn't know how to interpret your involvement with the orange grove."

"You know," Alan said thoughtfully, "they have this thick, tight hedge around the entire place. You know the one I mean?"

"The privet hedge?" Jim asked.

"Is that what it is?"

"It was planted probably sixty years ago. It's to keep out intruders, poachers, and the like. You know, like a fence."

"It's like she has one of those around her heart. It's like she sees me as the intruder."

"Can you blame her?" Linda said. "In a way that's what you are. And, your being here is threatening to her, Alan. Don't you see that? Her whole life is changing, right before her very eyes. You, dear friend, are the embodiment of that change."

"Would it be better if I left?"

"Don't you dare," Jim said. "We've come to like you around here. Are you going to give up this easy? Maybe during the picking she'll open up. Just you stay steady. Let her see that you're not the big bad guy she thinks you are."

"I heard you're going to help out," Alan said, nodding to Jim.

"Yeah, I'm not sure I can keep up with the more experienced pickers. But Sean offered me the chance and we could use the extra money."

"You saving up for something special?" Alan asked, then noticed the exchanged looks between the young couple.

"You know, Linda's been teaching nursery school. We'd like to have a family of our own and we'd like to get ahead so she can quit working when that happens."

Alan relaxed against the kitchen chair and crossed his legs, bringing one ankle to rest on the opposite knee. "You guys would make great parents."

"We hope so," Linda said. "We've been praying about it for quite a while now. We think we're pretty settled here in Summerwind. It's a nice place to raise a family. How about you? You interested in settling down and raising a family?"

"Now hold on there, honey," Jim said to his wife. "She thinks everyone should get married, you know."

"Well," Alan said. "I've thought about it a time or two.

Wanted to finish college and get some direction before I got serious about anybody."

"You leave a string of broken hearts in New York?" Linda asked.

"I doubt that very much," he said. "A few college romances. They didn't come to anything, though."

"Then you're a free man," she said with a teasing expression on her face.

"Watch out," Jim said, laughing. "You never want to tell a preacher's wife you're fair game."

"I get the feeling you'd prefer to not be considered 'fair game,' would you, Alan?" Linda asked more seriously. "You've got your eye focused on one girl at the moment, don't you?"

"Maybe so," Alan said. "Maybe so. But like I said, she's not giving me the time of day at the moment."

"At the moment," Jim encouraged. "But give her time, and, Alan, don't forget, give God time. Things can change. Can you be patient?"

"Do I have a choice?" Alan said.

Eighteen

A few mornings later, Alan was surprised to find light frost glistening on the top of his car when he went out to the sorting shed with Pat.

"Oh, oh," Pat said, running his finger through the dusting of glistening white. "Must have dropped lower than expected last night."

"It's probably freezing back home," Alan said, shrugging off the slight chill.

"You don't grow oranges back home," Pat said seriously. "We better turn on the radio."

"Unseasonably cool temperatures dropped an unexpected frosty curtain over the entire valley," the radio announcer said from the small plastic radio in the sorting shed. "Valley growers would do well to have those smudge pots ready. The cool temperatures look like they could be with us for a while."

"Well, Alan," Pat teased, "this is your lucky day."

"It is?"

"You are going to learn how to keep your crop from freezing."

"Freezing?" Alan, comfortable in only a light jacket, couldn't imagine that the grove was in any danger. "You must be joking!"

"Afraid not," Pat said. "We'd better get Retta out here. We've some decisions to make."

"Well, these are our options," Retta said as she walked into the shed a short while later. "We can pick now, but the fruit will be much better if we can let it stay on the trees another two weeks. Or," she continued thoughtfully, "we can put our energies into flooding or smudging."

"Or both," Pat said.

"Or both," she agreed. "And, as I see it, even if we picked, we'd have to smudge anyway. In saving our oranges—without smudging—we risk our trees."

"In other words," Alan said, "save these oranges, but risk next year's crop."

"You learn fast," Pat said.

"Guess we better round up some help," Retta said. "We're going to be busy for a few days a least."

"What do we do?" Alan asked, rubbing his hands together.

"You go out back of the tool shed and bring in the smudge pots," Pat said. "I'll check the fuel supply."

"I'll get on the phone—wonder if the *zanjero* is releasing any water for flooding?"

Suddenly a different schedule and focus was put into place. Each person was assigned a task, and the defensive strategy against the cold weather was initiated.

By midmorning Alan had gathered up the rusty, strange-looking fuel burners. He couldn't imagine trying to heat an orange grove. Pat announced they needed more fuel, just to be on the safe side. Retta came back with a list of men who would come and help. Paddy planted himself firmly in the tool shed and began the tedious task of examining and filling the pots.

At four in the afternoon, the group dispersed for a few hours' sleep in preparation for the long night ahead. Consuela organized her kitchen and began cooking and baking. At nine o'clock, everyone gathered in Consuela's large kitchen for a hot meal and last-minute instructions.

"Before we go out," Sean said, "I'd like to have the preacher, here, offer a word of prayer."

The group bowed their heads and, in a normal conversational tone, Jim simply and straightforwardly addressed the situation they faced. "You know better than anyone else the challenge we're up against, Father. We ask you for strength, wisdom, and above all else, your protection and favor—not only for ourselves, but for our trees. In Jesus' name we stand before you, boldly, unashamed, and convinced that you have not only our work, but us, in your care. Amen."

Retta took the team of workers and headed for the shed. Alan watched her as she expertly directed the placing of the large pots in their strategic locations throughout the grove.

"You keep an eye on these six," she said to Alan. "I'll be around later to check the fuel levels. Keep an eye on that one over there first. We've filled them to different levels so they won't all need refilling at once."

"How long will this go on?" he asked when she came by in the pickup an hour later.

"All night."

"I know that," he said, waving his hand through the thick smoke flowing through the air. "I mean, how many nights?"

"As many as it takes," she said flatly. "Put that one in the truck and take a full one to replace it," she said without looking up from the diagram in her hand.

"What's that?"

"It's my own system for keeping track of which ones we've filled and which ones will be going empty."

"Why don't you just bring the fuel out and fill it out here?"

"It's pretty hard to do that in the dark," she said. "Besides, the trees like water at their roots, not spilled fuel oil."

"But they like this smoke, I guess?"

"A lot better than ice, I assure you."

"Why don't you get taller chimneys on these things? Get that smoke up above the trees?"

"Because it's the smoke that keeps the frost down," she said, showing little enthusiasm for having to answer his questions.

"I thought it was the heat," he said, glancing with new appreciation at the smoke pouring from the tops of the stubby chimneys.

"You can't heat an entire grove," she said. "In case you haven't noticed, it's kind of wide open out here."

Alan watched her drive slowly between the trees to the next section and felt more than a little envy when he heard her friendly tone as she addressed Jim Henry.

Alan waited and watched his smudge pots all night, wishing he had worn his heavier jacket. His hands seemed warmer in his pockets than when he wore his gloves. In spite of the heavy smoke and acrid smell of the burning fuel, he kept moving between the pots, rushing to their warmth.

When dawn finally came, Retta came to get him, and together they loaded the smudge pots in the truck.

"I'm bushed," he said as he loaded the last pot on the truck.

"Well, in a couple more hours you can get some sleep. But first we clean the pots and get them ready for tonight."

The next five days and nights were a blur of activity in all the orange groves in the valley. High school kids, along with other available help, were hired to stand guard over the smudge pots all night. Alan barely showered the dirt and grime from each exhausting night before he tumbled into bed, awakening a few hours later to repeat the cycle all over again.

Just before dawn the last morning of the cold snap, Retta pulled the pickup truck into the grove where Alan sat in the dirt near a warm smudge pot, waiting for morning.

"It's over," she said, coming to drop beside him in the dirt.

"What?"

"The weather report says a high of seventy-two today and a low tonight of forty-five. The cold front has moved east. Look," she said, pointing toward the nearby mountains. "It's snowing up there now."

Alan squinted his tired eyes, trying to see what she saw. "How can you tell? All I see is dark clouds. You can't even see the hills." Alan hesitated to move from the warmth of the last burning smudge pot. "It still feels cold to me."

"No kidding?"

"It's not the same as back East. This kind of cold gets into your bones. Chills me clear through."

"It's still only about twenty-eight degrees," she said. "But once that sun comes up, it'll warm up."

He searched the overcast predawn sky. "Looks cloudy, doesn't it?" he commented.

"We might even get a little rain," she said. "It would really help wash the smoke out of the air."

"You tired?" he said, seeing the tiredness in her eyes.

"You're cold to the bone, and I'm tired to the bone."

"Do you have to do this every year?"

"Not every year. But then some years we've done it two or three times. It doesn't usually last quite this long. Five days is a long time to keep the pots going."

"Now you tell me," he said. "I thought I was just being—"

"You've been great," she said, smiling in his direction. "I watched you. You really aren't afraid to pitch in and work, are you?"

Alan shrugged and looked at the cloudy sky lightening with streaks of pink.

"I mean it, Alan," she said quietly. "You did a great job."

"Thanks," he said. "That mean's a lot coming from you."

"Oh?"

"You have to admit, you've been a little less than friendly lately."

"Have I?"

"Retta, have I done something to offend you?" he asked.

"Not really, I guess," she said, picking up a stick and beginning to trace randomly in the dirt.

"You know I had hoped—well, you know. I don't have to say it again, do I?"

"No, guess not."

An awkward silence fell between them, and Alan watched the young woman sitting near him in the dirt. He couldn't imagine a less—or more—romantic setting. Her long hair, pulled back into her usual braided ponytail, was covered with her dark, floppy-brimmed leather hat. She pulled her knees up and wrapped her slender legs with her arms as she leaned forward to rest her forehead on her knees.

"You are tired," Alan said, reaching to lay his hand lightly at the base of her neck. The last time he touched her, he had sensed her stiffen and resist. Now, she just sat beside him without moving.

"I'm so tired I could cry." Her voice was muffled and almost too low for Alan to hear clearly.

Sliding closer, he removed her hat, slid his other hand along her shoulder, and pulled her to lean against him. He turned his head slightly, bringing his chin to rest on the top of her head. In a few moments, he tipped her chin toward him with his finger and noticed the dirty smudges smeared on her nose, cheeks, and across her chin. Smiling, he could hardly resist kissing her.

"You're really something, you know that?"

"Oh yeah?"

"I've never met anyone like you before," he said. "In fact, I'm not sure there is anyone quite like you."

"Hmm," she said, putting her head back on his shoulder.

"Retta," he said softly into her smoke-filled hair. "Have you thought about—well, you know. I'd like to take you out some-time."

"I've thought about it," she said.

"And?" His heart was suddenly beating faster and he saw a glimmer of hope.

"And—" she said, then paused and turned her head away from him. "Listen, do you hear the porch bell?"

"Yeah, is that what that is?"

"Mama must have breakfast ready." Retta plopped her hat back on her head and stood up.

Alan scrambled to his feet, anxious for her to finish her sentence. "Retta McCarron," he said roughly. Grabbing her hand, he spun her around and pulled her into his arms. "Don't do this to me."

"Do what?" she smiled. She reached for her hat, trying to keep it from falling from her head.

Alan's blue eyes filled with tenderness as he pulled her closer and lowered his face toward hers. "As if you didn't know." His voice was a raspy, low whisper as his arms tight-ened around her.

"Alan," she said softly. Suddenly, she turned her head away from him. "Wait. Mama's still ringing the bell. Listen."

"I don't hear anything," he said.

"Listen!" she insisted. Her voice held a hint of alarm. "She doesn't just keep ringing it. Something must be wrong!" Pull-ing away from Alan's reach, she yelled over her shoulder. "Get in!"

Driving through the grove, she pulled up beside Jim Henry, already on a dead run toward the house. "Hop on!" she yelled out the window. Jim jumped onto the running board of the old pickup truck and swung himself up into the bed. By the time they got to the house, the pickup held half a dozen tired and dirty workers.

As they pulled around the tool shed and toward the house,

Alan spotted some commotion out by the carriage house.

"Oh, dear God! Retta! Your father has fallen off the roof!"

"The roof?" Retta sprang from the truck and gathered her mother in her arms.

Before the truck came to a complete stop, Alan opened the door and jumped out. He ran toward the carriage house, Jim right behind him.

"What happened?" Alan kneeled in the dirt beside Sean McCarron, who lay there grimacing in pain.

"I went to check the roof. The weather report said we could have rain later this afternoon or tonight." Sean's face was covered in beads of sweat. "I thought I'd better get the rest of the tar paper on before . . . I must have stepped on some frost . . . slipped."

Paddy's face was drawn and his eyes wide with panic. "He was up there," he said, pointing to the second story.

"It's barely light out," Jim said. "Sometimes that light pine can look wet when it's really covered in glaze."

"Go call a doctor," Alan ordered.

"He's on his way," Connie said. "Sean . . ." Connie came to kneel beside her husband.

"I'm all right, just twisted my leg a bit. Help me up."

"Sean McCarron," she said sternly, "you lie still. You're doing no such thing."

"No, I think I'm just shaken up a bit," he said. "Let me get into a more comfortable position then."

Alan and Jim exchanged glances. "Better get a blanket, Retta," Jim said. At the same moment, Alan and Jim stripped off their jackets and covered Sean the best they could. In the early morning light, they could see his face was pale and his lips were starting to tremble.

Retta returned with several blankets and they covered Sean with all of them.

"If we could just get him off the cold ground," Connie said.

"We don't dare move him," Jim said as he came alongside her. "Retta, go call Linda. Tell her to call the prayer chain." Jim looked into the stunned face of the ordinarily calm young woman. "Retta!" he said more forcefully. "Go call Linda!"

"Her number's in the little book by the phone," Connie

said. "Please, *m'hija*, do what Jim says."

Retta reluctantly went to make the call, and just as she was hanging up the phone, she heard the wail of the ambulance's siren in the distance.

"What's going on?" Glenna asked sleepily as she shuffled into the kitchen.

"Daddy's had an accident," Retta told her bluntly before returning to rejoin her mother at Sean's side.

Pat stood helplessly by, comforting and trying to reassure Paddy.

"Daddy! Daddy!" Glenna screamed as she ran across the yard.

"You better try to keep her away," Jim said to Alan.

"Jim, I—"

"We've got to try to keep him calm," Jim said. "The last thing he needs is to see his daughter in hysterics."

Alan crossed the yard to meet Glenna before she could upset Sean and Connie any more than they already were.

At first, Glenna tried to resist his attempts to restrain her. Then, catching a glimpse of Retta watching, she turned toward Alan and flung herself against him, sobbing uncontrollably.

Stunned by her reaction, Alan slid his arms around her, trying to calm her down. The more comfort he tried to give, the louder she cried and the tighter she clung to him. "Glenna," he finally said, "stop it! You're not doing anybody any good like this."

The doctor jumped from the ambulance and ran toward the carriage house. Within a few moments he determined that Sean had to be moved and waved for the attendants to bring the stretcher.

Alan wanted to return to Sean's side and assist with getting him into the ambulance, but he couldn't pull himself away from Glenna's hysterical clutches. All he could do was watch from a distance. Jim put Connie into the backseat of his car with Retta at her side, and Pat and Paddy crowded into the front seat for the ride to the hospital.

He could see the expression on Retta's dirty, tired face as they drove away, leaving him standing in the driveway with his arms around her sobbing sister.

As soon as they drove out of sight, Alan felt Glenna relax against him and her hands begin to move against his back. He grabbed her by both arms and pulled himself away from her. "You never miss a beat, do you?"

"I don't know what you mean," she said, wiping the tears from her face.

"Of course not," Alan said sarcastically as he stepped away from her and turned to walk to his car. "You better go tell Joanna what happened. Somebody will call you and tell you what's going on."

"Aren't you going to take me to the hospital?" she whined.

"You've got a car—take yourself," he said with disgust.

Nineteen

"For a man who fell two stories, he's very lucky," the doctor told the group huddled silently in the waiting room. "He has a nasty break in his right leg. In fact, the leg's broken in more than one place. We'll know more when we get some X-rays. There's an injury in the hip area—while it looks to be the most serious, we don't know how bad it is just yet."

Connie stood to face the doctor, and Retta rose to be as close to her mother as possible. "Is he going to be all right?"

"It's too early to say, but he doesn't seem to be in any immediate danger. He's never lost consciousness, and there doesn't seem to be any trauma to his head or upper body. He says he was able to break his fall somewhat by grabbing on to the roof just before he went over the edge. It appears he landed on his leg. He probably twisted it from the full force of his body weight. Like I said, Mrs. McCarron, he's a very lucky man. A fall from that height could have been much worse." He looked into the tired eyes of the small, attractive, dark-haired woman. "We'll be keeping him pretty busy for a while. Before we begin, why don't you come in and see him for a few minutes. He's been asking for you."

Connie followed the doctor and disappeared into an examining room in the rear of the emergency department.

"I think we should all go home and get some rest as soon as Connie comes back," Pat suggested.

"I can't leave," Retta said.

"You've been up all night, darlin'," Pat said, pulling her into a warm embrace. "Look at you. You're tired and dirty. You need some rest. Your mama's had a few hours sleep, at least. She and your daddy went up to bed around one or so. They got up at five—he wanted to get out to the roof, and she decided you all should have a good breakfast after smudging all night."

Retta looked down at her filthy clothes and rubbed a hand wearily across her forehead. "I guess you're right. But I want to wait for Mama."

As soon as Consuela came back, she smiled weakly at Retta, Pat, and Paddy. "He'll be all right," she said. "They've taken him for X-rays now. As soon as they know he doesn't have any internal injuries, they'll give him something for the pain. I hope it isn't too long." She remained calm, and though her face was lined with concern, she didn't appear to be panicked.

"Somebody, take Retta home. Pat, Paddy, you go too. I'll stay here; you can all come back later. Get cleaned up, and get some sleep. And," she added firmly, "you all need something to eat. Breakfast is on the stove. I hope it's still good—"

"Mama," Retta said. "Don't worry about us. Don't you want me to stay with you for a while?"

"Look at you, *m'hija*, you're dead on your feet. I'll need you more later. Send Glenna and Joanna back to stay with me."

"And you, Connie," Jim said, "you haven't had much rest either."

"I won't leave Sean," she said. "I'll rest once he does."

"Alan," Jim said, "take the family home. I'll stay until Glenna gets here. Besides, I called Linda. She's on her way."

Retta felt better knowing her mother wouldn't be alone, but still hesitated to leave her.

"Go on with you," Connie said. "The sooner you go, the sooner you'll be back. I've enough to worry about with Sean in there. I don't want to worry about all of you, too."

Alan crossed the small distance between him and Retta and put his arm around her shoulders. Pat came alongside, and together they urged her toward the door.

"You too, sweetheart," Connie said to Paddy. "Go on and get some rest. You can come back later."

Driving out of the parking lot, they saw Glenna's car just turning in. Pulling alongside, Alan lowered his window in response to her signal.

"You going to the house?" she asked. "Are you coming

back later?" She never took her eyes from Alan's face. He stared directly out the front window of his car and let Pat answer her questions from the backseat.

"You stay with your mama until we get back," Pat said.

"But I have to go to work," Glenna said. "I'll leave Joanna here with her."

Retta watched Alan's jaw tense and pulsate before he shot a glance in her direction, then quickly looked away.

"What about you, Alan?" Glenna said. "Will I see you later?"

"I'll be around," he said flatly.

"Good," she said with a flirtatious grin.

Back at the house, Retta could hardly conceal the anger she felt building within. Silently, she tended to the breakfast Connie had prepared earlier. Adding a little water, she absently stirred the oatmeal, thickened from standing in the pan. Alan reached around her and put a pot of fresh coffee on the back burner to perk. He poked a finger in the unbaked biscuits waiting in their pan and opened the oven door to find it still on. Slipping the biscuits into the hot oven, he turned to finish setting the table with the dishes Connie had abandoned at the sound of Paddy's voice when Sean fell.

Moving to Retta's other side, he lifted a lid on a frying pan and found bacon, now cold and stuck in thick, white grease. He found the right knob and turned on the heat beneath the skillet, hoping the meat could be rescued.

Pat and Paddy sat at the table, staring and silent. Alan poured fresh orange juice into four small glasses and put them on the table before returning to check the sizzling bacon.

Retta remained trancelike, her eyes fastened on the bubbling oatmeal as she continued to stir it. She wasn't even aware of Alan's movement around her and unconsciously responded as he gently moved her to one side, then the other as he worked around her.

"I think that's ready," he said, gently taking the wooden spoon from her hand.

"Oh, yeah, I guess it is," she said quietly.

"Come on." His voice was tender and patient. "Sit down and eat something."

"I don't think I can," she said.

"Now, Retta," Pat said, leaning toward her across the table. "If your mama comes home and finds all this food has gone to waste, she'll be as mad as a wet hen."

"Let's say a blessing, shall we?" Alan suggested.

"Go right ahead," Pat said and bowed his head obediently.

"Who wants to pray?" Alan asked.

"I think it's up to you," Paddy said quietly without looking up from his plate.

Alan swallowed hard, not knowing exactly how to begin. "Our dear heavenly Father," he said hesitantly. "We thank Thee for this food." His voice was halting and stiff. Taking a deep breath, he shut his eyes tighter. Then in a gush of words he let the rest of his prayer out. "And we are so glad that nothing worse happened to Sean. We ask for strength for this day, and the days to come. Amen."

Alan opened his eyes to see tears flowing down Retta's face, still stained and dirty from the night in the smoke-filled grove. Pat and Paddy began eating, silently. This meal was being eaten out of obligation to Connie and out of a physical need for nourishment—nothing more.

"I guess I really am hungry," she said in a low voice. Retta took a few sips of her orange juice and a couple bites of a hot biscuit before her appetite overcame her emotions.

After the four had finished breakfast, Retta stood to clear away the dishes. "I'll do that," Alan offered. He came to her side and steered her away from the table. "You go on upstairs and get some rest."

"What about you? You're tired, too."

"I'll be all right—I'll just put them in the sink. We'll do them later, okay?"

"Hello!" A friendly sounding woman's voice drifted in from the back porch. "Good morning, I'm Mattie Sloan. Linda Henry called earlier and told me what happened. After we prayed for Mr. McCarron, I told Ben I thought you might need a hand out here. Looks like I came right in time. I'll take care of these dishes," she said decisively. "Look at the lot of you.

You been up all night smudging? Get on with you. You'll be wanting to get cleaned up and some sleep before you go back to the hospital. Don't you worry about nothing else except to pray for that daddy of yours," she said to Retta. "I'll take care of things around here. You've got enough on your mind."

Alan remembered the grandmotherly woman from the few Sundays he had attended Jim Henry's church. He flashed her a thankful smile and returned his attention to Retta. "Go on. Do what Mattie says."

Taking her by the arm, he walked her to the bottom of the stairway. Just before she went up, he gently tugged on her arm and she turned to face him. "Retta, don't worry. It's going to be all right. Just don't worry."

Wanting to lose herself in his arms, Retta glanced away from his disarming gaze instead.

"I mean it, don't worry," he said. Lifting her chin gently, he forced her to look at him. "Don't worry about *anything*."

She took a step away from him and walked heavily up the stairs. Aware that he was still standing at the bottom, she paused halfway up and without turning said, "Not even about Glenna?"

"No," he whispered huskily, "*especially* about Glenna."

He waited at the bottom of the stairs, listening as she shut the door to her room. He heard the slight squeak of her bed, and then her muffled sobs. Putting one foot on the stairs, he felt a gentle hand of restraint on his arm.

"You go get some rest," Mattie said. "I'll go up to her." Mattie didn't wait for his response, but brushed past him and headed up the stairway. He didn't turn from his position at the bottom stair until he heard the bedroom door open and shut again.

Slowly, he turned and headed toward the back door. Tiredness swept over him, and for the first time he realized just how exhausted he was.

Heading out the back door, his mind already on taking a shower and climbing into bed, he was surprised to find a strangely familiar man walking around the carriage house.

"G'morning," the man said, extending his hand toward

Alan. "I'm Mark Andrews. Heard you had a little problem here this morning."

"Andrews?" Alan said, trying to make a mental connection. "Have we met before?"

"Sure. At church. Linda Henry called this morning and told me what happened. We're all praying for McCarron. But I wondered if there wasn't something else I might be able to do." Mark nodded toward the building project. "I have a crew that's standing idle today. I thought I might be able to send them over here and get that roof on."

"A crew?"

"What's that you say?" Pat's voice boomed from behind the two men.

"Pat, this is Mark Andrews. This is Pat McCarron, Sean's brother."

"Sorry to hear about the accident. I was telling this young man that I have a crew of men I could spare for half a day. I'd say we could have that roof covered in about that much time."

"Is that right?" Pat looked more than a little suspicious. "How much?"

"Mr. McCarron, I'm paying my men anyway. A load of materials was expected yesterday and it won't be in until late today. I'd rather the men be working than standing around. It won't cost me one cent more to have them come over here and put that roof on."

"I want to make sure I understand," Pat said. "You offerin' to come get that roof on for nothin'?"

"Have you had a lower bid?" Mark's face broke into a wide smile.

"No sir, can't say I have." Pat shrugged and looked at Alan.

"Good, then we'll have the job done by dark. And, I might add, not a minute too soon. Rain's coming in." Mark stuck his hand out to Pat, and Pat met it with his own. "I'll get things rolling. You guys look like you could use some sleep. Hope the noise doesn't keep you awake."

"It'll be as sweet as a lullaby," Pat said, slapping Mark on the back good-naturedly. "Come on, I'll show you the materials. Sean picked them up yesterday."

Less than half an hour later, Alan ran into Pat in the hallway of the small house they shared.

"What d'ya make of that guy?" Pat asked, his broad smile still in place. "Where'd he come from, anyway?"

"He goes to Jim's church," Alan said matter-of-factly.

"Oh," Pat said. "I guess that explains it."

Twenty

"Daddy," Retta whispered later as she stood beside her sleeping father. "Daddy, I love you so much."

"Retta," he said, his voice hoarse and drugged from the pain-killer administered earlier that evening.

"Shh . . ." She held a finger to his lips. Leaning over, she kissed his whiskered cheek and nuzzled her face into his neck.

"What did the doctor say?" he asked.

"Didn't Mama tell you?"

"I don't remember. Is she still here?"

"No. Jim and Linda took her home a few minutes ago."

"That's good. What time is it?"

"Ten."

"Night or morning?"

"P.M."

"It's late. Don't you want to go on home?"

"No, I've taken the night shift," she said. Pulling the bed-side chair nearer, she sat down and leaned forward, putting her head on the pillow near her father's. "I slept all day."

"You don't have to stay here all night," he said.

"My schedule is kind of messed up. Anyway, this is much better than working the grove all night." Then, remembering her father's pain, she said, "Oh, Daddy, I'm sorry. I didn't mean—"

"I know you didn't, sweetheart." Sean had no doubt about the love of his middle daughter. "Can I have a drink of water?"

"I'm not sure," she said. "I better ask a nurse." Retta found the button hanging from a long cord and pressed it to call for assistance. "Let's not do anything against the rules, okay?"

"I guess I really pulled a dumb stunt, didn't I?" he asked.

"I guess you did, at that."

"I knew better," he said. "I would have never let a carpenter up there under those conditions. I can't imagine what I was thinking—"

"Don't, Daddy. What's done is done. What's important now is for you to get well."

"Up until midnight," the nurse said when Sean asked about the water. "Nothing after that. We want his stomach completely empty. It's better for afterward."

"Afterward?" Sean asked.

"Your surgery," the nurse said, straightening his covers and checking the intravenous line.

"Surgery?" he asked, frowning in Retta's direction.

"Did you forget?" his daughter said. "They have to go in and set your broken ankle with a pin."

"Everything's kind of foggy," he said, rubbing his forehead. "I have only a vague recollection. . . ."

"You've a nasty break in your ankle, Mr. McCarron," the nurse said. "Among other things."

"Other things?"

"You have two other breaks, Dad," Retta tried to explain. She pointed to his immobilized leg suspended in a heavy temporary splint.

"No kiddin'?" he said. "No wonder I hurt."

"It's just about time for another pain shot. I'll see what I can do."

"Really hurts, doesn't it?" Retta said sympathetically after the nurse left the room.

"Yeah, it really does." He cast a sideways glance at his daughter. Her long, red-brown hair hung loosely around her shoulders. "You really goin' to stay the night?"

"Right here," she said. "I might have to get a cup of coffee later, but I'm here for the duration."

The nurse bustled back into the room and prepared to give Sean his pain shot. Retta looked away for a moment.

"The doctor says I'm a lucky man," he said as the pain medication began to take effect.

"He's wrong," Retta said softly. "We're the lucky ones. We could have lost you."

"I've been thinkin'," Sean said drowsily.

"You should've done that before you walked out on that icy roof," she teased.

He smiled his characteristic one-sided smile, his eyelids heavy from the drug. "No kiddin', honey. I think the doctor is wrong. Luck had nothin' to do with it. I shoulda been killed in a fall like that. I've been thinkin' God must've been up early this mornin', too."

"Shh," she whispered, stroking his silver-streaked red-bronze hair from his broad forehead. "Sleep now, Daddy." Watching her father's breathing deepen and his face relax, she knew the medication had helped him drift off to sleep. She turned off the overhead light and sat in a bigger, more comfortable chair in the corner of the room. Deciding to rest when he did, she leaned her head back and closed her eyes.

"Retta." She startled at the whisper of her name and the touch of a hand on her arm. "It's me."

"Alan," she said softly. "What are you doing here?"

"Same as you," he whispered, nodding toward the bed. "How is he?"

"Sleeping, I think. What time is it?"

"A little after midnight."

"How long have you been here?" Retta asked, rubbing her eyes.

"An hour or so, I guess."

"I didn't hear you come in," she said.

"I know," he smiled, almost feeling guilty for the wonderful feelings he felt being so close to her. "You were sleeping."

"And Daddy?"

"Sleeping," Alan said. "The nurse comes in and checks him every fifteen minutes. I guess we're all exhausted from working so hard this last week."

"Did you see Mama?"

"She's at the house. Mattie Sloan's sleeping over. Said she wanted to be nearby in case Connie needed her."

"She's a wonderful friend, isn't she?"

"I know how she feels," he said, his eyes tenderly searching Retta's lovely face.

"You do?"

"I wanted to be here for the same reason." Alan looked

away from her toward Sean. "He's resting quite comfortably, considering."

"He'll get another shot at two," she said looking at her watch. "I think they're trying to keep him as quiet as they can."

"Is he in a lot of pain?"

"More than he'll admit," she said.

"How about you?" he asked. "You doing all right? You need anything?"

"I'm okay. I'm thirsty, though. Maybe you could get me a drink of water?"

"How about a Coke?"

"Sounds good."

"You want to go down to the cafeteria?"

"It's not open this late, is it?"

"No, but the vending machines are," he smiled. "I checked."

She looked at her father. "I hate to leave him," she said.

"He won't even know. We'll tell the nurses where we'll be. If he needs you, they'll come and get us."

"It feels kind of good to stretch a bit," she said as they left the elevator and followed the directional signs to the dimly lit, deserted cafeteria. "I guess I had my neck bent wrong—it's kind of stiff."

"Here," he said. Slipping his long fingers under her hair and around the back of her neck, he began to massage her neck gently.

"That feels good," she said, closing her eyes.

Alan resisted the urge to pull her into the circle of his arms and capture the kiss he had wanted earlier that morning in the grove. "Come on now," he said, releasing her neck and taking her by the elbow. "Sit down and I'll get you a bottle of pop."

"I had an interesting conversation with Dad," she said when Alan returned, taking the frosty glass container and holding it between her long, work-roughened fingers.

"Oh yeah?"

"He said something I never thought I'd hear him say." She took a long drink from the small bottle opening. "He actually said that God must've been watching out for him this morning."

"You want a cup?" Alan asked.

"No, this is fine. You know, Dad hasn't had much use for the church, or God for that matter, for a long, long time."

Alan watched her as she stared at the bubbling liquid in the bottle.

"I've never been quite sure what happened, but he quit going to church a few years ago. He and my mother never discussed it with us kids. But I think he must have gotten offended or hurt in some way."

"At church?"

"We attended a small church on the edge of town," she said. "Dad helped get a new Sunday school building built. He was on the board, if I remember it right, and spent most of his time there during the building project. When he got involved, he got totally involved." Retta took a long drink of her Coke.

"My dad has mostly been a financial benefactor, rather than an actual participant in things like that."

"Your parents go to church?"

"Well, they attend, but really nothing more. But we're talking about your dad."

"Something happened at one of the board meetings. He came home very late and you could hear his voice all over the house when he came in. I've never seen him so mad—ever."

"Something to do with the building?"

"I'm not sure. He's not the type to have to have his way, unless they wanted to skimp on quality or use cheap materials. I don't think that was it, though. I can't put my finger on it, for sure. A visiting preacher was in town and wanted to come and pray for Paddy about that same time."

"When did Paddy get sick?"

"I was really little—about five or six, I think. Paddy was almost eight."

"That must have been scary," Alan said, shaking his head.

"Polio," Retta said quietly, "was always scary. Mama wouldn't let us go swimming at the pool or anything. Never quite knew where he got it for sure. He's never admitted it, but Bobby and Donny may have talked him into sneaking—"

"You mean going swimming without your parents' permission?"

"Maybe, who knows. They were always up to something. Always trying to get Paddy involved, then blaming him if anything went wrong. Anyway, this preacher wanted to pray for Paddy. Mama and Daddy had terrible arguments about it."

"What could that hurt if someone prayed for him?"

"Nothing, at least that I can see. But I did hear my father say that he didn't have much faith in the preacher's way of praying."

"What did he mean by that?"

"I'm not sure. Like I said, this was a few years ago. I was only about twelve. Paddy and Glenna were fifteen at the time."

"Did Paddy get prayed for?"

"I think so. But as you can see, it didn't do much good. All I remember that night is Daddy yelling at Mama that if he had sinned and done something that needed God's punishment, he's the one who would've been crippled, not Paddy."

"Do you think someone could have accused your dad of bringing on Paddy's illness?"

"I'm not sure. Someday I thought I'd ask Mama. But mostly I've just left it alone. Anyway, Daddy never went back to church again. He didn't stop Mama from going and taking us kids, but he said he wasn't about to listen to any of it—whatever he meant by that."

"Does your father feel responsible for Paddy's condition?"

"Sometimes I think so. But what parent wouldn't?"

"I see what you mean. Every parent probably feels responsible when something bad happens to a child. I know I probably would." Alan's face was shadowed by the thought.

"It wasn't anybody's fault," Retta said quietly. "I didn't get sick, and Glenna didn't either. Neither did Joanna. I just think that if God doesn't do things the way we think He should, we try to find excuses for Him. You know, other reasons. Doesn't anybody ever think that God might have His own reasons for doing things certain ways?"

"That's an interesting way to look at it," Alan said.

"I just think we ought to give God more credit than we do."

"More credit?"

"To see things we don't, to know things we never will."

Alan smiled, knowing she was sharing some of her deepest inner thoughts with him. "You could be right," he said, wishing she would say more. "You've given this some thought, haven't you?"

"Occasionally. It's not like it dominates my mind every day. But there are times when I think about it, yes."

"And?"

"And what?"

"What else do you think?" he asked, hoping for more.

She leaned toward Alan and motioned him to come closer to hear what she was about to say. "I have wondered if the visiting preacher didn't feel it was necessary to find a reason why *his* prayers weren't answered. Maybe he thought the people would blame *him* if he prayed for Paddy and he wasn't healed."

"Wow," Alan said softly. "So he dumped the blame on someone else."

"Is that a crazy way to think?"

"For the preacher, or for you?"

"Me," she said, locking Alan's gaze to her own.

"Have you ever talked to Jim about this?"

"I've never talked to anyone about this," she said with a slight edge of fear to her voice. "I probably shouldn't have told you."

"No, no. Don't ever think you can't talk to me, Retta."

"Maybe I'm crazy," she said, looking down to study the table between them. "I don't know anything. I quit church then, too. I didn't want to go if Daddy wasn't going with us. Mama finally ended up going alone or with Joanna. Glenna didn't want to go, and Paddy was pretty hard to handle without Daddy's help. Finally Mama quit going, too. But you could always tell she missed it."

"But she's going—"

"To River Place Community, I know. She met someone from there and they invited her. She likes it."

"I do, too."

"What's it like?"

"Different than any church I've ever been to before. Jim is quite, well, untraditional."

"That's what Mama says."

"Why don't you come sometime?"

"I don't know," Retta said. "You know, Paddy did all the poinsettia cuttings for the church's Christmas decorations."

"I know. I saw them. He's got quite a knack for growing things, hasn't he?"

"You ever see his room?"

"No, I haven't," Alan said.

"Get him to show you sometime. It's like a jungle."

A silence fell between them, and Alan was afraid to move for fear he'd scare her or that she'd want to return to her father's room.

"Alan?" she said, breaking the silence.

He looked into her dark eyes and found confusion and unspoken questions in her expression.

"I saw you with Glenna."

"What?"

"The day you left for River Hills. I heard your car and was trying to catch you before you left. I saw you talking out in the driveway. It looked like you were—well, I saw her waving as you drove away."

Alan felt the anger rise, leaving a dry, bitter taste in his mouth. "You didn't see anything," he said.

"I saw you again, last week. Talking to her out in the yard. I saw her lean into your window—"

"Retta," Alan said firmly. "Listen to me." He reached across the small table between them and covered her hands with his own. "You haven't seen anything. Do you understand what I'm saying?"

"But I did—"

"No, you didn't. You didn't see us—you saw Glenna."

The look in his eyes pleaded with Retta to understand. His expression had stilled and grown serious. Then putting the matter aside with sudden good humor, he smiled, tightening slightly the pressure on her hands.

"Are you going to tell me that if I had waited a moment longer, I would've been able to say goodbye to you?"

"Maybe" she said, even though she knew it wasn't true. "Probably not."

"Why not?"

"Because when I saw you with Glenna, I went back to work."

"Do you always let her get in your way?" he asked, tracing lightly along one of her fingers with his.

"Is that what I did?"

"After what we discussed the night before, what else could you call it?"

"I just didn't know for sure."

"Please, listen to me, Retta McCarron. I'm not the least bit interested in your sister. And she's not the least bit interested in me."

"Are you sure?"

"Of my interest in her? Absolutely. Of her interest in me? Now that's a question I'd like answered. She's not interested in *me*—but she is interested in getting to me."

"Is there a difference?"

"Oh yes. Definitely."

"What shall we do?"

"About Glenna?" he asked. "Nothing. Now, about us? Well, now, let's give that some thought, shall we?"

Retta looked at Alan, a thoughtful smile curving her mouth.

"What do you say?" he coaxed. "Do we have a deal?"

Her mouth broadened into a wide smile as she placed her hand in the one Alan offered.

"Deal."

Twenty-One

In the two weeks following Sean's surgery, the oranges grew heavy and sweet. Pat and Retta conferred about the best way to bring in the crop and even included Alan in their discussions.

"I know we pretty well shot the budget with the smudging help," Pat said. "But without some extra help, I don't see how we can manage without bringing in a crew of pickers."

"We'll have to hire out the work on the carriage house," Retta said, wishing immediately she could take back her words.

"I'm payin' for that, Retta," Pat said firmly. "It's for me to live in and I won't have Sean payin' for it. Never intended to let him in the first place. But he's such a stubborn man. Now he's not goin' to be puttin' up much of a fuss, is he?" Pat searched his niece's face. "Not unless you spill the beans."

"But your trip, Uncle Pat," Retta protested.

"Don't you worry none about that trip." A warning settled across his rugged features. "Ireland's been there a long time. It'll wait a while longer—that's my guess. I got my farm money. Besides, when we get paid for the crop, I'll come out all right."

"With his medical bills, we're going to be a little short. I know it worries him," Retta said. "But I don't know what to tell him."

"Tell him we're going to handle the picking ourselves. He doesn't really have to know *how* we're doing it, does he?" Pat asked.

"I'd like to get the crop in before he comes home," Retta said. "Then he can't complain too loudly when he hears about the crew."

"Good idea," Pat said, loving the conspiracy. "I'll call the

Santana outfit. Maybe they can fit us in."

————

"If we can take it in two parts, we can work you in," Santana told Pat on the phone. "We've got a four-day job, and a three-day job the next week. The men don't mind workin' long and hard, just before Christmas and all. We can be there Friday, Saturday, and Sunday this weekend and Thursday through Sunday the next."

"We don't work Sundays on our farm," Pat said.

"Well then, let me do some schedule shifting and get back to you. If I can't make changes, I'll need some extra men."

"We can give you three from here," Pat said, committing himself, Alan, and Retta. "Maybe four," he added, thinking about Jim Henry.

"You'll want some for your own roadside stand?"

"We'll mark the trees to leave; we'll do those later," Pat said.

On Wednesday Santana's crew arrived. Retta instructed them to pick around the big house first and leave the far end of the grove for the following week. Sean would be home by then, and he wouldn't be as apt to question or worry about paying the crew in Pat's—or rather, Alan's—portion of the grove.

Alan met the workers with a great deal of excitement and watched with interest as they picked the large orange fruit. Each man was equipped with a large canvas bag with a broad strap that he slung over a shoulder. Once the bag was filled, he took the bag to one of the large wooden boxes spaced throughout the grove. With a well-timed sideways swing, the picker hoisted the bottom of his bag over the side of the picking box, unsnapped the bottom of his bag, and emptied his load, resnapping it on his way back to the trees.

Each man took a set of four trees, sometimes four in a row, sometimes four square. When the skirt of a tree had been picked clean, the picker used a ladder to finish picking. Plunging his hand between the shiny waxlike leaves, he picked by feel, rather than sight.

Alan examined a pair of picker's clippers and turned them

over in his hand. The small plier-type tool lay easily in the palm of his hand, and Alan slipped the small strap over his third finger, securing it to his hand. Within a few minutes, he felt ready to give picking a try.

"Over there," Paddy shouted from the back of the flatbed truck. "In the tool shed."

Alan waved at Retta's brother and headed for the shed. Looking inside, he found a picking sack and an extra set of clippers and headed out to assume responsibility for his own set of trees.

"No," Pat said later, examining the fruit in Alan's bag. "The stems are too long. Here, you do it like this." With a quick rocking movement to the orange, he cut the stem off clean and dropped a softball-sized orange into Alan's bag. "The way you're going at it, we'd be doing the pruning and the picking all at once. Trees can't take that kind of shock," he said with a laugh.

"Just trying to be more efficient," Alan tossed back. "Never hurts to try something new."

"Better not let Retta hear you say that," Pat said just before disappearing between two trees.

Alan worked in silence, trying to master the quick, nimble movement Pat had so expertly demonstrated. He couldn't help but notice how quiet the grove was, even though it was teeming with busy men. Out here he seemed so far removed from the rest of the world. The full trees deadened any sound except those coming from the very next row, or maybe two. Each long row seemed more endless than the next, and a person could easily feel all alone in the trees.

"How's it coming?" Retta inquired, startling Alan as she suddenly appeared next to his ladder.

"I'm doing better now," Alan said.

"Better?"

"Since I snapped the bottom of the bag. Somebody should have told me to check that before I dropped several dozen oranges through it."

"Oh, that." She looked up at him and smiled. Removing her floppy leather hat, she wiped her forehead with the sleeve of her shirt. Casting a furtive look at the clouds overhead, she observed, "Rain's coming."

"Will that slow us down?"

"Maybe, probably just a duster though. The soakers will come later—if they come at all."

"Duster? Back home, water falls from the clouds. That's what we call rain."

"Yeah, well, California's different."

"You're telling me?" He stopped, turned, and leaned on his ladder. "So what's a duster?"

"Just enough rain to settle the dust. Not enough to make a difference. You'll see. Makes a mess of a shiny new car, though." She smiled at Alan, and he felt drawn to her and away from his task.

"Well, if you don't mind, miss. You're keeping me from my work."

"Sorry, sir," she said, bowing from the waist and sweeping her hat in a broad gesture. "Don't want to keep the hands from doing their job." She turned and walked down the row away from him. Before she got a half dozen trees down the row, Alan heard the shrill sound of a wolf whistle coming from somewhere not too far away. Immediately he felt hot anger creep up his neck and into his cheeks. Not taking his eyes from her back, he noticed how she didn't miss a step, nor did she turn around to look in the direction of the rude sound. Then he realized that though it was the first time he ever heard someone whistle at her, it probably wasn't a new experience for her.

At lunchtime, Alan stood back and examined his four bare-looking trees.

"Not bad," Pat said, coming to inspect his progress. "How about the inside?" he asked, thrusting both his hands deep within the thick green and spreading an opening in the leaves. "You check in here?" Pat stooped slightly and ducked into the interior of the tree. "Hey, Alan," he called, his voice muffled by the lush growth. "You missed a few!"

Alan pawed his way through the tree's branches. "You mean there's more? How do you expect me to get those?" he asked with a slightly raised pitch to his voice.

"Don't tell me you never climbed a tree?" Pat teased.

"Not like this, and not carrying an enormous bag."

"So, today you will." Pat's voice held a slightly parental tone. "Get up there and get at it." He backed out of the dense branches. "You wanted to learn the orange business—well, this is what you might call the heart of it. Every orange you leave to hang and rot is money out of your own pocket. And," he added, grabbing Alan's arm and pulling him closer, "you need to check the pickers, too. They get paid by the box, that's why I assign them a stand and don't let them move on until we've checked. You," he said, pointing at the clusters of bright oranges hanging overhead, "just failed inspection."

"How many boxes you pick today?" Retta asked when it was finally too dark to continue.

"Seven, almost eight," Alan said proudly.

"No kidding?" she said approvingly.

"That good?"

"Pretty good, I'd say. Tired?" she asked, trying to hide a smile.

"I never knew Californians worked so hard," he said. "Back East we see the posters hanging on the travel agent's wall, and we think all you do out here is have beach parties and barbecues."

"Sorry to disappoint you," she said.

Alan stopped in his tracks, grabbed her leather-gloved hand, and spun her around to face him. "I'm not disappointed, Miss McCarron. Not in the least." He looked deep into her dark eyes and liked the acceptance he saw there.

"Say," he said, although hesitant to break the moment. "How many boxes did you say you picked today?"

"I had a slow day today. Must be tired. I only picked forty."

"Right," Alan said sarcastically. "Forty. You expect me to believe that?"

"No," she said smiling. "But believe it or not, I picked forty."

"Anyone check your trees?"

"Check?"

"Did you only pick what you could reach from on the ground and around the outside?"

"With Uncle Pat breathing down my neck? Of course not."

"Forty boxes?" he asked, the reality sinking into his brain.

"Alan," she said patronizingly, "some of the men we hire pick eighty-five."

"In a day?"

"Every day."

"I'll have to get faster," he said.

"Okay, try for a dozen tomorrow."

———

After filling themselves on the stew Mattie Sloan had brought by earlier in the day, Retta excused herself to go see her father.

"I'll drive you," Alan offered.

"Alan," Pat stopped him, "do you mind? I've something I want you to do tonight."

"It's all right," Retta said. "I can go alone. I'll see you back here later."

"Not tonight," Pat said. "I'm planning to keep Alan busy for the rest of the evening."

"Well, then," she said shrugging, "I guess I'll see you tomorrow. Remember, we're going to double your quota."

"Gotcha!" Alan smiled as he watched her walk out the back door. "What's up?" he said to Pat, pulling his attention back to the man sitting across the table from him.

"Paddy?" Pat said before he addressed Alan directly. "You got any plans tonight?"

"No, not really," Paddy teased. "Thought I might meet the boys for bowling or take a spin around the skating rink, but I can do that some other night. What have you got in mind?"

"Get your coats," he said without giving a clue to either of the young men. "And come with me."

After they were a short distance from the house, Pat glanced at the two young men crowded into the seat of his pickup. He let out a low whistle and couldn't keep himself from smiling.

"Where are we going?" Paddy asked from his position in the middle.

"You'll see. Hang on to your pants."

"He means, be patient," Paddy interpreted, responding to Alan's puzzled expression.

Less than five miles down the road, Pat turned into a large, recently developed mobile home park. Paddy and Alan exchanged looks and Paddy shrugged. "You've got me," he said. "I have no idea what he's up to."

Pulling into a back area where the park manager kept his tools and equipment, Pat jumped out of the truck. "I'll be back in a minute. Wait here."

"Like we'd go anywhere," Paddy laughed.

In a few minutes, Paddy and Alan turned in the direction of a slight whining sound and saw Pat and a strange man pull up to the curb in a small electric cart.

"Come on, son," Pat said to his nephew. "Have a look at this."

Paddy stood with Alan's assistance until Pat retrieved his crutches from the bed of the truck. Together, they made their way to stand by the cart.

"Want to go for a spin?" the man said to Paddy.

"Sure," Paddy said as he turned and swung himself onto the seat.

"Hold on to your hat," the man said as he smoothly guided the cart away from the curb.

"What in the world?" Alan exclaimed.

"Think you could manage to help him learn to drive that thing?" Pat asked.

"No kidding?"

"I'm thinkin' of buyin' that contraption for the farm. Thought Paddy might be able to get around with it. The ground's pretty level between the trees. There's plenty of room. I'm not sure about going across the ditches, though. He'd have to be mighty careful."

"What a great idea, Pat!"

"Sean and Connie would kill me for this—if they knew." The last part of the sentence was more a warning than a request.

"My silence is guaranteed!"

Paddy was more than thrilled with the prospect of being more independent and mobile. Pat and the park manager shook hands and struck a deal that included keeping the motorized cart in the park for a week or two until Alan could teach Paddy to drive it on the smooth paved streets.

"So," Pat said on the way back home. "I guess I'll have to find errands for the two of you to run an hour or two each day. I don't want a single word of this leaking out, do you hear me? Mum's the word. And, Paddy," he added with a severe tone of seriousness, "I catch you on the street with that thing and I personally guarantee I'll cripple your other leg."

"Yes, Uncle Patrick," Paddy said soberly. Turning to see the wide-eyed expression on Alan's face, Paddy burst into laughter. "He's kidding, Al!"

Pat and Paddy shared an uproarious laugh and Alan finally joined in. By the time they turned into the McCarron driveway, their sides ached.

"You had me going there for a minute, Pat," Alan said with exaggerated seriousness before opening the door. "I thought you were serious!"

Gales of laughter coming from the truck reached Connie's ears as she was putting the finishing after-supper clean-up touches on her kitchen.

"I was," Pat said between hearty laughs. "I was!"

Paddy and Alan watched from the porch as Pat drove out of the drive. They could hear his laughter until he pulled out onto the street. They looked at each other in dead silence for a moment before they both burst into another round of uncontrollable laughter.

"What's going on out here?" Connie asked, coming to stand beside her son.

"It's just Uncle Pat," Paddy said, struggling to regain some composure. "He's just such a card!"

"What's he up to this time?" Connie asked suspiciously.

"Mom," Paddy said, wiping his eyes. "You know Pat—"

"Yes, I do," she said, looking at the two standing on the porch. "That's what worries me."

Twenty-Two

"McCarron?" the man's voice said from the doorway.

"Yeah," Sean said, straining to recognize the face.

"My name is Andrews. Mark Andrews."

"Andrews. Do I know you?"

"Probably not. We've never met."

"What can I do for you, Andrews?"

"Well, sir. I heard about your unfortunate accident. First, let me say how sorry I am. You doing all right?"

"Slow, but a bit better. So, what's on your mind, Andrews?"

"Jim Henry's a friend of mine. He said you might be needing someone to finish that carriage house project you started."

"You lookin' for work?"

"Might say that, I guess." Mark had been warned to approach Sean carefully. "I thought I might be able to get a crew together and finish it up in a week or so."

"A week or so? You must have a pretty fast crew—or a very large one."

"You interested in having it done?"

"Of course I am. But with the medical bills and all, I'm afraid it'll have to wait."

"We'll work pretty cheap," Mark said.

"Appreciate the offer," Sean said, "but I'm afraid that wouldn't help much."

"How about I make you a bid?" Mark asked, determined not to let Sean off the hook quite so easily. "I don't expect to do it for nothing," Mark said, "but I can guarantee you the best bid and work around."

"I don't know. . . ." Sean said.

"A bid," Mark said, almost begging. "That's all. It doesn't mean you have to accept it."

"I don't mean to be rude, Andrews. And I appreciate a man lookin' for work. But this accident . . ." Sean hesitated. "This happened at the very worst time. I've got oranges hanging ready to be picked, and Christmas is just around the corner. I'm afraid it wouldn't matter what the bid is, I'm just not in any position to go ahead with the project."

"Something like this makes you look at things in an entirely different light, doesn't it, McCarron?"

"Sure does."

"I know how that is, myself. Brings a man up short."

Sean searched the man's lined face, wondering if he was as old as he sounded. "Well, Andrews, I'll think about it. I'll be home in a week or two. Let me talk to my wife and my brother. We'll get back to you. Is there somewhere we can contact you?"

"Sure, Jim knows how to reach me." The two men shook hands. "I'll be looking for your call." Mark walked toward the door, then turned around again to face Sean. "I'll keep you in my prayers, McCarron," he said before turning and quickly walking away.

Sean listened to the sound of Mark Andrews's footsteps as he walked down the hospital corridor. *There's something about that man*, he thought. *Something I don't quite understand.*

Mark's visit left Sean somewhat shaken and uneasy. It wasn't his polite, even humble manner. It wasn't the fact that he was looking for work—Sean wasn't afraid to look for work either. Even coming right to the hospital to talk to him directly, instead of cornering Connie or his family, was an approach that Sean had to admire.

Maybe it was the sadness he saw in Mark's eyes. Every man knows sorrow sometime in his life. *No*, he said to himself, *there's something else. I can't quite put my finger on it.*

"Can you me get a phone in here?" he said to the nurse when she responded to his call.

"Sorry, Mr. McCarron," she said. "Doctor doesn't want you twisting to answer a phone, not just yet anyway. Is there someone I can call for you?"

"Jim Henry. I want to talk to him."

———

Retta came out onto the back steps just as Alan was about to leave. "Hi," she said softly. "You going home?"

"Thought I'd get to bed early. I've been told to increase my production tomorrow," he teased, reminding her of her earlier challenge.

"Oh yeah, I remember," she said smiling. "You'll need your rest, then."

"How's your dad?" he asked, leaning against the side of the house.

"Restless." She walked to the edge of the porch and sat on the seat next to the railing. "He hates being cooped up."

"He'll be a whole lot better once he can come home."

"I doubt it," she said. "We might as well enjoy the quiet while we can. He's coming home a day or so before Christmas."

"That soon?" Alan mentally calculated the days before the holiday. "That's only a couple of weeks away."

"I haven't even started my shopping," Retta said with a sigh. "I can't even think of it before the picking is done."

"Is it like this every year?"

"Nope. The navels are a little late this year."

"How did that happen?"

"It's hard to tell. It's not like we planted late or anything." She smiled and Alan could sense it, even in the semidarkness of the back porch. "Sometimes it's the weather in the spring. If the blossoms set early, we have an early crop—that is, if the weather in the fall is good."

"It's amazing," Alan said, staring into the darkness toward the trees. "These trees have been here for how long, sixty years?"

"Some of them."

"And you still can't predict what they'll produce or when."

"Or, how much."

"Pretty iffy business, if you ask me."

"Yeah, you have to be crazy to be a farmer, I guess," she said.

"I've heard that before." Alan came to sit beside her on the bench. "But tell me, Retta," he said quietly, "what is there in life that doesn't have its risks?"

"Not much," she said. After a short silence she looked at Alan. "Do you have to go so soon?"

"No," he said. "What do you have in mind?"

"It's raining," she said. "Would you mind taking me for a drive?"

"Not at all." He glanced toward the misting sky. "But do you really call this stuff rain?"

"I told you it would be a duster," she said.

"Come on," he said, grabbing her hand and leading her toward the pickup. "Let's go."

Pulling out onto the street, Alan scanned the dashboard for a heater knob or control.

"There's no heater," she laughed. "You cold?"

"I was looking for the defrosters," he said. "I can hardly see through the window."

"Sorry," she said, smiling. "But you'll have to roll your window down for that."

"Nothing doing, let's go get my car."

"This is much better," he said a few minutes later as he turned the defroster fan in his car on full. "Don't you agree?"

"This is better," she agreed.

"Where do you want to go?"

"I don't know, maybe just drive around awhile."

"You want to go to the drive-in for a Coke?"

"Something warmer," she said, rubbing her hands together. "Hot chocolate sounds good."

Alan reached for the heater control, sliding it to a warmer setting and turning the fan from the defroster setting to blow instead on the floorboard. "You know, it's warmer over here," he said. "Come on," he said, holding out his hand toward her. "I won't bite. I promise."

Sitting next to him, Retta felt her stomach tighten with uneasy excitement. As they pulled up to the drive-in, a couple of Glenna's friends walked by the car and waved. As the car hop came out to take their order, Retta scooted a little back toward the right side of the wide seat.

"Where are you going?" he asked. "You afraid someone will

see you out with me?" he said, nodding toward the people who were now staring at them.

"I just wanted more room, that's all. I'm not so cold anymore."

"Oh yes, you are."

"Alan," she said. "Don't do that."

"Don't you do *that*." His tone matched the slight irritation she saw in his eyes. "Are you ashamed to be seen with me?"

"No, of course not."

"You'd be hard pressed to prove it."

Taking a deep breath, she slowly let it out before she dropped her gaze to her lap and said quietly, "Maybe you'd better take me home."

Alan turned to rest his back against his door and slid his arm along the back of the seat. "No," he said firmly. "I don't think so." Glancing into the window of the restaurant, he saw the young people staring in their direction. "Who is that in there?"

"Friends of Glenna's."

"Oh," he said, "that explains it."

"Explains what?"

"Why you pulled away from me. Listen, Retta, I don't know what's going on between your sister and you, but leave me out of it, okay?"

"Nothing is going on between her and me," Retta said defensively.

"Yeah, right. You think I'm blind? She acts as if she hates the whole world, including the family, and expects every man she meets to fall at her feet."

"They usually do," Retta said. "Until now."

Alan looked at the lovely young woman sitting next to him. "Listen," he said sliding toward her. "I have an idea."

"Why does that make me nervous?"

"This is a small town, isn't it?"

"Very."

"And word gets around quickly."

"You're making me very nervous."

"Then let's give them something to talk about," Alan said. In one swift movement he had captured her face with one hand while encircling her with his other arm. Turning her to face him, he quickly smothered her mouth with a kiss. Anticipating her attempt to resist, he held her tightly. Releasing her, he caught her hand before it could leave her lap to slap him. "Don't spoil it, Retta. Let them think what they want. You and I know there was nothing to that kiss—don't we?"

Retta smiled sweetly and relaxed against him.

"That's better," he said, lowering his face toward hers again.

"Don't even try, Alan Conrad," she spat between lips held in a frozen smile. "Or you'll be sorry."

"I won't try," he said, releasing her and flashing the lights for the car hop, "but I'd never be sorry if I did."

Alan put the car in reverse when the tray was removed from his window. He checked out the back window, then turned to wave to the shocked patrons inside.

"I can't believe you did that!" she said, sliding as far to her side of the car as possible.

"Did what? Kiss you, or give some of Glenna's spies something to report?"

Wrapping both arms around her slender rib cage, she slumped slightly in her seat and stared out the window, pouting.

Alan pulled the car in beside the pickup alongside Pat's house. "Come on, I'll walk you home."

"It's raining, I'll take the truck."

"It's barely more than a heavy fog," he said as he held his face up to catch the moisture.

"You're crazy," she said.

"And you're mad at me."

"No," she said, tossing her long hair behind her shoulder with a quick turn of her head. "I'm not mad."

"Good. Here, take this sweater." Wrapping the warm sweater he had grabbed from the backseat of his car around her shoulders, he took the opportunity to pull her closer. His heart lightened at her nearness and skipped a beat when she didn't pull away. Together, they started along the dark pathway at the edge of the grove.

Walking in silence, Alan dropped his arm and found her

hand. "What is this?" he asked.

"What is what?" she could barely make out his profile in the darkness.

"This bushy thing." He pulled off a leaf from her arm and ran it along the length of her cheek.

"Oh that," she said softly. "The hedge."

"They're all over the place," he said. "I've noticed them growing everywhere."

"It's called a privet hedge," she explained. "It's really an olive tree that's been trimmed to bush instead of grow into a tree."

"They grow so thick," he said.

"That's the idea. When my great-grandparents came to California, there weren't any fences. I guess they used these trees to make fences. My grandparents must have learned that from their parents. Anyway, it keeps out intruders, poachers and the like. My grandfather had to be careful of squatters—you know, people who came and lived on your land without permission."

"Like me?"

"Alan," she said softly, stopping and pulling her hand from his.

"Isn't that how you see me?"

"Maybe at first," she said.

"Not anymore?"

"I don't know."

Alan stepped nearer to her and took both hands in his. "Am I an intruder?"

"You didn't mean to be."

"That's not what I asked. Have I intruded?"

"It felt like that at first."

"And now?"

"Not so much."

"Retta," he said, moving his hands to take her by the upper arms. "I have intruded, haven't I?"

Retta felt her mouth go dry and tried to still the beating in her chest by closing her eyes and swallowing hard. She stepped back, trying to escape his nearness, but he took the step with her and she felt the thickness of an orange tree at her back.

"You know, I did it on purpose," he whispered, holding his face only a few inches from hers.

"You did?"

"I most certainly did. How else was I supposed to get to know you? It didn't take me very long to figure out that you wouldn't come outside the privet hedge—I had to come in." He encircled her with his arms. "You know, back at the restaurant—that was just for show. This is for real," he said and touched her lips lightly with his kiss.

"Now," he said, lifting his face from hers, "I think it's starting to rain for real."

She held her hand out and let the warm pelts of wetness splash against her palm. "No, I don't think so. I don't feel a thing."

Alan tugged on her hand. Stubbornly, she resisted and he came to face her once again. She reached up slowly and touched his cheek with her hand and let her fingers wander up to his smooth, soft brown hair.

"Retta," he whispered hoarsely, then kissed her again.

Twenty-Three

"He's using you," Glenna said, coming into Retta's room before she could even get out of her damp clothes.

"Don't be silly." Retta didn't want to have this conversation with her sister. Not tonight, not ever. "If you'll excuse me, Glenna," she said, trying to be polite. "I'm very tired. I'll be out picking all day tomorrow. I want to go to bed."

"You're no match for him," Glenna insisted as she followed Retta's every movement with her eyes. "He's out to get what he can from you, then he'll be gone. You're so dumb when it comes to men."

"And you're not," Retta said angrily. "At least that's the word around town."

"You'll not get anywhere attacking me, little sister."

"Knock it off, will you? I don't give you advice about men, or the types you run around with, and I'd appreciate the same courtesy."

"You give me advice? That's a laugh." Glenna's tone was almost mocking. "Listen, dearie," she said, lying lazily across Retta's bed. "I know a man on the make when I see one."

"Glenna, please leave me alone. I want to go to bed."

"And what do you think he wants?"

"Get out of my room, Glenna. I didn't invite you in here and I want you to leave."

"Sharp, good-looking, Ivy League man. Tell me, Retta, do you think he's actually interested in *you*?"

"I'm not having this conversation with you." Retta bit her lip to keep from shouting at her older sister. "Get out."

"Rich man from the East meets farmer's daughter. He looks at you and sees *naive* written all over you. That's like waving a red flag in front of a bull."

"Stop it, Glenna, I'm warning you."

"He's setting you up for a fall, and you're so stupid you can't even see it coming. He's not interested in you—he's after Dad's land."

"You're wrong."

"Am I?" Glenna's eyes flashed. Maybe she'd get the argument she wanted with Retta after all. "Tell me, little miss *naiveté*, is that why he came on to me, because he was so interested in you?"

"He told me himself, Glenna. He's not interested in you."

"Anymore," she said, a mocking tone to her voice. "But that's because I knew how to put him in his place. What chance do you have against a guy like that, anyway? He's way out of your league."

"You're a liar," Retta shouted in her sister's face.

"Retta!" Consuela's voice cut through the room like a knife. "That's quite enough. Glenna, what in the world is going on in here? We can hear your voices all over the house."

"Maybe you can talk some sense into her, Mom. Heaven only knows she won't listen to me."

"Sense? About what?"

"Alan Conrad, that's what."

"Alan? What about him?"

"He made a couple of passes at me and I brushed him off. Now he's after Retta and she's too dumb to see it for what it is. She thinks he is actually interested in her. Any fool can see he has his own interests—and believe me, it doesn't make any difference to Alan Conrad whose face is on it—as long as there's a body attached."

"Glenna!" Connie was shocked to hear her daughter speak in such a manner. "That's a terrible thing to say."

"It's the truth," she said. "Ask her, Mom. Ask her—has he tried anything?"

"No," Retta said. She felt a blush begin in her chest and creep slowly to her neck.

"That's not what I heard," Glenna said triumphantly. "And," she said in a condescending tone as she rose, stretched, and walked slowly to Retta's bedroom door, "it's all over town."

Connie watched as her oldest daughter left the room and

turned to gather Retta in her arms just as she burst into tears.

"Do you know what she's talking about?"

"Yes," Retta sobbed.

"Do I need to have Uncle Pat have a talk with Alan Conrad?"

"Oh, Mama. No. I know what she's talking about, but believe me, she doesn't." Retta released herself from her mother's embrace and reached for a tissue on the dresser.

"Is Alan bothering you?"

"Mama, Alan's been so kind. I think he's one of the most wonderful guys I've ever met. Why can't she leave us alone?"

"Oh, poor baby," Connie said. Tugging her daughter gently by the hand, she led her to the bed and sat down. "Sit right here and tell me everything."

"There's not much to tell, Mama. You've been here, too. You've seen the way he's pitched in and helped. I've not tried to encourage him in any way, and he's been a perfect gentleman, always."

"Then what's she talking about?"

Retta quickly filled Connie in on the scene at the drive-in.

"Oh, my," she said. "No wonder."

"Mama, Alan said she's made, well, advances."

"Toward him?"

Retta nodded.

"And what does she say?"

"She says it was just the opposite."

"I see." Connie shook her head. "Maybe I'd better have a talk with Alan myself."

"No, Mama. Just watch. You'll see. Alan isn't interested in her. He likes me."

"I wish your father were here."

"Oh no, Mama. Please don't tell him about this. You know how upset he'd be. He'd throw Alan off the place. That's what Glenna wants. If she can't get him for herself, she certainly doesn't want me—"

"Hush, *m'hija*," Connie said. "Go on to bed. I'll pray about this."

"I'll keep my distance from him, Mama, would that help?"

"Will he keep his distance from you?"

"Oh, Mama, I hope not." Retta was surprised at her own words.

"I thought so," Connie said. Rising to her feet, she turned back the covers on Retta's bed. "Enough for tonight. You get some sleep."

As soon as Retta heard her mother's bedroom door shut, she turned off her light and lay in the darkness. Her mind was drifting back to Alan's kiss in the grove when she heard her bedroom door open slightly and Glenna tiptoe to the side of her bed.

"You better watch him." Glenna's harsh whisper almost whistled between her clenched teeth. "He can be snatched right from underneath your nose—so fast, you'll wonder what happened."

"Get out!" Retta yelled at her sister and threw a pillow in the direction of the retreating figure.

"Glenna!" It was Connie's angry voice in the hallway. "Get back to your room and stay there."

"I'm not a child, Mother," Glenna shouted back.

"Then stop acting like one!"

———

"What was all that about last night?" Joanna asked at breakfast.

"What was all what, honey?" Connie said cheerfully from her usual position at the stove.

"All that yelling."

"Just your sisters having an argument. It doesn't concern you. It's all over now, anyway. Eat your breakfast. Howie coming by soon?"

"What's Glenna up to now?" Joanna whispered to Retta.

"Never mind," Retta whispered in return.

"Girls, it's not polite to whisper in the presence of others. You're old enough to know that."

"Good morning, all." Glenna's false cheer made Retta's stomach turn.

Without a word, Retta pushed her chair back. Leaving half

her breakfast untouched, she grabbed her jacket and hat and hurried out the back door.

"What's eating her?" Glenna remarked with a sarcastic grin on her face.

"I heard you fighting last night," Joanna said.

"Joanna," Connie warned. "I told you this is none of your business."

"She's jealous," Glenna whispered to her youngest sister.

"Of who?" Joanna asked.

"Who else?"

"You?" Her attractive young face was scrunched in a mock frown. "I don't think so."

"Joanna, Howie's here. Tell him to come on in and wait while you finish your breakfast."

"Can't, Mom. We're late already. See you later," she said. Grabbing her books and heading out the back door, she almost collided with Alan on her way down the porch stairs.

"Good morning," Glenna called, gesturing for Alan to come inside. "Mom's French toast is going to waste if somebody doesn't sit down long enough to eat it."

"Good morning, Mrs. McCarron," Alan said.

"Alan, come on in. Sit down, you're just in time for breakfast."

"Listen, Alan," Glenna bubbled, "I'm glad I ran into you. Some of my friends and I are driving down to Palm Springs on Saturday. We'd like you to come with us."

"Sorry, no thanks."

"Don't say no," she pouted. "We'll have a ball. We're going swimming in the hot mineral springs and everything. It's wonderful. You should try it."

"I have plans," Alan said flatly.

"Oh?" Glenna asked, almost fluttering her eyes at him. "I could be talked into changing my plans."

"Glenna," Connie said, trying to contain her disapproval. "I don't think—"

"Oh, that's okay, Mrs. McCarron. Maybe Glenna would enjoy coming along with me this Saturday. How about it, Glenna, could you change your plans?"

"I'm sure I could. I can go to Palm Springs any Saturday. What did you have in mind?"

"We could use some more help picking. We're going to be in the far section by Saturday. We could use a truck driver and Paddy could use a little help out in his sorting shed."

"Oh, that," she said. "No, thank you. I work all week. Saturday is my day off. Working in the grove is hardly how I would choose to spend it."

"Just a thought," he said, smiling at Connie.

"Well," she said, getting up from the table, "I'll be late for work if I don't hurry."

Connie left the room to answer the phone, and Glenna took the opportunity to walk behind Alan's chair and wrap both arms around his neck. Leaning close, she whispered, "If you change your mind, just let me know," and brushed his ear with her moist lips. Connie came back in the room just as Glenna straightened. "'Bye all," Glenna said happily and hurried out the door.

"Why do I feel like I've just had a contract put out on me?" Alan asked.

Alan could see the embarrassment on Connie's face as she stood in the doorway.

"Alan," she said. "I'm so sorry about that. I'll speak to her."

"Don't bother, Mrs. McCarron. I can handle her. Really."

"I'm so embarrassed."

"Don't be. She's the one who's—" Alan decided not to discuss this any further with Connie, but he certainly wanted to take up the conversation with Pat. "Say, I didn't really come by to eat. I ate breakfast with Pat, but that coffee really smells good. Any chance. . . ?"

"Of course," she said, pouring a cup of the hot steaming liquid. "That was the hospital on the phone. Sean's asking for me. Says it's important."

"Well, then?"

"I'd better run along. Paddy's up, he'll be out in a minute."

"Good. I'll wait right here."

"Retta's already gone out," Connie said.

"Already?"

"She had something on her mind."

"She say what it was?"

"No, not for sure."

Alan hoped that he knew what she was thinking about. He'd see her later in the grove and find out for himself. Just the thought of her brought a smile to his lips, which he hoped was concealed behind his cup of coffee.

Paddy came into the kitchen and reached for the plate of French toast. "We're on for later, right?"

"Pat reminded me this morning. We're going after something, I think. He'll come up with our excuse."

"Can you believe this?"

"You are all determined to make Sean McCarron throw me off the place, aren't you?"

"Afraid of him?" asked Paddy as he smothered his French toast with butter and syrup.

"Aren't you?"

"Yeah," Paddy said, "sometimes I am. Not so much anymore, though, and once he's home and sitting in a wheelchair, we'll be eye level."

"Never thought of that." Alan smiled at Paddy.

"I didn't either until last night. I bet I get him to play chess."

"Your dad?"

"If it kills him."

"It might, you know."

"Didn't me," Paddy said, putting a bite of French toast into his mouth. Washing it down with half a glass of milk, he added, "You know, when you're sick of doing nothing, you'll do anything."

"You don't plan to make this easier for him, do you, Paddy?"

"Nope," Paddy said with a sly smile.

Twenty-Four

"Is that why you brought me over here at this hour?" Jim Henry asked.

"Look, Henry," Sean said, "I know it's late, but there's something about that man that bothers me."

"What, exactly?"

"I can't put my finger on it, for sure." Sean leaned back on his pillows. His thick eyebrows knit together in a frown and he rubbed his forehead. "I was hopin' you could shed some light here."

"Let me tell you a little about Mark Andrews," Jim said. Before he spoke to Sean about Mark, he took a moment to breathe a silent prayer. Walking toward the window, he searched for words that would speak deeply to Sean. Knowing Sean, he'd have to be very careful.

"Out with it, Henry," Sean commanded.

"Mark Andrews lost his son a while back—his only child. It's been a little over a year ago, now. He drowned. It was devastating to Mark, as you can well imagine. But the most painful part of it all was the knowledge that he had really lost his son long before the accident. Mark and his son were not close. Mark was ambitious, hardworking—too busy with his work for the good of his family."

Jim hesitated before coming around to face Sean squarely with the rest of the story. "Right afterward," he said, pulling a chair nearer the bed, "his wife divorced him and he's pretty much lost everything he worked so hard to get in life. He didn't put up much of a fight during the divorce. She got the house and a piece of the business. He had inherited quite a lot of money from his parents, but his wife had gone through most of that before the divorce. Anyway, his business was almost in hock and there wasn't much left except the house."

Jim noticed the momentary look of discomfort that crossed Sean's face.

"It made Mark stop and take stock of his life. Everything he had lived and worked for was suddenly gone. Unexpectedly alone, he turned to the Lord. Last spring, he started teaching at the high school. He had gotten a college education before going into business. Putting that together with his construction experience, he came up with quite an innovative program. He now does for other youngsters what he was unable to do for his own son."

"What's that?"

"He teaches them a practical skill. He's teaching carpentry at the school. He holds his classes in the evening—night school. Uses the wood shop. Most of the boys in his class are dropouts. Some have even returned to regular classes. Two will graduate this year. Twice a year he finds a project they can actually work on and gives them some on-the-job experience. They have a Christmas vacation project and an Easter vacation project. I'm thinking he's probably wanting your place for a Christmas vacation project. The kids will be out in a week or so, and they're off for two weeks."

"What does he get out of it?" Sean asked suspiciously.

"A way to get through the holidays without his family, for one thing," Jim said. "And it gives him a sense of accomplishment for another."

"Why didn't he tell me this himself?"

"He doesn't tell anyone. He just bids the job, hires the kids, and stands behind the work like he would any of his other jobs."

"Other jobs?"

"You don't recognize the name Andrews Construction?"

"*That* Andrews?"

"The same."

"I've read about him in the papers. We've been on opposite sides of most community issues."

"You mean ripping out groves for houses?"

"Yeah," Sean said awkwardly, fingering the sheet folded neatly across his stomach. "But then, things have really changed. With my brother selling out, and now this happening to me. Makes you take another look at things."

"That's what Mark said." Jim waited for a moment, then asked, "What things are you reconsidering, Sean?"

"My place, for one." Sean stared away from the young minister. "I've got to make some decisions where my orange business is concerned. You know, if my son were able—" Sean's voice broke. "Retta's interested in the business. But that isn't suitable work for a woman. Besides, she needs to get herself a husband, have a family and settle down."

"I don't think you better let her hear you say that," Jim laughed, imagining Retta's reaction.

"Well, she doesn't have any idea how hard it would be to run the grove alone."

"Would she be alone?"

"Someday. Her mother and I won't live forever. I realized that very quickly just a few weeks ago."

"What about when you've healed up? Has the doctor given you any reason to believe that you'll not be—well, has he said anything?"

"I haven't told my wife and family, Reverend. But the doctor says this break in my ankle is a nasty one. It could be some time before I'm able to walk again. Even then, he says I might need crutches or maybe a cane. It looks like my orange growing days are over."

"Sorry to hear that," Jim said. "That's got to be rough news to take." Jim Henry laid a hand on Sean's arm. "Any ideas about what you'll do?"

"I've thought of sellin' my place. You know the Conrads wanted to buy both places when they bought Pat's. Maybe I should have sold out then. Retta was pretty upset when her uncle sold out. I hate to think of what this would do to her. On the other hand, Glenna would be more than happy. She's been after us to sell."

"Why's that?"

"Wants to live on the other side of town. She's tired of bein' a lowly farmer's daughter. I don't know. Maybe she's right. Maybe a move to the other side of town would be good for all of us."

"You think all Glenna needs is a change of address?"

"No, of course not." Sean's expression grew thoughtful and serious. "I've been givin' her a lot of thought, too. Lyin' here, there's not much else to do. She's been kinda overlooked in our family. Paddy's gotten so much of the attention, bein' sick and all. He took so much of his mama's time, and the grove took all of mine. Always bein' part of twins, after he got sick she was mostly left out of things to her way of thinkin'. The others it didn't bother in the same way. They were used to the twins gettin' a lot more attention. There's somethin' special about bein' twins to start with. In a way, Paddy's illness crippled Glenna as much as it did him."

"Is there anything you could have done differently?"

"Maybe not. Maybe so. I guess I could have taken more time with her. But, I see it now—now that it's too late."

"I wonder," Jim said quietly.

"She's grown. She's old enough to be out on her own."

"But she isn't, is she, Sean?"

"What do you mean?"

"I'm not sure. Why hasn't she ever married and settled down—to use your own words?"

"She's not easy to get along with. Maybe you've noticed that."

"I've noticed."

"I was hoping some nice young man would come along and she'd—"

"Change?"

"Well, yeah. Fall in love and—"

"Live happily ever after?"

"That doesn't happen, does it?" Sean asked.

"Not very often. I wonder," Jim said cautiously, "how this has affected Retta."

"Retta?" Sean said, looking puzzled.

"Is that why she's so determined to carry on the family business?"

"She loves growing oranges."

"I'm sure she does. But have you ever asked yourself why?"

"You think—?"

"It's just a thought. I'm not a psychiatrist or anything. But

I wonder. Could she be trying to make up for Paddy's limitations as much as Glenna has resented them?"

"What reason could she have for that?"

"Same as Glenna's, is my guess—you."

"Me? I don't think so. I've never done anything to—"

"You misunderstand me, Sean. It's not what you've done. It's who you are. There's something very special between a girl and her father. Retta likes working outside in the grove. She found a way to be near you, didn't she? Glenna, on the other hand—?"

"Glenna hates working outside."

"You said yourself that you worked pretty hard out in the grove."

"Especially during Paddy's illness. It gave me a way to cope. Getting in touch with the green living trees. It helped ease my guilt."

"Your guilt? I'm sorry, Sean. Maybe I don't have any right to poke around in your own personal issues, but what do you have to be guilty about?"

Sean quickly wiped away an uninvited tear. "I wish I knew."

"Wait a minute," Jim said while breathing another silent prayer. "You're carrying a load of guilt and you don't even know why?" He shifted in his chair, leaning closer to Sean's bed. "I thought you were a Christian, Sean. Am I wrong?"

"I thought so, too." Sean said. "But—"

"You *thought* so?"

"I tried to be a God-fearing, God-serving man. As a youngster, I gave my heart to the Lord. My mother was a saint. Such a godly woman you'd never find anywhere else—except for Connie. My mother raised us kids right. Pat and me, we asked Jesus into our hearts right at the family prayer time."

"So what happened?"

"Paddy's illness happened."

"I don't get the connection. Maybe I'm a little dense, but where does it say in the Bible that a man's sick child is a sign that Christ has left a man's heart?"

"A preacher came through town—you know, one of them healers." Sean's tone lowered and his voice became thick with emotion. "He came to the house to pray for Paddy."

"And?"

"And nothin'—that's the point. This man had a pretty good record with healings and all. When Paddy didn't 'rise up and walk' when the man said to, he turned to me. He told me when I got the sin and doubt out of my own heart, my son would be healed. From that day on, I couldn't look my own son in the eye. Every time I looked at Connie I thought I could see the accusation in her face. She tried to assure me that it wasn't so. She even told me she thought the man was a fake. But it didn't matter. I know what I felt, in here!" Sean pointed to his chest, then covered his weather-roughened face with his hands.

"So you sought sanctuary in the grove." Jim stared at the floor. The tragedy of Sean's story left him feeling empty and alone. "I wish I could change what happened, Sean. But I can't. No one can. Is that when you stopped attending church?"

"Not right away. But right after that, they started havin' these long altar calls. Verse after verse, they sang and sang. Sometimes the altar calls dragged on longer than the sermon. I knew they were after me to come and confess my sin. I even gave in a time or two, thinking it would help things. I pounded the altar with both fists until my hands ached. I cried out to God to look into my heart and remove my sin. Somebody said I'd have to confess it so that everyone could hear my repentance. I confessed everything I could think of."

"And?"

"And they all looked at Paddy. Once there was this really big scene at the altar, and Paddy was right there watchin'. I was as empty as I could possibly get. I had confessed everythin' I could think of, but Paddy still didn't walk. When he looked at me, I thought my heart would break. He started cryin' and I took him out of there in his wheelchair. On the way down the aisle something inside me said, *That's enough, no more.*"

"Then what happened?" Jim asked.

"Then the next week they called a board meeting. I was on the board, so I didn't think too much about it." Sean wiped his runny nose on the back of his hand. Jim found a box of tissues on the stand beside his bed and handed him the whole box. "Thanks," Sean said after blowing his nose. "I didn't understand what they were sayin' for a bit into the meetin'. Finally, it got through my thick head. They gave this whole case for a man's walk pleasin' the Lord before he could lead others—"

"Stop! Don't say any more," Jim Henry said, "I can guess what comes next. This makes me so mad I could spit nails." Jim walked around the bed and stood silently at the window, staring into the darkness. He let his gaze fall on the lights of the small city, so clearly visible from the second-floor room. After a few minutes he turned to Sean McCarron. "But mostly," Jim said quietly, "it makes me angry with you."

"Me? Are you just like the rest of them, then?"

"How could you let them do this to you?" he said. Knowing full well his anger was showing, Jim threw away caution and firmly stepped closer to Sean. "How could you let them do this to your family? To Paddy? To your wife?" Jim turned and paced back and forth at the foot of Sean's bed.

"Reverend Henry, you still here?" said the nurse, coming in for a routine check on her patient. "You know, visiting hours were over long ago."

"I asked for him," Sean said. "He'll stay until I ask him to leave."

Without a word, she stiffened and made a hasty exit from the room.

"I'm sorry, Sean. I don't mean to take it out on you. But I've seen this before. Somebody sets themselves up as the infallible hand of God extended, and if what they demand—not ask, mind you—*demand* that God perform in response to their command doesn't happen, they have to find someone else to blame. It never seems to occur to some people that the real miracle may be in that Paddy didn't die. Or that He gave you the grace to bring Paddy up as normally as possible. Or even that Paddy's gifts may lie in other areas than orange growing." Jim stopped, feeling the surge of anger returning.

"I never saw it that way," Sean said.

"No, you were too busy blaming yourself to see that God's

miracle power can be expressed and be just as evident in the creative ways He gives His children strength to handle the tough things life so easily and quickly dishes out. You were so quick to accept the blame, you were unable to see the blessings in all of this."

"Blessings, is it?" It was Sean's turn to raise his voice. "You tellin' me Paddy's illness was a blessin'?"

"You'll have to lower your voices in here," the firm voice of the head nurse said from the doorway. "Or, I'll have to insist Mr. Henry leave, whether you want him to or not, Mr. McCarron."

"Yes, yes," Jim said impatiently. "We'll keep our voices down."

"Is that what you're sayin'?" Sean's voice was an angry whisper. "If it is, Preacher Boy, then no thank you. I don't want nothin' to do with a God who ruins a child's life, then calls it a blessin'."

"That's not what I'm saying at all, Sean McCarron. I have something to say, and I can only say it if you'll promise me you aren't already determined to misunderstand me. It's not something I was taught in Bible school, so I don't have some educated way to put it. I just have to speak from my heart. Maybe you can help me sort it out."

"I'm not much for this kind of thing—but go ahead. We've said too much now to go back."

"Do you think that God's blessings only come when everything is going good?"

"Well, certainly you can see God's blessings, then."

"And you don't think He can send blessings in the middle of adversity?"

"You surely don't mean that adversity is a blessin'?"

"No, that's not what I said. I'm asking you, can God send blessings in the middle of adversity?"

"I suppose He could."

"*Suppose?*" Jim said emphatically. "You *suppose*? Look at this hospital. Hasn't this place been a blessing to you?"

"You could say that, yes."

"And when do people need this place—if not in the middle of adversity?" Jim decided to carry his thought a little further.

Even though he knew he was stretching to make his point, he decided to risk it. "Maybe that's the way we think of the Lord," he murmured, almost to himself. "Let me put it this way," he said, turning to speak directly to Sean. "Having this hospital in town doesn't keep us from needing it, does it, Sean? No, of course not." He didn't wait for Sean's response, but continued with his train of thought. "What I'm saying is this: Having a medical facility isn't insurance against illness or injury, but an *assurance* of help and care when it comes. That's the way the Lord is for us. He doesn't guarantee that life in Him will be free of pain and injury, but that when it comes—as it does to all of us—He will be there. Otherwise, He would be giving us a life in which we wouldn't need Him." Jim searched his memory for an elusive scripture. "The Bible says, somewhere in Deuteronomy, I think, that when everything is going well, He commands the people not to forget Him. Why do you suppose He had to say that?" Jim gestured but didn't wait for Sean to answer. "Because, He knew that when things go great, we get dull. When things come too easy, we too easily forget where they come from."

"But why didn't he heal Paddy? Certainly we needed Him then."

"I haven't a clue," Jim Henry admitted. "I don't doubt for one minute that He could have. I believe with all my heart that He even died for our healing—that He made provision for it in the atonement. But why doesn't it happen every time? I don't know why. Furthermore," Jim said, coming very close to Sean, "I think anyone who says they know all the answers is a liar. There are just too many things we'll never understand as long as we live."

"There are certainly things I don't understand." Sean shifted in his bed, trying to get more comfortable. "Like, why did I fall off that roof?"

"That one's easy," Jim said.

"Oh really?"

"Yeah. You stepped on some ice."

"Then you don't think God had anything to do with that?"

"Did He make you get up on that roof?"

"No."

"Has He seen to it you got care since?"

"Well, if you mean the doctors and hospital—"

"Has your family been taken care of?"

"Yes," Sean said, wondering where Jim was headed with the conversation. "Don't cross-examine me, Preacher. Just make your point."

"If the same train of thought applied to this accident that you've believed about Paddy, then who're you going to blame for this accident? Yourself? You said you have cried out to God and asked Him to search your heart. Retta? Is she to blame for this? Connie? God knows that woman prays for you night and day. Or maybe it's Paddy. Maybe he's harbored resentment in his heart all these years and somehow is hiding a secret sin. Maybe if he confessed it and repented, God would see fit to heal you."

"That's ridiculous," Sean said. "Paddy's the most innocent person I've ever known."

"No, Sean. He's not. The most innocent person is the one who has sought God with his whole heart—the one God has forgiven and cleansed. Unless Paddy has accepted Christ into his heart, he's as guilty as anybody. He may not be to blame, but he's not innocent until the blood of Christ makes him so. Do you understand that?"

"I do." Sean was thoughtful. "Tell me, Jim. What possible blessings have you seen during this whole thing?"

"Well, for one, you've got a good roof on that addition of yours. Better than either of us could have done."

"What are you talkin' about?"

"Nobody told you?"

"Told me what?"

"The very day you fell, Mark Andrews came with his men and put it on. Not just the tar paper to keep it dry, but the whole roof."

"No kiddin'? Andrews himself?"

"Himself."

"Why'd he do that?"

"Because it needed to be done and he saw a way he could help."

"Why, I'll be—"

"Be what, Sean? Grateful?"

Sean McCarron's pain-filled eyes sought Jim Henry's. Jim watched as the realization of God's care and concern sank though Sean's calloused heart.

"If you think God's finished with you, Sean McCarron, think again," Jim said boldly. He took his jacket from the back of a nearby chair and slipped his arms into the sleeves.

"One thing I don't understand," Sean said before Jim could leave.

"Only one?"

"If God sent Mark to put on that roof, it's like He protected the building from the rain, but He didn't protect me by keepin' me from fallin'. How do you figure that?"

"I don't know," Jim said with a smile. "The roof—well, I'm thinking the roof wasn't His real concern. Maybe He did it for you. Maybe He hopes He can still teach you a thing or two."

"Do me a favor, Preacher?"

"If I can."

"Tell Andrews to get his boys and finish the thing, will you?"

"Sure thing."

"And," Sean said in a low voice, "tell him I'd like him to come by the house when I get home. If he wouldn't mind."

"He won't mind." Jim smiled at Sean. "I know that for sure."

Twenty-Five

"Been wantin' to talk to you, young man," Sean said as soon as he could get Alan alone.

"Yes, sir?"

"I see you've quite taken to the place," Sean remarked. "It's been a week since I came home. Andrews' boys are makin' right good time on that carriage house."

"I know, Mr. McCarron. I can't believe how much they've done in such a short time."

"It'll be ready for Pat before long. He says he'll move his stuff over before he goes on his trip. Won't really settle in until he gets back."

"Connie's been a real help. I don't think he had cleaned out any of the cupboards since his wife died."

"You may be right about that," Sean said. "But that's not the matter I wanted to talk to you about. You didn't see your folks over Christmas."

"I'll see them in a month or two. They always go to Hawaii for the holidays. After New Year's they'll fly home, and this spring they're going to spend a week or two in Palm Springs. Dad participates in a golf tournament and wants to look at things out here."

"He'll be by here, then."

"Possibly," Alan said. "We've discussed it."

"I was wonderin', Alan. You think he might still be interested in my place?"

"You can't be serious."

"Just a thought. He was interested when he bought Pat's place. You know I'm not going to make much of a farmer now—not with this leg."

"But I thought Retta—"

"This is no job for a woman. You've been here long enough to see that for yourself."

"But Pat's here. Even Paddy—" Alan dropped the subject of Sean's son. Sean still didn't know of the electric cart and just how mobile Paddy had become lately.

"I can't expect Pat to drop all his plans for me. He sold out of the orange business, remember? And Paddy—why the idea's out of the question! Retta's a capable woman, but for this place to run, it needs a man. Hiring workers is one thing, but havin' her alone out in the fields with them is quite another." Sean sat back deep into his overstuffed chair, his cast-covered leg propped up on pillows on the matching large ottoman. "Well, if your father's comin' by, I'll bring it up to him."

"What does Connie say about this?"

"Haven't told her."

"You are considering selling this house and you haven't even mentioned it to your wife?"

"That's a bit out of your way, isn't it, son?"

"If you mean it's none of my business—"

"That's what I mean, all right."

"You're right. It's just that I thought she might have something to say about it, that's all."

"A man's got to do what a man's got to do," Sean said matter-of-factly. "When it comes to takin' care of his family, he sometimes has to make decisions—"

"With no regard for their feelings."

"You're still out of bounds, Conrad."

"Maybe so," Alan said. "But, sir, so are you."

"Beggin' your pardon?"

"As much as Connie loves this house. Are you sure you want to do this?"

"As I look at it," Sean said, obviously irritated by Alan's intrusion into the personal side of his decision, "I don't have much choice. A family like yours may have all kinds of financial reserves, but this accident has cost me most of my savings. I might even be facing more surgery. Farmers like us, son, don't make a killing in the orange market like some do in the real-estate business."

Alan flinched under the subtle accusation.

"As we both know, the land is worth a bit more as real estate than it is in oranges. Once we start hirin' workers to do what we once did ourselves—well, the profits just aren't there."

"I just think your wife ought to have a say in this."

"Women want to take care of their homes and families," Sean said. "But they want their husbands to take care of the livin'."

"Times are changing, Mr. McCarron."

"People aren't," Sean said and immediately regretted the comment.

"Do you have to sell the whole piece, house and all?"

"Well, now. I never thought of anything else."

"I was just thinking, why not keep those few acres around the house? Paddy babies those trees, especially the tangerines out back. Couldn't you at least keep the house and grounds out around the sheds?"

"You know, that's an idea. I'll give it some thought. Wonder why I never thought of that before."

"Maybe it's because you didn't talk it over with your wife."

Sean grunted in disagreement.

"You think not?" Alan said. "Well, that's strange. Because that's where I heard it in the first place."

"How's that?"

"The day after you were hurt, when Connie began to realize how hard this would be for you once you were able to be up and around again, I heard her tell Pat she wished you'd sell, and just keep the homeplace."

"She didn't mention that to me," Sean said, rubbing his chin in disbelief.

"Perhaps she knows it's a subject she's not permitted to bring up."

"Permitted?" Sean's tone held a warning edge.

"Okay, maybe I'm wrong. You'd have to ask her."

"Maybe I will," Sean said. "Tell your father I'd like to see him when he comes."

"Does Retta know about this?"

"Retta?" Sean asked with surprise.

"No, of course not. If you didn't discuss it with your wife, you certainly haven't mentioned it to your daughter." Alan crossed the room and paused by the door at the sound of Sean's voice.

"And, young man, I'd appreciate it if you didn't mention it to her either."

"And I, sir," Alan turned to confront Sean, "would appreciate it if you did."

Without waiting for Sean's response, Alan walked out of the den, almost colliding with Glenna. The look of triumph on her face told Alan she had heard the entire conversation. Watching her run up the stairs, he knew Sean wouldn't be telling Retta of his desire to sell—Glenna would beat him to it.

"I told you," Glenna said later up in Retta's room, an arrogant smile spread across her face. "I told you he was only using you to get what he wanted. But no, you wouldn't listen. Now that he's convinced Daddy to sell, how much longer do you think he'll be interested in you?"

"I don't believe you," Retta said. Sudden fear gripped her insides and she felt sick. "You're lying."

"Whether you believe me or not, I heard them downstairs talking. Alan has persuasively convinced Daddy that the farm is too much for poor little helpless you to handle by yourself. And, how could he do this to his own family, his brother, his wife, his only crippled son—and to you? He's convinced Daddy that selling the place is in *your* best interest, my darling baby sister. If you don't believe me, ask Daddy." Glenna watched the pain send dark shadows through Retta's brown eyes. "You thought he was interested in you, and all this time he was only amusing himself with you while he waited for his chance to move in. Well, Retta, he saw his chance. And he moved in." Glenna turned and walked away, tossing mocking laughter over her shoulder.

"You know," Retta managed to say before Glenna walked through the door, "I'll ask Mama about this."

"Go ahead." Glenna's curt voice lashed at her sister. "But she doesn't know about it yet. Daddy hasn't told her. You mention this to her and you'll cause problems between her and Daddy. Is that what you want to do?" Coming back toward Retta, Glenna followed that threat with another. "You tell Daddy you know, and he'll think your precious Alan Conrad told you. And right after he told him not to."

"He what?"

"He told Alan he wanted to tell you himself. You spill the beans now, and you'll upset Daddy to no end. I suppose you could ask Alan, but then, he's lied to you all along. He certainly won't tell you the truth now." Glenna turned to leave the room once again. "No, little sister, this looks like a secret you'll have to keep all to yourself. Sleep tight," she called back cheerfully, "and don't let the bed bugs bite!"

Retta threw herself across the bed and turned off the light. She was surprised that she didn't feel anything. She wasn't angry, she wasn't scared. She had a sudden numb feeling. "Funny," she whispered into the darkness, "I can't even cry."

Early the next morning, Retta slipped quietly downstairs, trying not to wake her parents, who were still sleeping in the den and would be until Sean could once again manage the stairs. She glanced at the large pendulum clock in the center hallway. Five-thirty. Still dark outside. She grabbed her heavier jacket and slipped the hood over her head against the early morning heavy fog and chill. As long as the fog was moving, she didn't fear for the trees. Opening the kitchen doorway as quietly as possible, she walked tentatively across the graveled yard toward the grove—the only place she knew to find comfort for the pain that was beginning to gnaw deeply at her insides.

Only when Retta was out of sight from the house did her tears begin to flow—silently at first, but they soon gave way to deep, heart-shattering sobs. She had been disappointed and angry at Uncle Pat for selling, but this was different. Now she felt betrayed. For as long as she could remember, she had worked in the grove, cared for the trees, helped protect them from freezing in the winter and drying out from the heat in the summer. She had worked with her hands to maintain the irrigation ditches, clipped back dead twigs and branches. She had sounded the early alarm when a strange mite had infested a few trees along the privet hedge and helped apply the DDT, saving other trees and even the next crop. She had endured lurid remarks and steeled herself against the obscene catcalls of the itinerant workers and learned to ignore them, overcoming the very reasons orange growers refused to let their women into the groves during pruning or picking.

And now, it would soon be over. Was all her hard work and her faithful commitment to the family business really worth so little to her father?

And Alan. Could she have been wrong about him as well? Even lacking experience with men, Retta had thought she could tell when someone was lying. *How could I have been so dumb?* she thought.

No longer able to suppress her grief, Retta knelt in a long, empty furrow between the trees and pulled the hooded jacket around her. With her face near the ground, she released her sobs, as if the dirt could absorb her pain. Engulfed by her misery, she didn't hear Alan's approach.

"Retta?" he said softly. When she didn't answer, he reached down to try to take hold of one of her arms. "Retta," he repeated a little louder when she pulled away from him. "Please, Retta, look at me."

"Go away," she said, her voice muffled in the folds of her heavy, hooded jacket.

"I'm not going anywhere," he said, "until you talk to me. Please, Retta."

Alan circled around and sat in the dirt in front of her. He tried to lift the hood from her head.

Retta grabbed the hood and held it securely over her tousled hair. "I don't want to talk to you," she said between sobs.

"I want to talk to you," he said softly. "None of this is what you think it is."

"And how do you know *what* I think," she said, "or care?"

"Glenna told you, didn't she?"

"How did you know that?"

"I saw her yesterday when I left your father's room."

"Then it's true," she said, still without looking at him.

"I don't know if it is or not," he said. "I haven't the faintest idea what she said to you."

"Why don't you tell me, then?" she asked.

"Because I think I should stay out of family business. Your father should tell you himself."

"It's true, I know it is." Retta rose to her feet.

Alan wanted to reach out to her to ease the pain he saw in her eyes. "Retta, please, don't hate *me* for this."

"Who should I hate then? My father?"

"I think you should talk to him. But I don't think you should hate anyone." Alan reached out to her, but she jumped back from his touch. "None of this makes any sense to you right now," Alan said.

"I think it makes perfect sense."

"There are some things you can't even know, yet. Things I'm still working out in my own mind. Retta, please, will you listen to me?"

"You're not telling me, remember?" Retta stood a distance back and held her hand out in an effort to keep Alan from coming any closer. "Daddy's not telling me. You're not telling me. If Glenna hadn't told me, when would I have known? When you were signing the papers and giving us thirty days to get out of the house?"

Pat McCarron moved toward the young couple, wondering why their conversation was so animated. It was just past six A.M. In the heavy fog, he barely made out the figures in the darkness; only when he got within a few yards did he realize it was Retta and Alan. It was obvious they were quarreling about something. He would have turned discreetly away and left them alone, except he could hear the agitation in Retta's voice. When he saw her recoil from Alan's touch, he decided he would come nearer. He wasn't about to let any man force his attentions on Retta McCarron, not even Alan Conrad.

"What's the problem, kids?" Pat asked upon his approach.

"Retta's upset," Alan said.

"I can see that."

"I want to explain some things to her, but she won't listen."

"Retta? What's got you so upset?"

"I'll leave and you can ask Mr. Conrad—he's not allowed to talk to me about it, anyway."

They watched her run the length of the row, then disappear when she turned toward the house. "Alan?" Pat said.

"What a mess," Alan said. "You won't believe it even when you hear it, Pat."

"Try me, son." Pat put his hand on Alan's shoulder. "But let's go back and get some coffee, shall we? What are you doin' out here this early, anyway?"

"I came out to do some heavy-duty thinking and some serious praying."

"Well," Pat said appreciatively, "it's a good place for both."

"The voice of experience?" Alan asked the man.

"I guess you could say that."

Twenty-Six

"I can't believe it," Pat said when Alan told him about his visit with Sean the day before. "I take that back," he added quickly. "My brother's been known to be a stubborn man. Even thoughtless at times. But this. This is too important. He can't make a decision like this without talkin' to Connie. She's lived on the place most of her life."

"I'm sure he will," Alan said. "He can't make a decision like this without her signature, can he?"

"Not hardly. Grandpa McCarron made sure the property was put in all our names—wives included. Sean may make the decision, but Connie has to sign the papers." Pat looked over the top of his glasses at the young man sitting opposite him at the breakfast table. "What are you goin' to do?"

"I'd like to give it some more thought," Alan said. "I was hoping I'd have more time, but with my father coming out next week, I guess I'd better have my ideas pretty well lined up. I had hoped to talk to Retta about it, too."

"Retta?" Pat smiled his one-sided sly smile. "What's she got to do with this?"

"Everything," Alan said, leaning his chin in the palm of his hand. "Just everything."

———

"My land, *m'hija*," Connie said when Retta came in the back door. "What in the world is wrong?"

"Nothing, Mama."

"Don't you lie to me, young woman. Look at you. You're a mess. Have you been out all night? It's barely six-thirty."

"No, of course not. I went out early, that's all."

"Something wrong? It didn't freeze last night. The fog—"

"No, Mama. It didn't freeze. I went for an early walk. Isn't that all right?"

"Of course, honey. But look at you, your eyes are all swollen. You've been crying. Come here and sit down. Talk to me, please."

"I'm sorry, I can't."

"Sure you can. There's nothing you can't tell me, you know that."

"Mama?" Retta said reaching for the coffeepot. "You believe in prayer, don't you?"

"Of course I do."

"What happens when you pray and pray for something to happen and it doesn't happen? Then something else happens and you know it's too late for what you prayed to happen to happen because you need more time for it to happen in the first place?"

"Try that again," Connie said. "You lost me there someplace."

"It's just that I prayed for God to make something happen. I don't ask Him for much, but this was really important to me."

"I see." Connie turned the burner off under the oatmeal and pushed it to one side. Turning to face her daughter, she said, "Go on."

"Well, I knew that what I was praying for would take some time. You know, some things just take a lot of time. I knew that and I was willing to wait—as long as necessary. But then—"

"Good morning, Mama," Glenna said with a slightly overly friendly tone. "How's my lovely family this morning?"

"We're fine. Get yourself some coffee. Retta was talking about something important."

"Is that right? Well, little sister, don't let me interrupt. Maybe I can help." Glenna poured her cup full of coffee and came to sit at the table next to Retta. "What's bothering you? Maybe you need a big sister's shoulder to cry on."

"It's nothing," Retta said. "I think I'll go upstairs and shower."

Joanna came in as Retta left the kitchen.

"What's wrong with her?" Joanna asked. "She been crying?"

"Boyfriend trouble, if you ask me," Glenna said. "She's got all the signs."

"Boyfriend?" Connie asked. "I hardly think she's got boyfriend trouble."

"You mean you have to have a boyfriend first, don't you, Mama?" Joanna said.

"She has a boyfriend," Glenna said.

"Oh, come on," Joanna said in return. "You can't be serious."

"Listen, runt, if you had eyes for anything else that goes on in the world except Howie, you'd see that Retta has a king-sized crush on our little collegiate from Harvard."

"Alan?" Joanna asked with shocked delight.

"One and the same," Glenna said. "Too bad he doesn't feel the same about her."

"You sure?" Joanna said to her oldest sister.

"Positive." Glenna raised her eyebrows and gave Joanna a look she hoped would convey her meaning, "If you know what I mean . . ."

"No kidding? Has he—?"

"I wouldn't give him the time of day," Glenna said with a stuck-up tilt to her head. She fluffed her short, dark hair with her fingers, then examined the pale frost fingernail polish she had applied that morning.

"I would," Joanna said, "he's dreamy."

Connie turned her attention back to the pan of oatmeal and preparations of Sean's breakfast tray. Did he know anything about this? The question lingered in the back of her mind. *I know they're interested in each other. I couldn't have missed the signs of something so obvious happening right in front of my own nose. But does Sean know what's going on?*

————

Retta stood under the hot steaming water, letting it wash over her hair and warm her chilled body. She caught a washcloth by two corners and twirled it absent-mindedly. In a flash of anger, she snapped it at the tiled shower wall. "I can't believe this is happening!" she cried. "I ask you for one thing in my whole life—just one—" Retta's anger turned to disappointment. "Oh, God. What am I going to do with my life now?"

Within half an hour, Retta had dressed and slipped out the front door. Above all, she didn't want to see her father today—not today. With Glenna's taunting threats still ringing in her ears, she wasn't sure she wouldn't break down and demand to know what right Sean had to sell the family place. Unsure of her ability to maintain her composure, and with no particular destination in mind, she slid behind the wheel of the family car and headed toward town.

Checking her watch, she saw that it was still early. Driving aimlessly didn't appeal to her very much, but since high school she hadn't really maintained any close friendships. For the first time, she wished for a friend, a really close friend. Retta wanted to pour out her heart, not so much for advice or answers, but just to have someone hear her. Maybe it was just to be able to hear her own thoughts put into words.

Rounding a corner, she waited for a young mother to escort her preschooler to the curb. Glancing to one side, she caught sight of someone waving, trying to get her attention.

"Hi, Retta," Linda Henry said, running over to the car. Retta lowered the window and returned Linda's greeting.

"What brings you out so early on such a foggy morning?" Linda asked.

"Just had to get out by myself for a while. I needed some fresh air."

"Where are you going?"

"I don't know. Just for a drive." Retta turned, not wanting Linda to see the tears that filled her eyes.

"You okay?" Linda asked.

"Sure."

"I don't think so," Linda said, opening the door and sliding in the front seat. "Pull over to the curb and wait for me right here."

Before Retta could stop her, Linda jumped from the car, ran toward the building, and reappeared a moment later, slipping into her jacket as she came back to Retta's car.

"Come on," Linda said, "you can give me a ride home. I'll make some coffee."

"What were you doing back there?" Retta asked once they were inside Jim and Linda's modest little house.

"At Sunnydale? I work there part-time. I teach the kids music. I just love kids, don't you? Jim and I want a family of our own. But that doesn't seem to be happening at the moment. So I decided to teach little ones. It's really fun. I go two mornings a week."

"Then I'm keeping you from your job," Retta said.

"Don't give it another thought. Our morning routine is pretty flexible. We give and take for each other's needs."

"But won't they cut your pay?"

"If there was any pay. I volunteer."

"I see," Retta said, feeling guilty.

"Retta," Linda said gently, "what's the matter? I had to yell at you several times before you even saw me back there. Is there anything I can do?"

"I don't think there's anything anybody can do."

"Oh, boy," Linda said eagerly rubbing her hands together. "An impossible situation. I just love impossible situations."

Before too long, the whole story had tumbled out of Retta with a generous amount of tears. Finally, Linda handed her another fresh tissue and took both of Retta's hands in her own.

"We need to pray," Linda said easily.

"I did that already."

"You did? What did you pray?"

"Well, it was more like a complaint than a real prayer," Retta said, almost embarrassed at the tone she had used earlier in the shower.

"Oh, well," Linda said reassuringly, "don't worry about that. God doesn't mind."

"You don't think so?"

"Were you being honest with Him?"

"Very."

"Well then, there you have it. So you prayed already. And so. . . ?"

"So, what?"

"What did God say?"

"Say?"

"Yes. I assume you asked Him a question. So what was His response?"

"He didn't say anything to me. You talk as though God speaks back to us."

"You mean, you think He doesn't?"

"Wait a minute. . . ." Retta said.

"Why would you pray if you didn't think He could answer?"

"Well, I know He can answer prayers. But not like that."

"How then? If we can talk to God, but for some reason He can't talk back to us, how does He answer our questions?"

"Well, you know. By working things out. Changing circumstances, making things turn out okay."

"But, Retta. What if He wants to tell us no?"

"We have to wait. When it doesn't happen, we know He said no."

"But what if you need to know right away? What if you can't wait to come to a conclusion about His answer? What then?"

"Oh, Linda. I don't know. I just don't know." Retta put her head down on her arms and once again let her deep sobs surface.

Linda came around and knelt on the floor beside her young friend and soothed Retta's hair back from her wet cheek. "Shh. What is behind all these tears? I'm sorry you are hurting so. Can't we just tell God again what it is you want? Could we pray together?"

Linda began very simply telling God that Retta was confused and wanted to get some things straightened out, that things didn't seem to be working out the way she'd hoped.

Retta listened to the simple conversational way Linda addressed God and was impressed with how easy and natural it sounded. "You sound like God is your best friend," she said, lifting her face from her arms.

"He is," Linda said. "He really is."

"How is that possible? I mean, how can a person know *God* that way?"

"Wait right here and I'll show you." Linda retrieved her

Bible from a table in the living room and turned to a scripture passage underlined with a red pencil. "Right here." She pointed to the words. "John fifteen. Read it out loud."

"*These things have I spoken unto you, that my joy might remain in you, and that your joy might be full. This is my commandment, that ye love one another, as I have loved you. Greater love hath no man than this, that a man lay down his life for his friends. Ye are my friends, if ye do whatever I command you. Henceforth, I call you not servants; for the servant knoweth not what his lord doeth; but I have called you friends; for all things I have heard of my Father I have made known unto you.*" Retta finished reading and turned to Linda. "What does this mean?"

"Retta, have you ever given your heart to Christ?"

"Yes, a long time ago. In Sunday school."

"When you gave Him your heart, did He accept you as His child?"

"My Sunday school teacher said we were born again."

"And how were you able to accept this being born again?"

"Because Jesus died for my sins," Retta said. "He forgave me."

"You see, right here, it says, *greater love hath no man, than to lay down his life for his friends.* That refers to Jesus' death on the cross. You see, Retta McCarron, Jesus doesn't only want to be your Savior, He wants to be your friend."

"I guess I didn't realize that."

"Would your prayers sound different if you thought you were talking to a trusted friend rather than to a God you only were to obey and serve?"

"Of course," Retta said. "Like the way I talked to Him this morning—you know, when I was in the shower."

"So you said you were mad. Are you mad at God? Or are you mad at the way things are?"

"I don't know," Retta said slowly. "I'd have to think about that for a minute." She twisted the tissue in her hands for a moment before answering. "Both. I think I'm mad at God for the way things are."

"Don't tell me," Linda said. "Tell Him."

"Just like that?"

"Just like that."

Retta hesitated at first, then before long, she slipped into a very relaxed tone and poured out the confusion in her heart in the same conversational tone she had used with Linda earlier.

When she had finished, Retta sat back looking quite relaxed and almost peaceful, staring at her nearly empty coffee cup.

Linda hesitated to interrupt the moment, then finally broke the silence. "Well, what are you thinking?"

"Not too much of anything." She swirled the last little bit of coffee around in her cup. "You'd think that if we could imagine how God could work something out, He should be able to think of something that would help, wouldn't you?"

"And what do you imagine?"

"I can't even say," Retta said, her cheeks flooding with color. "I can't even say."

"What do you think God would say if He were sitting right here with us right now?"

"I haven't the faintest idea," Retta admitted.

"I do."

"You do?"

"You know, Retta. I think God would say, *Retta McCarron, trust me. Don't worry about anything. Just trust me.*"

Retta laughed a small, yet happy laugh.

"Is that so funny?"

"Yeah, it is. Because that's just what I was thinking I should do a few minutes ago." Retta looked directly into the smile-filled hazel eyes of the young pastor's wife. "You know, I never thought of prayer being a conversation before. I always thought of it as being, well, I don't know—a list."

"I did too, then I met Jim." Linda glanced toward the wedding picture hanging on the wall in the next room. "He upset everything I ever thought I knew about God."

"Is your church very different?"

"It's not your usual traditional service. Why not come and see for yourself sometime? I know your mother would be pleased. Paddy's been coming with her since Christmas. You know, Retta, his poinsettias were so beautiful."

"I know. I saw them before Jim picked them up." Retta's

eyes again filled with tears. "I can't imagine what my father's decision will do to Paddy."

"Oops!" Linda said quickly. "You forget already?"

"Forget what?"

"*Trust me.* I think we heard the Lord say that, didn't we?"

"I think we did," Retta said. "No—I know I did."

"Just one more thing, Retta." Linda said as she gathered up the cups and deposited them in the sink. "Just because you have made the decision to trust God, there's no guarantee it will be easy."

"Linda, could I call you sometime? I mean, I don't have many friends, it would be nice if—"

"You call me anytime," Linda said, encircling Retta in a warm embrace. "If I'm not here, come looking for me. I spend a lot of time next door. My neighbor lady is all alone, except for her housekeeper who comes once a week. She's pretty much confined to her house."

"Linda, I don't know if I have ever met anyone quite like you before."

"Look in the mirror, Retta." Linda laughed. "We're quite alike. Independent, stubborn, willful . . ."

"Oh, please." Retta moaned and pulled away from Linda.

In the living room, Linda paused at a large mirror hanging over a matching chest. "Look," she said, once again pulling Retta next to her, "two peas in a pod."

Twenty-Seven

"What's all that stuff out by the water main?" Retta asked. Pat looked up from his omelet and locked his gaze on his brother's face. Sean kept his attention on his breakfast.

"What stuff?" Connie asked from her usual position at the kitchen stove.

"Looks like pipes," Retta said.

"Oh, that," Paddy said, unaware of the warning in Pat's eyes. "That's Alan's new drip system."

"His what?" Sean said, almost choking on his food.

"Alan is putting in a new drip system at Uncle Pat's."

"It's not my place anymore," Pat corrected.

"You know what I meant."

"Well, the whole gang's here for once," Glenna said as she came into the kitchen. "Is there room for one more? What's this I hear about a drip system?"

"Alan's putting one in over at Uncle Pat's," Paddy repeated.

"It's not my place," Pat said, a little more forcefully.

"We hardly ever see you for breakfast anymore, Uncle Pat. To what do we owe this honor?" Glenna teased.

"He got hungry for real food," Sean said.

"I wanted some of Connie's fresh salsa with my eggs this mornin'. You know she won't let nary a spoonful off the place. Afraid someone will steal her recipe and market the stuff. You could get rich, Connie, I'm tellin' you." Pat ceremoniously took a bite of egg, laden with Connie's spicy Mexican tomato relish. He wanted to keep the conversation away from Alan's drip system if he possibly could.

"Well, now," Pat said to Paddy, "you start forcin' those lilies yet?"

"It's barely past Christmas," Joanna chimed in. "You guys thinking about Easter already?"

"I need some more plastic."

"More?" Sean frowned in Paddy's direction.

"I'm making sort of a greenhouse effect."

"You want black or dark green?" Sean asked.

"I'd like a whole roll of clear or white."

"Thought you said it was a greenhouse," Joanna laughed.

Connie kept plates of food coming to the table, loving to hear the friendly banter of her family at breakfast. She, too, was glad that Pat was able to divert the conversation away from Alan Conrad's plans. Without him here, it was almost possible to forget for a moment that Pat's place now belonged to an outsider. She hadn't told anyone of the empty ache that had been with her since Pat announced his plans to sell out.

"What's this about a drip system next door?" Sean asked.

"Next door?" Joanna wrinkled her nose, almost in disgust. "Isn't there some other way to refer to Uncle Pat's than next door?"

"What should we call it, then?" Glenna asked, eyeing Retta's serious expression. "Alan's? The Conrad place?"

"Will they really be building houses there, Daddy?" Joanna asked.

"I don't know, Jo-Jo. That's up to the Conrad people."

"I know what we can call it," Glenna said enthusiastically. "Conrad Estates. Can't you see it now? Little flat houses, three bedrooms, two baths. Their cute little roofs all covered with white stone. From your room, Retta, you'll be able to see down into everyone's backyard. Wow!"

"Excuse me," Retta said, scooting her chair back and hurrying from the room.

"Was it something I said?" Glenna asked innocently.

"Eat your breakfast, girl," Sean said.

"I'll be off. I'll go see if Alan needs any help," said Pat, leaving the rest of his breakfast to get cold on his plate.

"I'll be outside," Paddy said as he reached for his crutches.

"There's Howie," Joanna said cheerily. "See you later, alligator!"

"Get my crutches, will you, Connie?" Sean said, scooting his chair away from the table. "I'll be in the den with the morning paper."

Glenna stared at the food on her plate. "You'd think somebody hollered fire or something."

"You," Sean said between clenched teeth, "have got a big mouth. Will you ever learn when to keep it shut?"

"All I said was the truth. Nobody's facing the truth, Mama." Glenna was clearly defensive, yet Connie read a glint of defiance in her daughter's eyes she didn't like.

"You know it's a sore spot with the family, Glenna. Think how you made your uncle Pat feel just now."

"He's the one who sold out," Glenna whined.

"You don't have to rub his nose in it." Connie tried to keep her tone soft when what she really wanted to do was paddle her grown daughter. "You know, daughter, not everyone finds this as easy to take as you do. Can't you remember other people have feelings too?"

"Everybody's so touchy around here," Glenna said. "Nobody's any fun anymore. Can't anyone even take a joke?"

"Nobody's forcing you to stay," Connie said.

"What do you mean by that?" Glenna asked, looking at her mother in surprise.

"You are almost twenty-three, Glenna. You have a good job. I would think you could afford a place of your own. Maybe a roommate, another girl at work, perhaps?"

"You telling me I have to leave home?" Glenna could hardly believe what she was hearing come from her mother.

"I'd never tell you that," Connie said, "but I would remind you that if you don't like it here—"

"I didn't say that," Glenna retorted.

"You could have fooled me," Connie said as she turned to leave Glenna alone in the kitchen. "Clear the table before you leave for work this morning. I'm going in to join your father."

"But I'll be late," Glenna complained.

"Not if you hurry," Connie replied as she left the room.

Connie and Sean sat without speaking. A casual observer would have guessed them to be engrossed in their newspapers. Several minutes went by, however, and neither had turned a page.

"Any more coffee?" Sean asked without looking up from his paper.

"I think so," Connie said without moving.

"Would you mind getting me some, then?" Sean lowered his paper and looked over at his wife.

"Yes. I would mind."

Sean folded his paper and put it to one side and reached for his crutches. Moving awkwardly toward the hallway, he was stopped by Connie's voice.

"We have to talk about this sometime, Sean McCarron."

"That's what you keep sayin'," he answered.

"And I'll keep on until we do," she said.

"Not today."

"When?"

"Not today." Turning toward her, he felt his heart fill with both love and longing. "I'm expecting Mark Andrews after a while."

"I'd better get dressed then."

"I'd appreciate that."

"I'll make fresh coffee."

"Thanks."

———

Mark sensed the tenseness between Sean and Connie the minute he walked through the door. He wondered if he should come back another time. Connie always seemed so friendly and warm at church. Somehow this atmosphere wasn't at all what he expected to find in her home.

"How's the leg coming?" Mark asked.

"Not much change. I'll know more when the cast is changed."

"When's that?"

"Another month yet."

"Time going slow, cooped up like this?" Mark asked, aware that Sean was used to being outdoors.

"You can only watch so many game shows, you know."

"I bet. I don't know how you do it, McCarron. I'd be half crazy by now."

"Connie thinks I was half crazy before this all happened," Sean smiled.

"You asked me to drop by, you have something on your mind?"

"Yeah, I do, Andrews. I want to know about your boys."

"My boys?"

"Pat tells me they've done a very respectable job on the carriage house. I can't tell you how much I appreciate it. But I'm curious. How did you get started? Why do you do it?"

Sean listened with interest as Mark shared his personal journey from the tragedy of his loss to feeling productive and useful once again. When Mark finished, Sean sat back quietly—almost lost in his own thoughts.

"I'm afraid I haven't cheered you up with my story, have I?"

"It's not a cheerful story. But you may have helped me more than you know. Maybe even more than those boys of yours."

"Are you close to your son?"

"Paddy?" Sean asked. "Not as close as I would like—but that's my fault, not his. I'd say we're getting much closer these days. This leg has really given me more of an understanding of him and how he feels. Sorry to say, I have only looked at him knowing how *I* feel about what happened to him. I'm starting to think I almost needed this accident—isn't that a sorry admission?"

"Well, look at it this way, Sean. God says He works all things together for the good of those who love Him and are called according to His purpose."

"I've failed miserably in that area, too, I'm afraid."

"Who hasn't?" Mark didn't know how far he dared push Sean McCarron on that point. "But, just as I am sure your son would welcome a closer relationship, I am convinced God would."

"You know, it's my daughter Glenna I'm most worried about."

"I didn't have any other children," Mark said sadly. "I would have really wanted a daughter, too." Mark stood to leave, then turned back to face Sean. "Don't let anything drive her away, McCarron. I have a daughter-in-law and a granddaughter. God has given me a second chance—He'll do the same for you, if you let Him."

Long after Mark Andrews left, Sean remained alone in the den with his own thoughts. His situation couldn't compare with the tragedy Mark Andrews had suffered. Yet Mark said he had more peace now than at any other time in his life. How could that be?

Losing your only son would be bad enough, but to lose your wife as well. And then your business.

What was it Mark had said? "I had no choice but to start over. To begin again from scratch. So I decided I might as well choose a new attitude, too. And with Jim Henry's help, I found a new beginning—a second chance with God."

Sean struggled to his feet. It was terrible when a man had to have help just to stand up. Something disturbing tugged at his heart. How long had his spirit been as broken as his body had become? A sense of overwhelming failure swept over him. Being closed up in the room made him long for the outdoors. He made his way toward the window and pulled back the curtain, trying to get as close to outside as possible, yet the nagging in the back of his mind refused to be stilled. It wasn't his body that felt cooped up, but his heart and spirit.

A new beginning with God, Sean wondered. *Is it really possible when you've shut Him out this long and for such selfish reasons?*

"It's not too late," Mark had urged with regard to Paddy. Sean recalled the other words Mark had spoken about his own son. "I had provided a living, but hadn't given him life. I gave him everything but a father. And worse than that, I didn't let him have himself."

Let him have himself. Sean turned the words over in his mind. Had he been guilty of that as well? *Have I let Paddy be himself?* Sean let his tears flow unchecked down his face. *Do I have the courage?*

Lost in his own thoughts, Sean barely noticed his older brother drive the golf cart up the driveway and pull around the side of the house.

"Sean," Connie's voice interrupted the quietness of the room. "Pat wants to show you something out back. You want the wheelchair?"

"I think I'll try the crutches."

"I don't mind getting the chair."

"No, I think I'd rather stay on my feet."

"Here, let me help you," she said, coming to stand closer.

"Thanks, but I think I can do this on my own."

"Why do you have to be so stubborn?" Connie asked, her hands on her hips.

"Consuela," Sean said, "stop smotherin' me, will you? I'm a grown man. I can make it to the back door, for heaven's sake."

"Now you're starting to sound like Paddy," she said. Without meaning to, Connie struck a nerve of understanding deep within Sean's heart with her words.

"Is this what we've done to our son all these years?"

"What?" Connie's eyes flew open and a soft gasp escaped through her mouth. "What did you say?"

"Have we so protected Paddy that we've not let him have any sense of independence at all?"

"Sean McCarron, how can you say that? We've only looked out for him. We've only done what we thought was for his own good!"

"His own good? Or ours?"

"Sean," she said softly. "Don't, please."

"I mean it, Connie. What I wonder is why he doesn't resent us for it."

"Oh, please," Connie said with disgust. "Glenna does enough of that for the both of them."

She heard Sean's quick intake of breath and turned to find her husband pale. Shock and surprise had siphoned the blood from his face.

"Sean!" she cried. "What's wrong?"

"Oh, Connie. I can't believe what a fool I've been all these years. A busy, overbearing, unfeeling, unloving fool." He held his arms as wide as he could and still maintain his balance between the crutches. "Come here, darlin'. Please, come here, I need you so much."

Stepping between his arms, she slid her hands around his waist and up his back. "What, sweetheart?" she whispered. "Tell me what's wrong."

"Me, that's what's wrong." Sean bent his head into the soft

crook of her warm neck and wept without shame. "But it's not too late," he said. "Thank God for new beginnings."

"Sean!" Pat's voice rang loud through the house.

"He's got something to show you," Connie said.

"Coming!" Sean yelled back. "Hold on to your hat!"

"What's this?" Sean said, trying to carefully maneuver the back steps with his bulky cast and awkward crutches. "Where'd this come from?"

"I bought it," Pat said, grinning from ear to ear. "Thought you might like to get out in the grove a bit now and then." Pat moved around the cart, then back toward Sean and Connie. "See? It's quite a bit more open—easier to get into than the truck. Don't you think?" Pat pointed to the back and urged Sean to turn around and sit a little sideways with his casted leg propped on the bench-style seat.

"You in?" Pat asked.

"I think so," Sean said excitedly.

"You ready, then?"

"You bet!" Sean looked around at the efficient battery-powered machine. "Cushman, huh?"

"What?" Pat said. "Oh yeah, a Cushman."

Paddy came across the gravel yard, much more expert on his crutches than Sean, but still dragging his left leg laboriously behind him.

"Hey, Paddy," Sean said, "what do you think of this contraption?"

"It's great isn't it, Dad!"

"Uncle Pat's takin' me for a ride. Want to come along?"

"Did I say *I* was takin' you?"

"Hold on, Dad," Paddy said, positioning himself behind the controls. "This could be a wild experience. Get ready for the ride of your life."

"Paddy!" Consuela said, objecting to what she saw happening. As she moved toward the cart, Pat stepped in her way and grabbed her by both arms.

"Go on, Paddy," Pat ordered. "Connie, you stay out of this."

Paddy put his strongest foot on the bright silver accelerator button on the floor board and the cart moved smoothly forward.

"I hope you know what you're doing!" Sean yelled to his son.

"I bet you do," Paddy laughed. "You just make sure you're holding on tight."

"Pat," Connie cried, "please go with them. If they should have an accident out there. Oh, please, Pat."

"They'll be fine."

"Pat," she begged. "What if they turn over, or if one of them should fall?"

"Tell you what," Pat said, trying to soothe his frantic sister-in-law. "If they don't come back by lunchtime, I'll go out lookin' for them."

Within fifteen minutes, Connie was relieved to hear the whine of the cart as it approached the nearby edge of the grove. She quickly wiped the tears of relief that welled up in her eyes.

"Get the camera!" Sean yelled as they came into view. "Let's get a picture of this!"

"Let me help you out of there," Connie said as Paddy brought the cart to a halt.

"Absolutely not," Sean said. "My son has promised we'll inspect the whole grove. Isn't that right, Paddy?"

"Come on, Mom," Paddy pleaded. "Get on."

"Not on your life," she said. "You two are crazy."

"It's her loss, son," Sean said with a laugh. "On with it, then. To the grove!" Sean gestured widely with one hand while slapping Paddy on the back with the other.

"Yes, sir! To the grove!" Paddy repeated as he once again urged the machine forward.

Standing a little distance away, Pat could barely contain his emotions. He closed the distance between himself and Connie and reassuringly slipped one arm around her shoulders.

"They act like two kids!" she said in a scolding tone.

"They're celebrating, Connie. Freedom is a precious thing when you've been cooped up so long."

"This has been hard on Sean, I guess—"

"I wasn't talking about Sean," Pat said as he moved away.

Twenty-Eight

"I don't understand why you're doing this!"

Alan jumped, losing his grip on the awkward wrench he was using. "Do you think you could give a warning shot before you come in here blasting the cannons?"

"Sorry, I thought you knew I was standing here," Retta said.

"No, I didn't know you were within miles of the place. You've been keeping your distance lately."

"Why are you going to all this trouble?"

"What trouble?"

"All this," she indicated the pipes lying helter-skelter around Alan's feet.

"Why should you care?" he asked sarcastically.

"I didn't say I cared," she shot back. "I'm just curious."

"As you can see," he said, "I'm busy. I don't have time to satisfy your curiosity. Now, if you'll excuse me."

"Listen, Alan, you don't have to be rude. I came all the way over here to find out what in the world you think you're doing."

"And I walked all the way out to the far end of the grove to find out what was wrong that morning, remember?"

"Forget I asked," she said, turning to retreat into the grove.

"I'll do my very best," he called angrily after her.

Watching her walk down the row between the trees, Alan wanted to run after her. If he had any indication that he would be able to penetrate the cold cloak she had pulled between them, he would have tried. Instead, his feelings of futility toward her added to the frustration he was having with the pipes, and he squeezed hard on the handle of the wrench in his hand, then forcefully sent it flying into the dirt.

"Hey, Alan! You got troubles with that?"

At the sound of Sean's voice, Alan spun around to see the two men watching him from the cart.

"Over there, son." Sean tapped Paddy's shoulder and pointed in the direction of Alan's project.

"I see you finally sprung it on him," Alan said, his dark mood suddenly lifting.

"We may be sorry we did this," Paddy said. "Now he talks like I'm his chauffeur."

"Well, aren't you?" Sean laughed good-naturedly.

"It's good to see you out and about, sir," Alan said, extending his hand in a gesture of friendship.

"It's good to *be* out and about, Conrad," Sean said. "Isn't it, Paddy?"

"Sure is," Paddy answered. "But if we don't check in now and then, Mom will be worried sick."

"She'll learn," Sean said. "What's the trouble here?" he asked, pointing toward Alan's disassembled sprinkler system. "Anythin' we can do?"

"It's that pipe there," Alan said. "It won't stay where it's supposed to."

"Pull it up here and let's have a look."

Alan hefted the difficult section of pipe for Sean's inspection.

"What do you think, Paddy?" Sean asked, holding it where Paddy could see it.

"Looks to me like the threads are stripped," Paddy said.

"That's what I thought. Listen, Conrad. There's a pipe threader in the tool shed. Go on over and help yourself. But if it were me, I'd put that pipe aside and take care of it later. Find another one with good threads. Don't let a little thing like that stop you. Any idea when you'd like to have this ready to run?"

"I thought I'd like to have it ready to go by the next watering schedule."

"I figured as much," Sean said. "Then you've got your

work cut out for you. Pat helpin' out any?"

"Not much," Alan said. "He's getting ready to move out this weekend."

"Oh, yeah, I forgot."

"But don't worry about me, Mr. McCarron. I'm doing fine." Alan shot an unspoken message to Paddy through exchanged glances.

"I'd help you myself," Sean said. "But I'm not much good with this cast on."

"It's okay, Dad," Paddy said. "I'll give him a hand. Now I'd better have you home before Mom sends out the militia. See you later, Alan. I'll come back while he takes his nap."

Sean thumped the back of Paddy's head with his finger. "Don't give me any of your lip, sonny. I'll dump you off out here somewhere and make you crawl home."

"At least I'd get home," Paddy retorted with a grin and waved to Alan as they drove away.

After struggling to connect the pipes, making sure the drippers were strategically placed near the trees, the last thing Alan wanted to do was go near the McCarron house. However, if he were to use the needed tools to rethread not only the one pipe, but two others, he had no choice.

Once inside the tool shed, Alan relaxed and concentrated on the task. He hadn't run into Retta, and Paddy had agreed not to tell her where he was.

"How's it going?" It was Glenna's sultry voice that brought him around in surprise.

"What are you doing here?"

"Just coming to see if you needed any help," Glenna said as she moved closer.

"I can manage."

"You sure?"

"Positive," he said without looking up from the pipe in his hands.

"Well, then," she said softly. "I'll just watch."

"Suit yourself," he said.

"I intend to."

As Alan turned to stand the finished pipe in the corner,

Glenna saw her opportunity and slipped between him and the wall. Eagerly, she turned her face up to his and quickly planted her kiss on his lips.

Alan, though taken by surprise, felt completely calm. With a great deal of restraint, he took her firmly by the arms. But before he could unwind himself from her clutches, the door opened. Suddenly his calm gave way to panic, and he took a large step backward away from Glenna. Without even looking toward the doorway, he knew who was standing there.

"Well, Retta." Glenna's dark eyes sparkled, even in the dimly lit tool shed. "I see you found us." Turning to Alan, she moved closer to him and ran her one manicured finger across his chest. "I'll see you later," she purred.

Retta stepped out of her sister's way, then turned to follow her out the door.

"Retta!" he said.

Caught off guard by the sharp tone of his voice, she spun around to face him.

"This is not what you think," he said.

"You don't know what I think!" she said, choking on her words as if a strong hand had closed around her throat. "I came out here to apologize for the way I acted this morning. But I've changed my mind!"

Alan stood and helplessly watched as she disappeared into the house. Turning back to the bench, he grabbed his pipes and slammed the door to the shed as he left.

Halfway through the grove, he stopped dead in his tracks and turned back toward the family home. "This has to stop," he said resolutely. "Right now."

Dropping the pipes, he walked with heavy, determined steps through the grove, up the back steps of the McCarron home, and into the kitchen without knocking.

Retta, standing at the sink with her mother, tried to leave the room when she saw him.

"Wait!" Alan commanded. "Stay right where you are. Stop running away from me!"

"Stay away from me!" Retta said and burst into tears.

"Don't worry," he said, his tone of voice revealing his depth of defeat. "Where's Sean?"

"In the den with Paddy. Jim's in there too," she said, but Alan was already storming into the den. "What is wrong with him?" Connie asked Retta.

"He's having a little trouble making up his mind," she said between tears.

"About what?"

"That's something you'd have to ask him." Retta quickly dried her hands and threw the towel onto the counter. Running through the dining room, she mounted the stairway and hurried upstairs, covering her ears against the raised voices coming from the den.

"You're what?"

"You heard me," Alan said, standing over Sean, clenching and unclenching his fists. "I said I'm not recommending my father consider the McCarron place any longer. In fact, I'm going to suggest he put Pat's place on the market as soon as possible. I'll be leaving for New York as soon as I can wrap up any business he has for me."

"But, Alan," said Jim, leaving Paddy at the chessboard, "your father is going to be here in a week or two, isn't he?"

"He's coming to California, yes. But he doesn't necessarily have to come here."

"Now wait a minute, son," Sean said. "Sit down, will you? What's behind all this? Surely a little problem with a pipe isn't causing all this grief."

Alan faced the older man and wanted to scream the truth at him. *I'm in love with one daughter*, he wanted to yell, *and I hate the other!* How could he tell Sean the truth and make it believable? "It's a personal matter," Alan said simply.

Sean watched Alan leave the room and heard the back door slam behind him. "It's Retta, isn't it?" Sean asked to no one in particular. "Why can't they just admit they're in love and be done with it?"

"Alan," Connie pleaded as she followed him out the door, "don't leave like this."

Stopping in the driveway, he let her catch up to him.

"Come back in the house. We can work this out. Whatever it is, please come back and talk about it."

"I don't think so, Connie," Alan said.

"You're upset. Let us help you. We're your friends. Come on, now. Whatever it is—Jim's here. We can sort this all out together."

Alan let Connie lead him back into the house. Coming into the room she said simply, "I think it's time we got to the bottom of this."

Alan Conrad faced Sean McCarron and squared his shoulders. Feeling strength well up within his chest, he took a deep breath and said, "Mr. McCarron, I want to talk to you about your daughter."

"I thought so." Sean smiled and shifted to a more relaxed position. "But I want her here. I don't talk about my girls behind their backs. Not when it's this important."

Alan shut his eyes, knowing the smile on Sean's face would fade the moment he realized the truth.

"Connie," Sean motioned to his wife, "call Retta down here, will you?"

Alan's voice called Connie back. "No," he said. "This isn't about Retta."

"Oh?" Sean's chin dropped and a hint of concern flashed through his deep blue eyes.

"It's Glenna, isn't it?" Connie asked.

Alan nodded solemnly.

"I thought so," she said.

Glenna came in response to her mother's voice. Immediately, she sensed the tension among the people waiting in the room.

"I can leave," Jim said.

"Me, too," Paddy offered.

"No, stay. Everyone stay," Alan said. "Glenna, I need to say something to you and I want your father to hear it. I've said it to you before, but I guess you haven't understood what I said—or maybe you haven't believed I meant it. I don't want to embarrass you, but you leave me no choice."

Shock and fear registered for a second on Glenna's face

before she forced a frozen smile to her lips.

"I want you to stay away from me. I'll do my best not to come around when you're here. I have no romantic interest in you whatsoever. Please, leave me alone."

Closing the distance between them, he stood facing her, locking her gaze into his. "Do I make myself clear?"

She stared, openly devastated with embarrassment. A tense silence engulfed the room. The chill between them began to swell into a volcano of anger on the verge of erupting. Glenna clenched her hands until her nails dug painfully into her palms.

"Do you understand what I'm saying?" Alan's hoarse whisper shattered the tense silence in the room.

"Perfectly," she said, turning on her heel and leaving the room.

Alan remained motionless until he heard the bedroom door upstairs close with an angry thud. He shut his eyes momentarily and opened them when he felt Connie's soft touch on his shoulder.

"I'm sorry, Mrs. McCarron," he said quietly without turning around. "I'm really sorry about this."

Connie sent her forgiveness to him through a gentle pat on his shoulder before she left the room to follow Glenna upstairs.

Sean sat speechless, feeling both sadness and anger toward his daughter. He had no idea she had gone this far. No wonder Retta was so angry she couldn't think straight. "I'm the one who should be apologizin'," Sean said at last. "Don't you worry about this, Alan. I'll speak to her."

"I didn't mean to cause so much trouble, Mr. McCarron."

"You didn't cause it, Alan," Sean said huskily. "The trouble was here long before you showed up. You just helped bring it out into the open."

Sean watched Alan retreat from the room and turned to Jim Henry. "Maybe you better go have a talk with him, Jim."

"I don't think so, Sean." Jim turned back to the chess game with Paddy. "Some things a man has to work out alone—just him and God."

"You're right about that, Preacher," Sean said. "Found that out myself."

Jim and Paddy exchanged smiles.

"My move, Paddy?" Jim asked.

"Don't you wish?" Paddy said, moving a piece and challenging Jim's secret weapon move. "Check," he said triumphantly.

Twenty-Nine

Sleep didn't come easily to Retta after her confrontation with Alan in the tool shed. Long past midnight, she crept as quietly as possible down the stairs and into the kitchen to heat some milk.

"What are you doing up at this hour?" Connie said when she came to investigate the noises coming from the kitchen.

"I'm sorry, Mom," she said, "I couldn't sleep."

"*M'hija*," Connie said tenderly, "what is bothering you?"

"I'm not sure, Mama," Retta said. "I just want everything to stay the same for our family and the farm. But that isn't going to happen, is it?"

"No, sweetheart, it isn't."

"What's going to happen to us?" Retta's eyes filled with tears, and she searched her mother's face for an answer to her question.

Connie opened her mouth to speak just as they both heard a gentle knock at the back door.

"Who could that be—at this hour?" Connie exclaimed, glancing at the kitchen clock. "It's two-thirty in the morning!"

Opening the door, Retta faced a uniformed police officer.

"I'm sorry to bother you, ma'am," the polite young man said, "but I saw your light on back here. Otherwise, I would have come to the front."

"Is something wrong?" Retta asked with Connie standing close behind.

"It's your water, ma'am. May I speak to the owner or manager of the farm?"

"He's—" Retta paused, remembering her father's injury. "I'm in charge of the farm. What's the problem?"

"Your irrigation water is running down the street. Something must be wrong up at the main. I've put a call in to the water department, and they should have someone out within the hour. I just thought you ought to know."

Retta didn't wait for the policeman to finish his explanation before she turned to run upstairs and get dressed. "It's that ridiculous drip system of Alan's," she called over her shoulder. "He probably forgot to turn the main faucet back on. I can't believe this—oh, yes I can!" she muttered angrily.

Within minutes, Retta had pulled on her jeans and a heavy sweater. She pulled her boots over her bare feet and didn't bother with her hair. Grabbing her hooded jacket from the hook on the back porch, she jumped in the pickup truck and headed toward the water main at the corner of the property.

Consuela turned to the officer and said, "My husband's brother and the new owner of the farm next door live on the other side of the farm. Would you mind going and—"

"I wouldn't mind at all, ma'am," the officer said.

By the time Alan and Pat joined her, Retta was frantically trying to turn the main water valve by hand. "It's stuck," she cried over the sound of the rushing irrigation water. "I can't get it open!"

"What do you mean? It *is* open!" Alan said, trying to pull her away from the spigot.

"It's stuck shut," she yelled. "Can't you see that? Look at all this water rushing down the street. If it was open that water would be running into the ditches, not down the storm pipes! You idiot! Didn't you even know to open it after you finished hooking up this, this—" Retta ran to the main joint of Alan's new system and kicked it hard with her boot. "Of all the stupid ideas!"

"Retta!" Pat's voice carried above the sound of the gurgling water. "Stop it!" Pat took hold of her arm and she tried to yank herself free. "The main's broken just above the shut off. Can't you see that?"

"I can see that Mr. Orange Grower here, with all his fancy ideas about change and making things better, has just cost me some of my water. Maybe he can afford to send the water down the street, but I can hardly afford to pay for what I get now, let alone more! No telling how long this has been running like this!" Retta's expression of rage and anger matched the high pitch of her voice. She stamped angrily toward the water flowing freely down the street.

Alan had never seen her like this. He knew she felt possessive of the farm, but her intensity shocked him.

"Let me tell you something, Mr. Alan Conrad!" she said as she shook her fist in his face. "You *will* pay for every drop of my water that you have sent down that street. Do you hear me? Every last drop!"

Alan took a speechless step back away from her anger.

"I mean it," she shouted, pointing at the water gushing down the street. "Let it run, for all I care! I'm not in the least bit worried. You will pay for it. I'll see to that!"

Turning in the darkness, Retta headed back toward the dimming lights of her pickup. Alan watched her and saw her stumble, falling headlong over one of his pipes. Rushing to her side, he tried to help her up.

"Don't touch me!" she shouted. "Don't even come close to me. I don't want to see your face ever again—" Her voice broke in angry sobs as she moved away.

"Retta, please," he said.

"I mean it. Get away from me and stay away." She scrambled to her feet and climbed into the truck. Alan stood by helplessly as the truck engine moaned before it sprang to life.

Shoving it into gear, Retta's mud-caked boot slipped off the clutch. The truck lurched and the engine died. This time, the battery refused to turn the engine over. Trying a few times before she would admit defeat, Retta finally put her head forward on the steering wheel and wept openly.

"Let her be," Uncle Pat said, placing a restraining hand on Alan's arm. "I don't think this is only about the water."

Alan's attention was drawn away from Retta's tears by the headlights of an oncoming truck.

"What's the problem here?" Owen Jones called as he approached the men.

"Broken valve, I think," Alan said, pointing the way. Alan barely noticed the second man slipping through a small opening in the privet hedge.

"Mel's going to turn it off up at the next valve. Let's see if we can spot the trouble."

Owen knelt down and easily turned the faucet that Retta had been struggling to open. "It's already open," he said. "Nothing wrong here. I see you're installing a system. Wish more farmers would. It would really save water. Money, too, in the long run."

"Here's the trouble!" they heard the voice of Owen's partner calling from the other side of the hedge. "Looks like the old pipe finally gave out. It's happening more and more. Those old pipes are just getting too old to handle the pressure anymore. We'll have somebody out here first thing in the morning. By noon we should have your water running again. You get any at all before this thing gave way?"

"Not much," Alan said.

"I don't see any," Jake said. "That'll be easy to figure. No telling how many acres got away from us tonight. Good thing that patrolman was in the neighborhood. It could have been much worse."

"I don't see how," Alan muttered.

"Oh, young man," Jake said. "I've been with the water company for almost forty years. I've seen much worse things than this."

But Alan Conrad wasn't listening, he was heading in the direction of Retta's truck. All he cared about was her. She hated him; he was convinced of that now. She had tried to be polite, even made an attempt or two at liking him. But it was no use. Alan came around to her side of the truck and saw that it was empty. She had probably decided to walk home. Just as well, he knew the grove would give her some comfort. He didn't feel like facing her anyway. Chilled to the bone, Alan turned his own steps toward the small, modest house at the edge of the farm, the place he now knew would never be home for either of them. Stepping into the yard through an opening in the privet hedge, he stopped in midstride and turned. Breaking off a twig from the thick, thorny hedge, he crushed its leaves in his hand.

"No wonder," he whispered angrily into the darkness. "This house isn't inside the privet hedge. She'd never agree to live here anyway."

Moving through the dark grove by instinct rather than by sight, Retta's steps slowed as she remembered the cutting, accusing words she had hurled at Alan. She had wanted them to hurt him. For a moment she didn't even care that the diverted water wasn't his fault. She had used the moment to lash out at him. Abruptly, she was caught by the elbow and turned around to face Pat McCarron. Even in the darkness, Retta could sense his intense anger.

"Are you pleased with yourself, Retta McCarron?" His tone of voice was seldom if ever this sharp—especially when it was directed toward his favorite niece.

"I don't want to talk about it, Uncle Pat."

"No, I wouldn't think you would at that. So then, just listen to me, young woman."

"I'm tired," she said, trying to pull away from his grip on her arm.

"I don't care, you'll hear me out. That young man back there is heartsick. Not about the water, not even about the angry words you said. He's heartsick because he likes it here. He's found something he could really love doing—being an orange farmer. He's ready to pack in all his claims to his family's money if he has to. But this is where he wants to live, and this work is what he wants to do. He could do anything in the whole world, go to the finest schools, and marry some beautiful rich girl from the East."

"Then why doesn't he?" she shot back angrily.

"Because he doesn't want to. He wants to stay right here."

"Well, then, let him. I don't care anymore. Let him buy the whole farm. He can have the entire place as far as I'm concerned." Retta was crying, and she hoped Pat couldn't see her tears in the moonlight. "That's what he's been after from the beginning. Glenna was right all along."

"Your sister? Is that what she told you?"

"She heard Alan pumping Dad to sell. What's he supposed to say? He's not ever going to be able to be out in the groves like he was before. We all know that. Dad's accident was just what Alan Conrad needed to make his move. He couldn't get to Dad through any of us, but the accident . . . how much more perfect could it be?"

"You are so wrong, Retta," Pat said, shaking her roughly, "and so stubborn. Don't you trust anybody?"

"Not Alan Conrad," she said between sobs.

"But Glenna?" he asked with surprise. "Come on, let's get you home."

"I can make it on my own," she said, freeing her arm from her uncle's grasp.

"You only think so," Pat said as he fell into step at her side.

Coming back into the house, Pat and Retta came face-to-face with a frustrated and angry Sean McCarron.

"Simmer down," Pat told his younger brother. "No harm done."

Retta, silent and obviously upset, tried to brush by her father. All she wanted was the privacy of her own room. Sean caught her arm and restrained her.

"It's not easy for a man to stay in the house and let his daughter go out into the night to take care of a problem that he should do himself," Sean said. "Next time, you get on the phone and call Alan. That grove's no place for a woman any time of day, let alone in the dead of night!"

Retta shut her eyes tight and clenched her teeth and pulled away from her father. "I want to go upstairs," she said.

"What happened out there?" Sean insisted.

"Let Uncle Pat tell you," she said, stepping toward the kitchen door.

"No," Pat said as he settled into a chair at the kitchen table. "I think we need to hear your version first."

"The pipe gave way just before our connection. The water company will have it fixed by noon tomorrow. We won't be charged for any of the wasted water."

"So that's good. Then what took so long out there?" Sean asked.

"We had to walk home, the pickup has a dead battery," she said, avoiding Pat's glare.

"So then, no harm done," Sean said.

"I'm going to bed," she said firmly.

Turning to Pat after Retta left the room, Sean noticed his

brother seemed unhurried to call it a night. "Is there something else, Pat?"

"I'm probably not the one to tell you this, Sean. But she made a complete fool of herself out there tonight." Pat motioned his brother to sit down and waited until he was settled in a chair opposite him before he gave him the details of Retta's outburst and accusations of Alan.

"She couldn't turn the valve and assumed that Alan had closed it too tight—and all the time it was open, just like he said." Pat rubbed his hand across the stubble on his face. "He just stood back and let her rant and rave. He didn't even try to defend himself. She was so angry. I've never seen her like that before."

"Well," Sean said, "after Jake explained the problem—"

"She didn't hang around."

"You mean she didn't even apologize?"

"Nope. By the time we got back to the truck, she was gone—already headed for home."

"And Conrad?"

"High-tailed it back to the house. Can't blame him, either. Might have done that myself. She can be a real spitfire, that one."

———

Alan rambled around in the empty house, grateful for the chance to be alone. Wanting something to help him get warm, he put on a pot of coffee, then pulled a heavy sweater over his T-shirt. He checked his watch and decided Pat must have stayed at the main house to fill Sean in on the details of the water situation. Images of Retta's angry face flashed into his mind, and he struggled to fight back his growing emotion.

"Dear God," he prayed quietly, leaning over a steaming cup of coffee. "I really need your help on this one. Maybe you don't want me to stay here. I want your will for my life, Lord. But I can't for the life of me figure out what that is." Alan shoved his cup away and lay his head down on his arms. "I know that what you want for me is best. And if Retta isn't it—" he faltered. The very thought of not being with her was almost unbearable. "Then I know," he prayed hesitantly, "I should be grateful this is not working out the way I wanted it to. But I have to confess, I'm not grateful. Not at all. I'm sorry, God, but I'm only being honest with you." Alan straightened himself and then with a deep breath slumped again in his chair. He sat perfectly still for a while, then refilled his cup. Walking around the small kitchen, he remained silent—waiting, listening. He didn't know just what he expected to hear, maybe Pat's steps on the small back porch. But not really, because Alan Conrad was listening on a much deeper level—he was listening with his heart. "I want to hear your voice," he finally said aloud. "I want to see you do something." Alan stopped in front of the small old refrigerator and folded his arms across its yellowed top. Lowering his head until his chin rested on his arms, he let his emptiness escape with the kind of emotion a man doesn't want anyone to see. Then, like a small boy begging his father for mercy, he tearfully uttered three desperate words: "Please, God, please."

Thirty

"What are you doing out here so early?" Retta's voice cut through the silent, fog-shrouded grove, startling Alan.

"I came out to change the battery," he said, pointing to the place under the hood of the pickup. "Pat had another one in the small shed back at the house."

"Why?"

"Because, Retta McCarron, I had nothing better to do with my time," he said, clipping his words. Alan resumed his task beneath the hood of the old pickup.

"It's not even six o'clock," she said quietly.

"I'm aware of the time." He didn't look up from working on the battery.

"Do you always get up so early?"

"I'm not up early, I'm up late," he said, lifting the old battery from its place. Stepping toward the back of the truck, he placed the battery in the bed. He picked up the spare battery and returned to the front of the truck, setting it into place. "Hand me the wrench, will you?"

Retta picked up the indicated wrench and turned it over in her hands. "I want to talk to you."

"You said plenty last night," he said. "Are you going to hand me the wrench, or not?"

"I was angry last night."

"No kidding. And I'm angry now. Give me the wrench or you can finish this yourself."

Slowly, she extended the wrench toward Alan's out-stretched hand. She searched his face for some small encouragement to continue the conversation.

Alan carefully avoided looking into her eyes. "Thanks," he said, perfunctorily taking the wrench from her hand. When the battery was connected, he stepped away from the raised hood and pointed toward the cab. "Try it now," he ordered.

Retta walked toward the truck and placed her hand on the handle. She paused and turned slightly to face him. "Alan," she said quietly. "I've been doing some thinking."

"You should have done that last night before you opened your big mouth."

"You're not going to make this easy for me, are you?"

"Like you have for me?"

"You couldn't sleep either." It was more a statement than a question.

"Just try to start it, okay?" He moved her aside and opened the door of the pickup.

She tensed and shut the door before he could stop her. "I said I'm sorry."

"No, you didn't. You said you were angry. That's not the same."

"It is to me," she said quietly.

"Not to me. An explanation is not the same as an apology."

"Okay," she said forcefully. "I'm sorry. What else can I say?"

"Nothing," he said. "Now get in the truck and see if it starts."

"Do it yourself," she said as she spun around and headed away from him.

"Retta McCarron!" his tear-thickened voice stopped her in her tracks as if he had physically restrained her. She dropped her head and studied her work-roughened hands. "I think it would be best if I left, don't you?" he whispered.

She remained where she was, motionless for a moment.

"Isn't that what you want?" His tone was insistent. "I have only succeeded in making you hate me, haven't I?" he continued, his tone somewhat softening. "That isn't at all what I wanted."

She took a step forward and he stopped her again. "Don't go. I might as well tell you everything. Then go to your father if you want. I don't care anymore."

She turned, waiting—afraid to hear, but afraid not to.

"I like it here, Retta. I really do. I can't believe the beautiful weather, the deep blue of the clear winter sky, and the fact that things grow here all year. I sat in class after class in college thinking I'd forever be stuck in a three-piece suit and some executive suite shuffling papers, attending meetings, and transferring money between accounts. Then I came here. I couldn't believe what I found. Whether you believe me or not, I like it here. I even thought I wanted to live here." He turned away from her, not wanting her to see the tears swelling in his eyes. "But I don't think that anymore."

"Why not?" she asked.

"It doesn't matter why not. I'm leaving. I have already told my dad your father's place wouldn't be a good investment—for us, anyway."

"You did what?"

"He wants to put Pat's place back on the market," Alan said, and turned to face her again.

"Why?"

"Because, without your Dad's place, it isn't much good for anything other than orange growing, Retta. Surely you realize that?"

"But I thought you—"

"I what? Wanted the whole thing? I did." Alan looked away.

"Then what happened?" she asked, digging her toe into the dirt self-consciously.

"I changed my mind." Alan leaned against the pickup.

"I don't understand," she said.

"I don't either."

A deafening silence fell between them and the early morning fog began to lift. Retta took a small step toward Alan, then abruptly turned and started walking away from him, down the long row between the trees.

"It's funny," he called after her, slowing her steps. "I almost thought I'd get what I wanted. I even had these crazy thoughts it just might be what you wanted too."

She froze.

"You might as well hear this, Retta McCarron." Alan kept his deep voice at a level loud enough for her to hear clearly.

She didn't turn around—but waited.

"No matter what your dad wanted—or my dad wanted—I had my own plans. Mine were a little different than his. I wanted to buy his place, sure. But not all of it. Just the grove. And I wanted to add it to this place, to make it one farm again."

Retta dropped her head and her tears fell freely down her cheeks.

"I even thought," Alan said, his voice wavering with emotion. "Can you believe this? I even thought I would make a good farmer. Maybe not right away, but in time. Isn't that the most insane idea you ever heard?"

She shut her eyes, bracing herself against Alan's outburst.

"No," he continued, his voice getting louder. "It's not the most insane idea I've ever had. I can tell you one even crazier than that. I thought you might be interested in helping me. Now, there's a crazy idea for you. You, of all people. Know what else I thought?"

Retta wrapped her arms around her rib cage and took a few quick steps forward, wanting to escape the heartbreaking impact of Alan's words.

"I thought that you—get this—" Alan's voice cracked with emotion and Retta broke into a run. "That you might even marry me!" he yelled after her.

She halted suddenly and spun around to face him. Suddenly she felt the shell she had built so carefully shatter within her heart. "You what?" she screamed.

"Now you know the whole crazy story," he shouted. "Now you and your sister can have a good laugh at my expense."

"What did you say?" she yelled.

"I said you and Glenna can—" He stopped and purposely kicked loose a connection of his sprinkler system.

"Not that!" she shouted. "Before that."

"What? That I wanted to marry you?" Alan began kicking wildly at the pipes on the ground. "Is that what you want to hear?"

Before she could answer, water gushed out of the broken connections of Alan's sprinkling system and rushed wildly everywhere except the irrigation ditches meant to control it. Lunging for the loose joint, Alan slipped in the water and sat squarely in a rapidly filling puddle. Seeing the comedic tragedy of his situation, Retta grabbed the wrench from the pickup, ran to the water pipes, and quickly disconnected the pipe from the main supply, letting the sparkling water flow along familiar irrigation ditches.

"What did you do that for?" he screamed at her angrily.

"Because, you idiot," she screamed back, "I didn't think you could put it back together with the water running through it at full force."

Scrambling to his feet, Alan glanced at his mud-soaked pants and hands. "Who cares? It doesn't matter anyway," he said, his voice filled with defeat. "Take the whole thing and . . ." Alan left his sentence unfinished and with heavy steps turned to walk toward the house.

"Alan Conrad!" Retta called after him. "Come back here! I love you!"

This time is was Alan who froze in his tracks.

Retta remained where she was, afraid to move—afraid to even breathe. When Alan turned, she saw the broad grin on his mud-smeared face.

"You do?"

"Why else am I so miserable?" she said, laughing.

Alan quickly closed the distance between them with long strides. He opened his arms and Retta McCarron flung herself against him. He searched the depths of her dark eyes and smiled.

Retta threw her arms around his neck and pulled his face toward her own. "I want that kiss now," she said.

"Me, too," Alan whispered just before their lips met.

"Say it again," he said softly when she pulled away. "I want to hear you say it again."

"On one condition," she teased.

"Anything, just name it."

"Will you tell me again all those crazy ideas you have?"

"I love you, Retta," he whispered hoarsely against her ear. "Will you marry me?"

"And where do you plan on living?" she asked.

"Well," he hesitated, then gazed into her dark, sparkling eyes and seemed to gather courage. "It would take some fixing up, but I thought we might live in Pat's house."

"Really?"

"I know it's outside the privet hedge, but maybe we could—"

"Maybe it's time I stepped out—you know—beyond the privet hedge."

"Retta, I don't want to make a mistake about this. Are you saying yes?"

"I'm saying yes."

After he kissed her again, he held her close and snuggled his face into the richness of her long, dark red-brown hair.

"Can we get married today?" he whispered.

"No," she whispered back.

"Why not?"

"Because today we have to repair the sprinkler," she laughed.

"How about tomorrow?"

"Probably not," she said softly. "But soon, very soon."

"Promise?"

"I will if you will," she said.

"I'd promise you anything," he said, and once again found her lips and covered them with his own.

Walking back toward the house, the two young people, so in love, forgot the pickup truck sitting deep within the grove.

"You think he'll sell it to us?" Alan asked.

"He probably will," she smiled up at him. "Do you think we can afford it?"

"I think we can. If we work real hard and keep our minds on our work whenever we're in the grove together."

"Will we be able to do that?"

"I doubt it," he said, smiling down at the beautiful woman at his side.

"There may be another way," she said shyly. "It's a crazy idea, though."

"What's that—another one?" He squeezed her hand and pulled her closer. "I really like the ones we've come up with to-day so far."

"I just thought maybe I'd give up the grove," she said quietly.

"You would what?" Alan's face echoed the shock in his voice. "But, Retta, I thought you loved the grove."

"I do," she said. "I love every part of it. But there's more to life than just working in the grove, isn't there?"

"For you?"

"For us," she said.

"Like what?"

"Well," she said, looking down, away from the uncomfortable look in his eyes. "I'll have to do some redecorating at the house, of course. But—"

"But?"

"Oh, Alan, maybe it's too soon to discuss this. But, well . . ." She couldn't bring herself to finish her sentence. "Let's just say that I don't want to only grow oranges all my life."

Alan smiled in understanding and delight. "Nothing would make me happier, Retta. Is that what you want?"

She looked down and nodded.

"I couldn't agree more—there's much more to life than growing oranges." He tightened his arms around her and tenderly kissed the top of her head. "And we'll discover what all that means, together."

When they reached the gravel driveway beside the main house, Alan said, "I want to ask your father myself, Retta. Do you mind?"

"Of course not," she said. "Can I at least be there?"

"I think he'd insist on that, and in fact, so would I."

"Then can we tell Jim and Linda Henry?" she asked.

"I know what they'll say," Alan said, smiling.

"You do? What?"

"Jim will say, 'Praise the Lord,' " Alan said.

"Would you mind getting married in the school where they meet for church?"

"I can't think of a better place, can you?" Alan said. "Especially since it will be our church." Alan grinned and straightened his shoulders, then nudged Retta toward the house. "Let's go find Sean, shall we?"

"Can we wash up a little first?" she said, touching the dirt on Alan's cheek.

"Nah, let him see us this way. Then he'll know we mean business."

Retta turned slightly toward Alan and he pulled her once again into the circle of his arms. Retta could feel the warmth of the gentle California winter sunshine on her back and marveled at how easily she fit against him as he kissed her, how right his arms felt around her.

"What are you looking at?" Connie asked her husband, transfixed at the scene in the driveway. "Oh, my," she said as she caught sight of Alan kissing Retta.

"They ever gonna get in here?" Sean said, grinning broadly. "Now, to top it all off, we'll have a wedding to pay for. I really don't think we have any choice but to sell, do you, Connie?"

"No, Sean. Maybe we don't at that," she said, smiling.

"I suppose he'll expect a decent price—now that Retta's in the picture."

"And, you'll give it to him, too. If, that is," she said, snapping a towel toward her husband, "you know what's good for you."

Sean caught the towel and pulled Connie onto his lap. "I sure do, sweetheart. I most certainly do."

"I love you, Sean McCarron," Connie whispered before lowering her face into his kiss.

"I know you do, Consuela. And I couldn't have made it without you. You, your love, and your prayers—and I'm mighty grateful."

"Sean," Connie said thoughtfully, "I was wondering. As soon as you're rid of that cast. I mean, when you're back on your feet. Will you please come to church with me again?"

"What? Your church has somethin' against a man on crutches?"

"Of course not. Why would you ask such a thing?"

"I just wondered why I had to wait, that's all," Sean said.

"Wait? You don't have to wait!" she said excitedly.

"Good," he said. "I don't intend to."

Non-fiction Books by Neva Coyle

Abiding Study Guide
Daily Thoughts on Living Free
Diligence Study Guide
Discipline tape album (4 cassettes)
Free to Be Thin, The All-New (with Marie Chapian)
Free to Be Thin Lifestyle Plan, The All-New
Free to Be Thin Cookbook
Free to Be Thin Daily Planner
Free to Dream
Freedom Study Guide
Learning to Know God
Living by Chance or by Choice
Living Free
Living Free Seminar Study Guide
Making Sense of Pain and Struggle
Meeting the Challenges of Change
A New Heart . . . A New Start
Obedience Study Guide
Overcoming the Dieting Dilemma
Perseverance Study Guide
Restoration Study Guide
Slimming Down and Growing Up (with Marie Chapian)
There's More to Being Thin Than Being Thin (with Marie
    Chapian)